Love on the Run

BARBARA DONLON BRADLEY

This is to my family – my husband who put up with my growling when he interrupted me, and my son who would ask me if I was done every five minutes but tried so hard to respect my writing time.

I also want to thank Satin Romance for allowing me to find another home for my first two books. I love these books and hope my readers do to.

LOVE ON THE RUN

ISBN: 978-1-68046-725-3

Published by Satin Romance
An Imprint of Melange Books, LLC
White Bear Lake, MN 55110
www.satinromance.com

Published in the United States of America.

Cover Design by Ashley Redbird Designs

CHAPTER 1

Southern Louisiana, 1878

Beth Boudreaux wandered around her parents' home. Her father had headed to the general store, but she had begged off. She was tired of the questions and sad looks from their customers at what she had been through. Alexandra was the only one who didn't do that to her, but she had been beside her when Beau Manning kidnapped them. That was a frightening experience. One she had trouble putting behind her. Perhaps it was time to go visit her friend.

She spoke to her mother, then headed to the Dalton plantation.

Alex met her on the front steps. "Beth! I wasn't expecting you."

"I know and I'm sorry, but everyone keeps asking me if I'm okay and giving me those big sad eyes."

"Cow eyes," said Alex. She gestured for Beth to come into the house. "I've been getting them too."

"How do you stand it?"

"I have Trey to give them dirty looks when they step over the line."

"[illegible]h I had that."

"What about Andrew? I thought you two were a bit of an item." Alex brought her into the sitting room. She knew Fleurette would be in with something for them in a few moments.

"He did call on me a few times, but he's been out of town recently." She shrugged. "I don't know, maybe there's nothing there."

"Now that doesn't sound like you. You've never been one to give up like this." She gave Fleurette a slight nod as she came in with a tray. "You can't let what happened get to you."

Fleurette set a small plate of cookies and some tea for the ladies to drink, then headed back to the kitchen.

"I'm trying not to." She picked up her tea. "Mama has been giving me something to help me sleep."

"Is it helping with the nightmares?"

"Yes. I haven't had one in over two weeks."

"Yet, you don't feel like doing anything, do you?"

Beth shook her head. "What is wrong with me?"

"Nothing." She looked up as Trey entered the room.

"Afternoon, ladies." He bent down to give his wife a quick kiss. "Perhaps Beth should spend some time with us? Maybe a change of scenery will help."

"Oh." Beth shook her head. "I don't want to intrude."

"You don't mind?" asked Alex, ignoring her comment. "You know I would love to have a little company. I've had my own demons to battle since Beau kidnapped us."

"You have?" asked Beth. Alex's comment surprised her.

"She jumps at every sound she doesn't expect. It's no fun to be hit in the face when all I want is a hug." Trey leaned against the fireplace. "You might be good for each other."

"I'll need to make my parents aware."

"I'll send Jacob."

~

Andrew stomped up to the door to his ancestral home. He wanted to spend more time with Beth, but his work the last few weeks had him running back and forth from New Orleans. He finally found someone who made him see that there was more to life than work and it was getting in the way. The door opened easily and he shook his head when he found it unlocked. Even though he practically begged his mother to lock her doors at night, she refused.

He found an envelope propped against his bottle of bourbon. The one place his mother was sure he would see it. He snorted. His mother knew him better than he thought.

You received a telegram while you were out.

Love you,

Momma

Andrew poured three fingers of bourbon into a glass and downed it.

He had just left the office this morning. What could be so important? He walked over to his desk and sat in his chair. Andrew poured more bourbon into his glass and opened the telegram, consuming the fiery liquid while he read.

Beaureguard Manning has escaped Stop Return immediately Stop

His gasp caused the alcohol to slip down the wrong pipe. Coughing and choking, he tried to clear his throat. Gulping in air, he fought to regain control of his breathing. Coughs still escaped after he finally could breathe again.

Quickly he scribbled a note for his mother, explaining he had to go back to New Orleans unexpectedly and would be back as soon as possible. Grabbing his coat, he dashed down the front porch steps into the humid night.

~

Beth wandered around the study at the Dalton plantation. She did feel better being with Alex and Trey, but she still didn't feel like her old self. She feared this was the way she was going to feel the rest of her life.

The study door squeaking open brought her a reprieve from her tangled thoughts.

"Looks like we're going to get company," said Alex as she walked into the room. "Trey says it's your mom. Jacob is escorting her in."

Her heart jumped. Why was her mother coming? Had something happened to her father? "My mom?"

"I know, I was worried too, but Trey said she wasn't racing here so he doesn't think anything is wrong. Perhaps she just missed you."

"Mama?" Beth had to grin. "She is far too busy to admit something like that."

Fleurette came in and set down a large tray filled with fruit, cheeses, and small pastries that were Beth's favorites. By the time she came back with drinks for everyone and had set the small table that Alex used when she worked on the ledgers Trey walked in with her mother.

"Elizabeth." Her mother hugged her and kissed her cheek. "You got a telegram."

"I did?" She looked at the envelope her mother pulled out of her reticule. "Who would send me a telegram?"

"Aunt Martha."

That got her moving. She took the envelope and opened it. "You have already read this, haven't you?"

"I'm sorry." She pulled her bonnet from her head. "It came to the store and your father opened it before he read who it was to. She's not feeling well and would like you to visit. We think you should go. It would give you a change of pace."

"I don't think I should leave right now."

"Beth." Alex took her hands and gave them a gentle squeeze so she could have her attention. "I think it would be good for you."

"I—I don't know."

"Everything here reminds you of what happened. You need a break," added Trey.

She sighed. They were right. Beth looked at Alex. "Will you be my chaperone?"

"I would love to, but I can't." She looked at Trey. "My students need me, so does Trey."

Beth's brow crinkled. How was she supposed to get to her aunt without a proper chaperone?

"How about we ask Aunt Rose? She has been worried about all of us and this will give her a chance to get away for a little while."

"I think that will work," said Beth's mom.

~

Hoofbeats pounded along the dirt road. Birds screeched as they fluttered out of the way of the racing horse.

Andrew ignored the land as it flew by. How could he have been so stupid?

He knew Beau Manning better than anyone else did, and he should have been the one to escort him to trial. If he had, Beau wouldn't have escaped, and now seven days later they lost any trail they had on him.

His horse skidded to a stop in front of the Dalton plantation. Andrew threw himself onto the porch, through the carved oak doors, into the house, and down the main hallway, shouting for Trey in the process.

"Trey! Where are you?" he bellowed.

"Andrew Leroux, stop your hollering! We're in the study." The soft, feminine voice caught his ears, and he spun around and headed in that direction.

He gripped the doorframe, fighting for breath as Alexandra and Trey Dalton stared at him.

"Not quite ready for the Olympics are you, Andrew?" Alexandra asked. She sat behind a small mahogany table, covered with several ledgers of different sizes.

Although he knew the ancient Greeks had held games called Olympics, he assumed she meant it as a joke when her lively green eyes filled with humor. Alexandra used some of the oddest phrases, but he actually thought they suited her.

Trey shot his wife a quick glare.

Alexandra smiled at Trey before shrugging her shoulders, causing her light green day dress to lift up and down.

Ignoring Andrew, Trey watched as the taut material molded against her.

She shot Trey a glare of her own before nodding toward Andrew. Picking up her steel-nibbed pen, she proceeded to work on the numbers in the ledgers.

"What's the matter, Andrew?" asked Trey.

Andrew still couldn't speak, and dragging large gulps of air into his lungs caused him to choke instead.

"Perhaps a drink will help." Trey crossed to the mahogany cabinet in one corner, pulled out some brandy and a crystal snifter, and poured two fingers full.

Andrew downed it in one swallow and hoped he wouldn't start choking again. The fiery brew worked its way down, allowing him to catch his breath and calm his hammering heart. "Beau Manning has escaped," he wheezed.

"Good God, how?" Trey set the decanter down a little too hard on Alexandra's desk.

Andrew had never seen Trey's face so white.

"Shit!"

Andrew stared at Alexandra, who was trying frantically to wipe up the ink she'd just spilled all over the blotter and the ledgers.

Her expletive went unnoticed as Trey knelt by his wife, gently rubbing his hand on her bare arm.

She placed her hand on top of his and tried to give him a smile. "I'm sorry, Trey. I didn't mean to spill it. It's just..."

"It's all right, Alex."

"No it's not. Everything is such a mess now."

"Alex."

She looked up at her husband, love shining in her eyes, and something else, too—a touch of fear.

Andrew found his voice again. "Beau was being escorted to court in New Orleans seven days ago when the four guards surrounding him were attacked. Three were killed instantly, but the fourth lived long enough to tell us what happened."

"Do you know where he's run to?" Trey led his wife to the couch next to the unlit fireplace.

"We're trying to pick up his trail, but right now, no. That's why I came to warn you. He's threatened to kill everyone involved with his capture."

"You honestly think he'd try to come after us again, after what we did to him the last time?" asked Alexandra.

"Not right away. First, he'll lick his wounds and hide out, but the longer he's free, the greater the danger to you."

"And you?"

"It comes with the job, Miss Alexandra."

The frown on Alex's face told him she didn't like his answer.

"Will you stay for lunch, Andrew?" Trey eased himself away from his wife's side and stood.

"Thank you, but no. I must warn Mr. Boudreaux and make sure Miss Elizabeth is safe."

"Oh dear."

"What?" Andrew looked at Alexandra, who had turned a pasty white.

"Well, Beth isn't here right now." She glanced up at her husband. "She's gone to visit a sick aunt."

Andrew stilled for a second. The thought of her being in danger sent a chill of cold dread down his spine. "When did she leave?"

"Yesterday."

"That shouldn't be a problem." He cleared his throat. "I'll catch up with her in no time."

"There is something you don't know. Her aunt lives in Wichita, Kansas."

~

Of all the luck!

Beth looked down the dusty railroad track before checking her timepiece again. If it hadn't been for the odious man on the last train, she would be resting in a nice hotel room with Miss Rose. But he'd kept staring at her so blatantly, it had made her do something she now considered foolish, hide out until the train left. She knew her emotions were in control instead of her brain, but after her dealings with Beau, she'd learned to trust her gut instincts and they'd told her to get off the train. So instead of a hot bath and a meal, she stood in a decrepit old train depot in the middle of nowhere waiting for a train over two hours late.

It wouldn't have been so bad if she'd had something to occupy her time. She had been scared at home. Everyone felt if she got away she could find herself again. Right now she was wishing she was home, wandering the house and wishing Beau had left her alone. The fear filling her right now had her wanting to find a small hole to hide in.

What she wouldn't do for one of her books. She had always loved reading and after her ordeal with Beau she had lost herself in her dime novels. The stories she read pulled her right along with it. She could see the dusty streets of the Western towns. She wanted to have an adventure like the ones she read about. But if this was the way it was going to start she might not want that adventure now.

Once more she looked down the empty tracks. Dust swirled down the wooden ties in the slight breeze. It was going to be a long wait.

~

Andrew pushed his horse harder than ever. Mr. Boudreaux gave Andrew the information he needed, including her itinerary. Now Andrew was racing to catch up with her.

A loud piercing wail filled the air.

The train he wanted to be on was leaving without him. Andrew swore under his breath. If he missed this train, he'd have to ride another three hours at breakneck speed to catch up with it at its next stop. His horse wouldn't survive the ride.

Rider and horse cleared the station, racing toward the slowly moving train.

"Find your way home, boy. Back to Trey's house, you hear?" Andrew patted his horse twice on the neck before vaulting off his back and onto the train. He hoped the train didn't suddenly pick up speed, or he'd end up slammed up against the side instead of slipping comfortably inside.

His luck stayed with him. Climbing the three steps into the car, he found himself face-to-face with the conductor.

"Ticket?"

Andrew drew out his badge.

The conductor took a few steps back. "Who you chasing today? He's not on this train is he?" He said it loud enough for the whole car to hear.

Andrew slapped the man on the back and headed toward the back. Inwardly he smiled as the sea of people parted to let him pass. It didn't take them long to figure out what he was. He found the people's fear of his job amazing. It was easier to let them think the worst, since many of his associates were ex-criminals themselves. He found being able to intimidate people very refreshing at times. He played on that fear to get people to do what he wanted, and he'd saved many lives in the process.

Claiming a vacant seat next to the door at the rear of the car, he made himself comfortable and waited. Before long, the whole train would know there was a Pinkerton man on board, and sooner or later, someone with no brains would come hunting.

He never understood why these green kids would want to confront him anyway. Half the time he was after bigger game, but if they were dumb enough to try to take him down, he'd be smart enough to make sure they paid for their crimes.

Stretching his legs in front of him, Andrew crossed his ankles and closed his eyes. The soft murmur of passengers floated to him. He knew they all wondered what he was doing there and who he was after.

The rattling jerk of the train caught him off guard and almost sent him sprawling to the floor. Stomping his boots on the floor stopped him from falling. It also stopped all conversation in the car. Once the other passengers realized he had no plans to move, they relaxed and started to chat among themselves again.

The rattling of the train along the tracks grew louder as the door at the other end of the car opened. Andrew opened one eye. In walked a kid, more scared than he was smart. The young man looked around the car, not sure who he was looking for.

Andrew waited. Unless the boy was here looking for a relative, the passengers would direct him in the right direction. Every time this had happened in the past, everyone ended up looking at him, making it obvious none of them knew the newcomer. This crowd would be no different.

With a sigh Andrew opened his eyes, sat up in his seat and crossed his arms over his chest.

The stranger who entered the car couldn't have been older than sixteen. Wild, white-blond hair tufted over his ears. His coat was badly wrinkled and patched on one shoulder.

"Wh-who's the Pinkerton man?"

No one spoke, but all eyes turned to Andrew.

The kid fumbled for his gun. One of the women screamed when he dropped it before finally gaining control and pointed it at Andrew with a shaky hand.

"You're going to hurt someone with that." Andrew nodded toward the gun flailing in the air.

"Only you." The kid gripped the gun in two hands, trying to steady it.

"I was thinking you'd hurt yourself, like shoot your foot off." Andrew stood up slowly. "Why are you doing this anyway?"

"My pa was killed by a Pinkerton man."

"So any one of us will do to even the score?" Andrew slid his coat back to give him easy access to his gun. "You do realize I can draw this gun, shoot your gun hand, and sit back down before you could even pull the trigger."

He watched the kid's Adam's apple bob up and down. Beads of sweat popped up on his forehead. "What's your name, boy?"

"Edward."

"Edward what?"

Edward swallowed hard. “Cross.”

The train lurched as it hit the brakes.

Oh, great. They were nearing a depot. The new passengers were going to love seeing a standoff the moment they got on the train.

Edward glanced around as he felt the train slow down. Pulling a dirty bandana out of his pocket, he mopped his forehead, not watching where he pointed the ever-shaking gun.

“Well?” Andrew’s temper grew short as the train pulled into the station. He didn’t like the wild look that had entered Edward’s eyes. A frightened boy could do a lot of damage with a gun in his hand. “Look, Edward, we can either have it out right now, right here, or we can talk about this. I don’t know who your pa was or why he was shot.”

“He was shot because he didn’t want to be arrested.”

Andrew’s brow shot up. “Then your pa was running from the law?”

“Yes. I mean no. He had been forced to help some of his old friends rob a train.”

“Forced?”

“Some of the men from a gang held me and my ma hostage.” The boy’s face turned scarlet. “If Pa didn’t help them, they was going to kill all of us.”

“So your pa ran with them before.”

Edward broke eye contact and his gun drooped toward the floor of the train. “Yeah, but that was before he married my ma! She made him give up his old ways. He’d been a farmer for fifteen years before his friends found him.”

Andrew braced his feet for the sudden jerk of the train stopping. He hoped to use that moment to grab the gun from Edward.

“They killed my ma and my pa got killed helping them rob that damn train!” Anger had replaced the fear. “If those men had been able to pull off the robbery, both my ma and pa would still be alive.”

“Are you sure about that? Those men probably planned on killing everyone once they finished.”

“No!” The gun snapped back up toward Andrew’s chest. “They promised!”

“Edward, since when did criminals keep their word?”

"My pa did! He gave it all up for my ma!"

"Your ma must have been a special woman." The train skidded to a halt. Andrew threw himself at Edward, knocked the young man down, and wrestled the gun from his grasp.

Gun in hand, he rocked back on his heels, staring down at Edward.

"Boy, do you know what I should do to you?"

"Perhaps you should start by getting off that poor child?" The soft, feminine voice washed over him like honey. "Or have you decided accosting children would be better than courting me?"

Andrew looked up into the eyes of Elizabeth Boudreaux.

Wonderful. Now he had to keep the boy from doing something stupid while trying to explain to Beth that she was in danger.

CHAPTER 2

"Miss Elizabeth." Andrew's heart pounded in his chest. He couldn't believe his luck, or lack of it. Of all the times for her to come upon him. This wasn't it. She didn't need to see the seedier side of his job.

She held herself stiffly as she watched him. How did she end up on this train anyway? She should have had a half day head start on him.

It was fleeting, but he saw the shocked look that filled her eyes. He wanted to know what she was thinking. Maybe he'd have been better off slamming into the side of the train instead of making it through the doors.

But he also wasn't about to let this kid get away so Edward could try to shoot him at another time. Andrew swore under his breath when Edward struggled to rise. "Don't even think about it, boy."

"Andrew!"

"Miss Elizabeth, this is none of your concern." He knew how sharp his voice sounded, but he had to maintain control. He winced when he saw the hurt look leap back into her eyes.

"Obviously." Her spine stiff, she marched over to the seat he'd abandoned, and perched primly on its edge.

Not wanting to ignore her, but knowing he had to, Andrew turned his attention to Edward. "Now. Tell me why you decided to shoot me, and I don't want to hear the story about your pa again."

"But—"

"Your ma and pa are gone. As sad as that is, it's a fact of life. One you're going to have to live with. How would killing me make everything better? Would it bring back your family?"

Edward shook his head no.

"Then why?"

"It would stop people from pitying me." The words burst from the boy's lips.

"Why? Have you tried this before?"

Edward dropped his gaze to the buttons on Andrew's shirt.

So he had tried this before and unsuccessfully. And that agent had felt sorry for the kid and didn't lock him up. Why else would he be trying it again?

"Did they ever catch the men who killed your pa?"

Edward looked up at him. "No. Why?"

"Wouldn't it be better if you went after the men who caused all of this instead of those who tried to stop them?" Andrew relaxed a little.

"I..." Edward paused. A myriad of emotions raced across his face. "Never thought about that."

"You should have." Andrew studied the boy's face. "If I let you up, you have to promise not to shoot me."

"You took my only gun."

Andrew rose carefully before offering Edward his hand.

After a few seconds of hesitation, Edward clasped his hand and pulled himself off the floor.

The whole car seemed to breathe a sigh of relief.

~

"We need to talk about how you can go after the men who killed your father," Andrew said to Edward.

"But you have to take care of something first," the young man finished for him. Edward's eyes strayed toward the young woman who made his palms sweat since he was a boy.

"Yes." Andrew grabbed the boy by the shoulders, propelled him back toward the seat Beth occupied, and pushed him down to the floor. Pulling a pair of handcuffs from a pocket, he secured Edward to the legs of the bench. "And you'll stay nearby until we have a chance to talk."

"With me or that pretty lady?"

"Both." Andrew wanted to smack the kid. "Just be quiet."

He rubbed his hand over his face, wondering how he should approach this. Trying to explain the danger she could be in while some green kid was handcuffed to their bench didn't make his job any easier. And Beth sure didn't look happy to see him but she had been that way since he started calling on her.

That beautiful smile that had made him act like a green kid around her was gone. So was the sparkle in her eyes. He was worried that the knowledge of Beau' s escape would send her over the edge. Her kidnapping had changed her.

"I am surprised to see you, Mr. Leroux." She clutched her purse tight in her hands.

Andrew lowered himself slowly to the bench. His lips upturned for a second when he saw her frown. Good. His closeness was affecting her and might keep her off balance enough to get her to do as he asked.

"You sure are a pretty sight."

"What do you want, Mr. Leroux?" Elizabeth turned away. If she didn't, he'd see how his words affected her.

"Just to look at you for a minute." Andrew's gaze traveled up and down her slender form, taking in every curve. He wished he knew how to make her smile again.

"Maybe I should move." Elizabeth rose, reticule still clutched tightly in her fingers.

Andrew placed one hand on an arm. He cupped her chin with the other, urging her to look at him. "Not until we talk."

"What is so important that you came all the way out here, unless you just happened by." Beth fought to keep her voice aloof. "I'm traveling to my aunt's right now."

Andrew's six feet two inches towered over Elizabeth's five foot four. Not knowing an easier way he was direct. "Beau Manning escaped."

Fear flickered across her face as color drained from it. Maybe he should have let her sit for this. It took her a second before she regained her composure. "Good thing he doesn't know where I am."

"Beth, I don't want to make this worse than it is but you know he's threatened to kill everyone involved with his capture. That includes you, darlin'. You need to go home."

"Home?" A shiver slid down her spine when he called her darlin'. "No, he knows where my parents' house is, but not my aunt's."

"Are you sure about that?" Andrew crossed his arms over his chest.

He could see her hesitation. "No."

"Then you need to go back home where you'll be safe."

"Home?" Another frown creased her pretty face. "No. I won't sit and wait for him to attack."

"I'm not asking you to do that."

"Really? Because it sure sounds like it." Lovely brown eyes looked up at him.

"I want you to be safe."

"I'm not going home." She crossed her arms over her chest. Andrew had to admit that she looked a lot better doing it than he did.

"Beth."

"No!" She shook her head. Andrew watched as something changed in her. Anger filled her. "I will not let that man fill my life with fear anymore."

"Look, Elizabeth, Beau is out there somewhere looking for each of us." He looked over at Edward, who sat watching them with rapt attention. "I've warned the Daltons. I'm here to escort you back to your father."

"I'm not going."

"What do you mean, you're not going?" He stepped closer. "You have to. You know what Beau is capable of."

"And the first place he'll look for me is at home. He'd never expect me to leave home to visit a sick aunt. Papa knows I'm perfectly safe right now. He wouldn't have let me travel with Miss Rose if he was afraid I'd be harmed."

"Where is Miss Rose? I was told she was your chaperone, but I didn't see her get on the train with you."

Elizabeth blushed. Tugging on the sleeves of her dress she mumbled an answer.

"I'm sorry." He tilted his head close to hers. "I didn't catch what you said."

"I said I got off the train at the last stop without her." Angry little gold flecks danced in her eyes.

"You got off the train without your chaperone? Are you daft, woman?" Didn't she know how dangerous it was for a woman to travel alone?

"No, I'm not daft. There was a man." Her voice faded to a whisper once again.

"Someone you recognized?" Cold fingers of dread wrapped around his spinal cord. Was Beau after her already?

"No. He just kept staring at me. After the ordeal with Beau I guess I've gotten a little skittish."

"I'd say you did the right thing. Does Miss Rose know you left?"

"Didn't get a chance to tell her."

Andrew nodded. If she had, Rose would have gone straight to the conductor and had the man arrested. But then he wouldn't have caught up with Elizabeth so quickly if she had, so he should be happy. "You did the right thing."

"Really?" Those beautiful brown eyes looked up at him, shining with hope. He could tell his praise made her feel so much better. "I wondered about that as I stood at the depot waiting for this train."

"You got away from a potentially dangerous situation. We'll catch up with Miss Rose at the next stop. Then I'll take you ladies home."

"I don't want to go home."

"You must."

"You can't make me." She blinked, her gaze glassy from unshed tears.

"Elizabeth, your life is in danger. You need to be protected from Beau. Your father will shoot first and ask questions later. You need to heed my words." Andrew wished he could take back the words the moment they left his mouth.

"So you think I can't take care of myself?" She rapped him with her parasol. "I'll have you know that Alexandra taught me her Taekwondo. I'm black belt recommended." She rapped him again. "I might not know how to use a gun, but I believe I'll be fine."

"Elizabeth." Why did she have to fight him? The woman found her backbone at the wrong time.

"It's Miss Boudreaux to you." She swept past him, heading toward the front car.

Andrew watched her leave. What a mess he made of that.

Edward looked up as Andrew turned to look at him. "Girlfriend?"

"That's a personal question." He knelt down beside Edward to undo the cuffs.

"True." Edward watched as she struggled to open the door of the car. "She sure is pretty."

"I want you to tell me everything about the men who forced your pa to help them." Andrew needed this to get Elizabeth off his mind. Somehow he'd protect her, but right now he couldn't think of how.

"Gosh, there were eight in the beginning. They acted like they were friends of Pa's. They just came by to catch up on ol' times. At least that's what Pa told Ma. Everything was fine for a while. Then this other man came to the house." Edward shivered a little. "That's when everything changed. He started talking about old times when Pa used to run with them. At first he was nice—like when he spoke of those times, but he started to talk about getting the ol' gang together again. That made Ma nervous. I heard her beg Pa not to start up with them again, and he promised her he wouldn't.

"Then the new man..." continued Edward.

"Do you remember his name?" asked Andrew.

"Yeah. It was a fancy one. Beaumont."

Andrew tried to remain calm. Edward was talking about Beau. He was sure of it.

"Anyway, he started to threaten Pa. Saying if he didn't help them, he'd turn Pa over to the authorities."

"When did this happen?"

"They showed up about a year ago."

So then it was long before Beau had taken Beth and Alexandra captive. Andrew waited for Edward to continue.

"Pa didn't seem to mind. I guess Ma was a good influence on him, 'cause he said that he knew he'd have to pay his dues sooner or later and guessed that now was as good a time as any."

"But this Beaumont didn't like his answer, did he?"

"No. Although he didn't say anything then, Ma and I knew he was really mad. His face turned bright red just before he excused himself and retired for the night." Edward stared out the train window. "That's when Ma tried to send me to stay with her sister in the next town. I think she knew what was gonna happen and she wanted me safe."

"But you refused."

"I had to protect her. Pa was starting to act strange. Don't know how else to describe it. He practically ignored us. He even beat me the one time I snuck away from Ma to talk to him. I wanted to help him, but he didn't want my help."

"It sounds more like he was trying to protect you and your ma." Andrew rubbed his hand on the back of his neck. "How'd you get away?"

Edward hung his head. "I was a coward. Pa and those men had saddled up and headed out. Only one man was left behind to watch me and Ma. The knots that tied my hands and feet together weren't done very well so I slipped out of them pretty easy. I wanted to free my ma too, but she wouldn't let me. She was right by the door so the guard could see her each time he walked past. I left to go get help."

"But you were too late."

"I should've stayed," he snapped. Andrew could practically see the anger rolling off him. "If I'd thought about it, I probably could've knocked the man out and freed my ma, but I went to my aunt's instead. By the time we got the sheriff and went back to our little ranch, it was deserted.

"Anyway, my aunt wouldn't let me stay at the ranch. The sheriff helped me pack up my stuff and he asked about any valuables Ma might've had." Edward released a shaky breath. "I didn't even want to think about that. That was her stuff and my ma would come back, but my aunt must have been thinkin' the same thing. She came out of my ma's room just as the sheriff and I stepped into the hallway.

"She gave me a small box Ma must've hidden at the bottom of her closet and a journal. At first I didn't want them, but I'm glad my aunt forced me to take them. I feel like she's right here with me at times." From under his dirty shirt, Edward pulled out a small booklet, hand-bound with a calico cover to help keep it together. "This here tells the whole story, at least most of it. Ma wrote in it every day."

"Can I read that journal, Edward? It would help me know what really happened."

"I don't know. This is all I have left of my ma."

"I'll read it right now and only the section about the gang, if you'll let me, and I'll give it back the moment I'm done reading it." Andrew knew he was asking a lot of this boy. Fifteen minutes ago Edward had tried to kill him, and now Andrew was asking him to bare his soul to him. But if it was Beau, there might be something in the journal he could use.

Edward clutched it to his chest for a few moments more before thrusting it at Andrew.

Andrew opened the book carefully, finding crushed flowers, tickets to special events, and other personal effects gently placed between the pages. With a little guidance from Edward, he found the spot where the eight men first showed up.

The story came to life on the handwritten pages. Edward's family had been happy. They'd worked hard to make a living off the land, but didn't regret a moment of that hard labor. The first inkling of fear showed up in the journal the day the eight men showed up.

Edward's ma didn't tell her husband how she felt, but she poured out her emotions on the pages. So many men showing up at once didn't bode well to her. She knew they were there to take her Henry back.

Andrew looked up at Edward. Now he had a name other than Pa.

She made sure the men had food to eat and alcohol to drink, but stayed out of sight as much as possible. As much as she wanted to send Edward to her sister's, she knew she could cause a stir if the boy just up and disappeared. Ma was smart, though. She sent her sister a letter, letting her know what was going on, and to expect Edward sometime in the near future with explicit instructions he had to stay away from home until she or Henry came after him themselves. The journal took a more fearful turn when the last man showed up about a month after the first group.

Andrew sat up a little straighter as he read the description. Tall, blond, and extremely handsome, he'd seemed charming at first. She found the handlebar mustache he sported intensified his looks, and she never saw his mustache arch in a smile. Nor did she see the cold, calculating look leave his eyes. She knew he was the leader and, no matter what, these men would do what this Beaumont wanted.

Andrew smiled as he read those words. Now he had hard evidence Beau had been involved with some of the train robberies. If he kept Edward around, he might recognize some of the other men and Andrew would be able to build a case against Beau so strong he would hang.

"Edward, I want to help you, but I need your help as well." He knew he could be very wrong, but he wanted to see if he could keep Edward with him for a while.

"Nothin' bad, right?"

"Not at all." Andrew drew out a slip of paper from his breast pocket and handed it to Edward. "When we stop at the next station, I want you to go to the livery station there and get us two fresh horses. This'll get you everything we need."

Curious, Edward flipped the paper over. "Just this little piece of paper?"

"Just show it to the owner when you walk in the door."

"Okay." He stuffed the note deep in his pants pocket. "Don't know what's so special about a silly piece of paper anyway."

Andrew just smiled. That silly piece of paper would let the livery owner know the boy was there on official business for the Pinkerton Agency, and Andrew had more of those if Edward got off the train and never looked back.

"I'll meet you at the platform when you're done." He looked toward the doors that separated this car from the others. "First, I need to see a certain young lady."

Andrew worked his way through several cars before he found Elizabeth. She sat rigidly in the seat, flanked by a mother with a screaming baby and a heavyset elderly woman, who had fallen asleep and proceeded to snore. She didn't look very happy.

"Miss Boudreaux, I wish to speak with you."

Her eyes widened when she saw him standing so tall, proud, and virile in front of her.

"I have nothing to say to you."

"Then you won't heed my words?" He didn't think her back could get any straighter, yet she stiffened in the seat.

"You've had your say and I listened to you. Have a good day, Mr. Leroux."

Andrew wanted to yank her out of the seat and make her see reason, but knew it wouldn't do any good. She could be as pigheaded as her father when she wanted to be. So instead, he inclined his head and walked away. If he couldn't get her to do what he wanted by reasoning with her, he'd force her to do what was necessary.

CHAPTER 3

Andrew remained in the car with Elizabeth until it rolled into the next town. As the train slowly pulled into the depot, he made his way to the doors. Looking back at her once more, he tipped his hat before stepping down onto the platform.

He wondered what she thought of him now, watching him leave. Relief probably. Too bad she didn't realize how soon they would see each other again.

~

Of all the nerve!

Elizabeth sat in her seat, watching Andrew leave the train in disbelief. She knew he wouldn't just walk away, would he? That didn't seem like the man she fell in love with.

She fell against the stiff seat, not understanding why this bothered her. What did she want him to do? Stay where he wasn't wanted? Beth shook her head. *Of course not*. This was her chance to see the world. Her one chance for adventure, like the heroines she read about in her dime novels.

"Thank God! Elizabeth Boudreaux, you scared about ten years off my life!" A thumping cane, drawing closer, accentuated each word.

Beth looked up to see Rose Dalton. Her black hair, touched with silver tendrils of curls, danced about her face. The sight of Rose snapped Beth out of her thoughts quickly.

"Miss Rose!" Beth stood and hugged her. "I'm sorry. I missed the train at the last stop."

Rose sat her ample frame down next to her, examining Beth's face. Resting her hands on her silver-topped cane, Rose smiled knowingly. "And it was no accident, was it?"

"Of course..." Beth couldn't lie to Rose. Besides the woman had the uncanny ability to know when someone lied to her. "No. I became nervous when someone on the last train kept watching me."

"But a lot of men watch a pretty young thing like you, Elizabeth." She pushed the large violet plume from her lavender hat out of her face.

"This was different. His stare made my skin crawl." Beth shuddered at the memory.

"The rotund man with the gray beard?" Her bright blue eyes watched Beth intently. Rose was in her fifties, but didn't look a day over thirty-five.

"No. The younger man…the one who sat several rows away. He was constantly around me. He even followed me to the powder room one time." Beth patted Rose's gloved hands. "I didn't mean to worry you, but I reacted instinctively."

"Once I figured out you didn't get back on the train, I knew there had to be a reason. I did ask the conductor to check and make sure everyone but you was still on board. You'd be safe enough if no one had followed you."

"And you decided to wait for the next train to come in?"

"Well, the train coming from Dresden anyway." Rose stood up to dust off her dress.

"What happened to that young man?" Beth could imagine what Rose looked like in her lavender gown, that ridiculously large plume and that ever-present cane swinging as she demanded the train be searched.

"I don't know." Rose smoothed down the folds of her expensive gown.

"If he truly was following you, he could be getting on this train too. He knew we were together."

Beth glanced around nervously. Now that she knew Beau had escaped, her fear grew stronger. *What if the man had watched Rose? Maybe he worked for Beau?*

Where was Andrew when she needed him?

"Are you all right, chile? You look a little pale."

"I'm fine, Miss Rose. Better, now we're back together." Beth looked around one more time, wondering if it had been such a good idea to make Andrew leave so quickly.

~

Beth breathed a sigh of relief when she saw the next depot come into view. She had kept waiting to see the man from the first train show up. Rose tried several times to draw her into a conversation, but she only answered in monosyllables, all the while on guard for any sign of the man.

The train jerked a few times as it slowed down, then finally came to rest next to the platform. Soot blew in the open window, smudging Beth's dress. Thankfully she'd taken her mother's advice and worn black.

"Should've known better than to wear this light color." Rose batted at the dirt on her ample bosom.

The conductor informed them they would have two hours before their connecting train arrived.

"Oh, that should be plenty of time for us to enjoy a good meal. It would do you good to get off this train and away from those dark thoughts you've been having," said Rose.

"I haven't had any dark thoughts."

"My chile, you've been as surly as a grizzly." Rose leaned heavily on her cane as she stepped onto the platform. "Sir? Where might we find a nice restaurant?"

"Sorry, ma'am. Don't know this town, but you could ask the ticket taker. He'd know which ones are the best," said the conductor.

"Thank you." Rose dashed straight for the ticket booth, moving quickly for a woman with a cane.

Beth and her friends had wondered just how much the cane was for show. There were times when Miss Rose acted like she needed it, but most of the time, the cane was Rose's way to emphasize her point.

She made her way back to Beth in a few minutes. "That sweet young man said the best restaurant was next to the bank, about a block down."

"Sweet young man? Were you flirting again?"

Rose laughed. Cane thumping against the boards, she led the way toward the restaurant.

They walked along the boardwalk when they could. Thank goodness this town hadn't seen rain in a while or else their dresses would've been soiled beyond repair, Beth mused idly. They spent more time on the dirt-packed road than they did on the boardwalk.

Beth stared around in awe. Marion, Kentucky, was nothing like Jennings, her hometown near New Orleans, which boasted of five buildings. Marion had several hotels, more bars than she cared to count, a bank, a livery, the mercantile, the church, the sheriff's office, and a rather large jail. The restaurant was in the mercantile. A huge plaque dangled from the overhang, touting the glories of the soda fountain.

"Wonder if they use ice cream or sweet cream?" Rose nudged Beth. "I know you've feasted many times on those wonderful treats, but old ladies like myself don't get out that much. When we do, we splurge."

Beth wanted to laugh. Rose was one of the most traveled people she knew.

"I wouldn't mind having one either." She did like the soda better with the ice cream, but it was hard to come by at home, so the treat was special when they did have it.

A quick movement out of the corner of her eye caught her attention, but when she looked again, she found nothing. She thought for an instant that she had seen the young boy from the train. The one who pointed the gun at Andrew. Then Beth shook her head. It was probably just nerves.

The small bell attached to the door of the mercantile tinkled when Rose opened the door.

~

Andrew hid in the alleyway, waiting for Edward. The moment the boy returned with the note and horses, Andrew had put him to work. He felt the sooner Edward thought he was tied to the Pinkerton Agency, the sooner he would straighten himself out. He couldn't go around trying to shoot every agent he found.

Edward would have walked right past him if Andrew hadn't grabbed him by the coat and pulled. "Well, what did you find?"

Edward stared at Andrew for a moment before answering. Andrew didn't mean to startle him, but he didn't want Beth to figure out he was having her followed.

"I followed her like you asked. She and some lady just went into the mercantile."

Andrew frowned as he let go of Edward's coat. So Rose had been able to catch up with Beth. That wasn't good. "Did anyone see you?"

"I don't think so."

"Good. Head on back and keep an eye on the mercantile. See if they go anywhere else, but stay out of sight. I'm going to the depot for a moment. Then I'll catch up with you near the store."

Edward nodded before sauntering out of the alley and back up the boardwalk.

Andrew didn't want anyone remembering him so he took his time walking to the depot.

"When is the train to Saint Louis due to arrive?" he asked the ticket agent once he entered the little building. Andrew knew that would be the next big stop Beth would have to make before heading on to Wichita.

"It should be here in about an hour. Need a ticket?"

"No. Have some friends coming in on that train." Andrew tipped his hat, headed back out of the building, then turned toward the mercantile. Too bad Rose Dalton was traveling with Elizabeth. Knowing Rose would take her duty seriously could put a kink in his scheme. He'd wait until the train met its next destination before deciding if he had to alter those plans.

~

Beth and Rose strained their necks to see out the grimy window as the train pulled into St. Louis.

"Are you sure you'll be safe for a little while?" asked Rose. "I hate leaving you here while I go and send a telegram to your father."

"Miss Rose, I'm sure I'll be fine. We haven't seen any sign of the man, and there are so many people here no one would dare try anything."

"Humph." Rose's cane pounded the floor of the train. "I'd feel much better if you came with me."

Beth looked out the window again. "I don't feel like dealing with the crowd out there. You go and tell Papa everything is fine. You've already asked the conductor to keep an eye on me. What can happen in a few minutes?"

~

Andrew watched as Rose exited the train and headed toward the center of town. He didn't understand why Rose would leave Beth alone, but now he could put his plan into action.

~

Beth debated on whether or not to get off for a while. The stifling heat of the Pullman car was getting to her. They would be in St. Louis for several hours, and her body was stiff from the hard horsehair seats. She needed to stretch and get a breath of fresh air.

Rose might be angry with her for getting off the train, especially since she said she didn't want to leave it when Rose had first asked her, but she planned to stay on the platform until Rose came back. Then they could walk around a little.

She sighed as she stood up and stretched. Stepping down from the train, Beth looked around. The breeze was almost as hot as the interior of the car, but feeling its caress on her face had a calming effect.

The townspeople bustled around her, making her wish she had stayed on the train. A woman alone in an unknown town wasn't very smart. She turned back toward the train and she would have climbed back up the few stairs to the car if she hadn't heard someone crying.

Beth looked around. No one in sight was crying, so where did the sound come from?

Glancing down an alley, she saw a huddled figure. She hurried toward the form, hoping she could help. As she came closer, she could tell it was a young boy.

Just as she reached him, a strong arm wrapped itself around her waist while another hand closed over her mouth. Without a sound, she was dragged farther into the dark alley, tied up, and thrown unceremoniously on the back of a horse.

CHAPTER 4

Beth wanted to scream, but having the wind knocked out of her when she slammed against the saddle prevented that.

At least she knew whoever kidnapped her was a gentleman. She heard him mumble an apology when her loud *oof* filled the air, and although her hands had been tied, he had been thoughtful enough to place her small handbag on one of her wrists before tying them together.

Hanging upside down, she could do little more than take in her surroundings. Her view of the underside of the horse wasn't very pretty and she could hear a strange buzzing in her ears. Beth stared at the now unruly mass of hair hanging in the dirt. A burst of hysterical laughter shot from her mouth when she realized her hair came to a point, much like the onions growing in her mother's garden.

Finally regaining her breath and her senses, Beth struggled to slip to the ground, but a restraining hand forced her to remain slung over the saddle. Not something she was happy with.

One dusty black boot landed in the stirrup inches from her face. She tried to jerk away, but found she'd lost her ability to move once again.

Strong hands lifted her up a little, and then Beth felt her body being dragged backward. Before she could react, she found herself draped across well-muscled legs encased in black, and at least one of those legs belonged to the boot she had seen up close and personal only seconds before.

Her restricted vision forced her to watch as her captor's sculpted legs flexed, tapping the horse on the belly with the stirrups. The moment the horse took off, she realized what hell must be like.

Her body bounced against the thighs that held her, making her flop around like a landed fish.

A scream tore from her throat when she started to slip toward the ground that sped by.

She felt those strong hands grab her, stopping her descent before she heard an oath escape her captor. "If you promise to behave yourself, I'll sit you up in the saddle with me."

Beth nodded vigorously. She'd agree to anything if it meant she'd be safer.

She felt her dress tighten against her neck as she was pulled up by the back of it. Steel-like arms wrapped around her waist before she was maneuvered into the saddle properly.

Using her tied hands, she pulled at her neckline, relieving the pressure and allowing her to breathe better.

Now she had to figure out how to get herself out of this predicament.

"If you return me to town now, I promise I'll never mention any of this to a soul. No harm done."

She felt a deep chuckle vibrate against her back.

"I doubt that very much, Miss Elizabeth. That's why I did this in the first place. You never listen to reason."

She twisted sharply in the saddle to stare at Andrew Leroux's face. "You—"

"Yes. Me. Since you wouldn't go home to the safety of your family voluntarily, I decided to take matters into my own hands."

"You have no right." She swung her bound fists at him, throwing off her equilibrium. Almost in slow motion, she started to slide off the horse. Unfortunately, her descent accelerated when Andrew slid with her.

He hadn't released his grip on her waist and although he struggled valiantly to keep them seated, he lost the battle before he could even start fighting it.

They fell to the ground in a heap.

Beth leaped to her feet first. Pulling her skirts from under Andrew's sprawled body, she started marching toward where she thought town was.

"You know, you won't get very far."

"Ha! I'm not some weak and helpless female, Mr. Leroux. Something you should remember." She shook her tied hands at him.

"A horse has always outrun someone on their feet, Miss Elizabeth."

"Then run me down, Mr. Leroux, because I won't come back willingly."

"Yes, you will."

That stopped her. She spun on him. "You are wrong, sir."

"Even if you're going in the wrong direction?" Andrew stood near his horse, arms crossed over his chest. A very fine chest, she noted. "Then there're the Indians."

"Most of whom have been driven onto reservations. You can't scare me with that one." Brave words. Too bad she didn't believe them.

They hadn't ridden very long, yet she couldn't see any sign of civilization. What if Andrew had lied to her and she ended up wandering around out here forever? Or worse, she might meet some of the few renegade Indians roaming around these parts. She'd never see her aunt or home again.

"Come, Miss Elizabeth, let me take you back to your father. You can visit your aunt after the danger has passed."

"No, I can't. I have allowed Beau to make me afraid for too long. I promised my family that I'd go to my aunt's. You aren't going to stop me." Did she just see him wince? "The telegram my family received said she was gravely ill and she needed me." She pushed a few strands of brown hair out of her face. "I must go to her now."

"Then you leave me no choice, do you?"

"The choice was never yours to have." Beth started walking toward Andrew, giving him a wide berth as she skirted around him. "I must make that train."

A piercing whistle filled the air.

"Oh no!" Beth stopped. That was the signal that the train was leaving. She wouldn't make it back in time.

She dropped to her knees, ignoring the tears making tracks in the dirt on her face. All her belongings were on that train. Her father had made her hide the bulk of her money in the false bottom of her trunk. All she had with her was what was left after lunch. It wasn't enough to buy another ticket. She was stuck and she didn't know if she'd ever see her belongings again.

Andrew watched Elizabeth fall to the ground, then frowned when he noticed her shoulders shaking. He hated it when women cried. He always did something stupid, like agreeing to do whatever they wanted or asked. Anything to stop their tears.

Pulling the horse with him by the reins, he walked slowly toward her. Maybe by the time he got there, she would've stopped crying and would yell at him again. That he could handle.

He stopped beside her.

"Go away."

"Miss Elizabeth."

She looked up at him with a tear-streaked face. "This is all your fault!"

"My fault! If you had done as you were told—"

"Who appointed you my protector?" Beth struggled to her feet and looked him in the eye.

"I did." He placed his hands on her arms.

"What?" That stopped her. He had been so polite she thought he was only courting her because of his friendship with Trey. Alex had been pushing them together since she met her. "Why would you do that?"

"You need my protection."

"You are wrong, Mr. Leroux." Once again someone wanted to control her life. No more. She pulled away from him.

It was obvious she didn't like his answer. "Elizabeth. Beth, I know what Beau is capable of. If he were to harm you I don't think I could live with myself."

"Then you understand why I can't go home."

Now he was confused. "I'm not sure I do."

"If I go home I put my parents in jeopardy."

He frowned. "And you won't do that at your aunt's?"

"Beau doesn't know about my aunt. I'd be safer there than at home."

"I don't agree." Andrew shook his head. "Your father would shoot first and ask questions later."

"My father would stuff me in some tiny room and throw away the key." Beth shook her tied hands at him. "If you were in my position you wouldn't want to go home either."

"And I won't be able to do my job properly if you're not someplace safe."

"Oh please. I know better. My papa can ignore my momma and me whenever he wants. The moment I leave your presence you will forget all about me."

Andrew fought a laugh. "You are unforgettable, darlin.'"

"I'm going to my aunt's," said Beth.

"You're going home."

"No I'm not."

"Yes you are." He really should have been paying attention, but when it came to Miss Elizabeth, he never seemed to do anything right. Her small bag clipped him in the ear.

"Ouch!" The rope restraining her hands hadn't stopped her one bit.

"Serves you right! I don't care what you do or say, Andrew Leroux, I am going to my aunt's. It doesn't matter if you take me home because I'll sneak out of the house and catch the next train going to Wichita."

"Really wish you hadn't said that, Miss Elizabeth."

"Why?"

He loved the way her brow crinkled up when she didn't understand. "Because you've made me realize I'll have to keep you safe myself."

"What about recapturing Beau? I thought that was your main goal right now."

"Keeping you safe is the most important thing. Once I'm sure of that, I'll go after Beau."

Beth glowered at him.

"Please don't try to fight me on this." He could almost see the wheels turning in her head. He could throw her in jail while he went after Beau but feared she'd find a way to get free. "I don't think your father would appreciate it if you came home with your hands and feet tied."

Beth blew a stray hair out of her face as she contemplated his words. She gave him a sweet smile. "All right."

Andrew didn't like the determined glow in her eyes. It spelled trouble.

~

Several hours later, Beth wanted to scream again. They hadn't moved an inch. Well, that wasn't completely true. They had moved to a small rise closer to town. Of course not close enough for her to be able to figure out where it was, but enough to make her contemplate escape. The only thing stopping her was Andrew's ever-alert gaze. They stopped on the rise as if Andrew was waiting for something.

A small plume of dust headed their way.

Beth thought Andrew would hide them when he knew they were going to have visitors, but he remained where he was, watching the cloud of dust grow closer.

After a while, she could make out the shape of a wagon with a team of two horses.

Andrew never moved.

It turned out to be a buckboard, slowing down as it veered toward them. Beth could only glare in anger when she realized Andrew knew the driver.

A young man leaped from the seat as he pulled the team to a stop. "I got everything you asked me to get, sir. I also have some news."

"What's the news?"

"A man fitting the description of who you're looking for has been through this town recently. He robbed the bank here about a week ago."

"You're sure?"

"Near as I can tell." The young man shrugged.

Beth gasped as she recognized the young man. "Aren't you the one Andrew fought with on the train?"

"Yes, ma'am." He blushed. "Nice to see you again. The name's Edward. I gathered your things from the train."

"My trunk?" She raced to the buckboard, sighing in relief when she spied her precious trunk.

She half listened to Andrew and Edward talk about the bank robbery as she forced the lid up and worked her way through her things. Beth had to make sure nothing had been stolen. She dug through her clothing, making sure none of her essentials were seen by the men. Something she found hard to do with her hands still tied. Her knuckles scraped against the bottom of the trunk.

"Miss Elizabeth?"

His voice caressed her like velvet before she realized Andrew stood beside her. She jumped a little as she looked up. Heat from a blush spread across her cheeks as she tried to hide her underwear from prying eyes.

Andrew didn't speak. He just held up a very large and sharp knife.

She stared at the large knife and gasped. What did he plan on doing with the knife?

He arched an eyebrow. "Wouldn't you like me to cut off your bonds?"

Blushing deeper, she offered her wrists. The blade sliced through the rope like it was butter. She swallowed hard as the ropes slithered to the ground.

Andrew, it seemed, had dismissed her as soon as he cut her bonds because he was already back by Edward, speaking in hushed tones once more.

A quick glance over her shoulder let her know the two men were still deep in conversation. Beth pressed her hand against the corner of the wood, giving her fingers a small space to wiggle into. A quick push slid the floor back just enough for her to get her hand inside to feel the small purse of coins she'd put there. She sat back on her heels, saying a quick prayer of thanks to God. Now she had the money she needed to get to her aunt. All she had to do was get away from Andrew.

Pushing her clothes back into the trunk, Beth started to formulate a way to escape. She could take off now, but Andrew would chase her down on that horse of his before she could get ten feet, then probably tie her back up 'for her own good.'

Sitting on the back of the buckboard, one elbow wrapped around her knees, she watched the two of them, wondering how she was going to get to her aunt's. Maybe she should wait until they fell asleep and tied them up. As appealing as that seemed, she knew she'd never be able to do it. She wasn't quick enough to bind Andrew before he'd realize what she was up to.

Andrew would definitely be her biggest problem. How would she be able to slip away without him knowing for a while? Or keep him from following her?

~

Rose Dalton stood at the counter of the mercantile. This was something she dreaded, but knew it had to be done.

"May I help you, ma'am?"

"Yes. I need to send a telegram."

The young woman behind the counter pulled out a pad and a pencil.

"It's to go to Jennings, Louisiana. To William Boudreaux and it's to say your daughter's been kidnapped."

CHAPTER 5

Her chance to escape came quicker than she expected.

Two days of travel brought the threesome to a small town…if Beth wanted to call it that. The five buildings that comprised the center of town barely qualified. The church, bank, mercantile, sheriff's office, and bar looked like clapboard dwellings badly in need of paint.

Beth couldn't understand why they stopped there, but when she questioned Andrew, all she got was a curt, 'I have my reasons.'

He locked her in one of the rooms he rented above the mercantile the moment they arrived, then maintained a vigil at the bar across the street.

She paced her small prison, wondering what she should do. Through her open window, she could see Andrew sitting near the big pane of glass that dominated the front of the bar, but he seemed preoccupied.

Was he paying attention to her? Could she walk out in broad daylight and slip away before he realized?

Pacing the bedroom floor Beth thought about this. She could go for a walk and see if Andrew noticed her leaving the mercantile, but what if he did and confronted her? How would she explain how she got out of a locked room?

A soft knock startled her out of her thoughts.

"I have something for you to eat, miss," said Edward.

"Thank you." She watched the lock turn before Edward elbowed the door open.

He smiled at her shyly as he set the tray down on a small table. "Mr. Leroux noticed you pacing in front of the window and thought you might be hungry."

So he was watching her. "How very thoughtful."

Beth sat down at the table. After shaking out the napkin that covered her meal, she placed the napkin on her lap. Tantalizing aromas drifted up toward her. Her stomach growled. "My goodness."

"You did miss your lunch today, ma'am."

She nodded as she retrieved her fork and speared some of the mashed potatoes covered with brown gravy. A sigh escaped her as the food melted in her mouth. Just a hint of pepper remained on her tongue. Several slices of beef also lay on the plate.

Beth made short work of the meal.

"That was heavenly." She dabbed her lips with the napkin.

A crashing sound sent her running to the window. Across the street a chair fell onto the boardwalk, which was quickly followed by more glass breaking when a body hurled through another section of the bar window. Whoever had been thrown out of the window didn't seem to be bothered by it. He picked himself up and marched back into the bar.

"Wow! Sure hope that window ain't too expensive." Edward stood beside her. In all the excitement, she didn't even realize he had come to the window too.

"Oh dear." Beth bit her upper lip. "Do you think Andrew has been hurt?"

"Doubt it, ma'am. He strikes me as a man who always lands on his feet."

A shot rang in the air.

Elizabeth's body turned cold. She was going to use her fear for Andrew as an excuse to get out of the room. But it wasn't an excuse anymore. She had to know for herself. He might not feel the same way, but she cared for him and didn't want anything to happen to him.

Beth turned around and quickly walked to the stairs that led down to the street. Edward's boots pounded on the stairs as he followed her.

"Ma'am, that's no place for a lady."

"Maybe not, but I can't sit up there waiting to hear if Andrew is all right." They made it to the front of the building, only to find their way barred by gawkers. Slowly, Beth made her way forward until she could get a clear view of the interior of the bar.

Andrew stood there unscathed, shouting orders and threatening to throw everyone in jail if they didn't listen to him.

Beth glanced around. Edward was nowhere to be seen. She scooted over just a little so Andrew couldn't spot her from inside the bar.

She scoured the crowd again.

Now or never.

Ducking her head down, she walked quickly down the boardwalk. Shouts filled the air as the fight gained more spectators.

Beth kept walking. She was lucky the train depot stood right on the other side of the sheriff's office. She stepped up to the window and ordered a ticket.

"When will the next train arrive?"

"Tomorrow morning." The man behind the counter slid a ticket toward her. "That'll be three dollars."

"Tomorrow? Never mind." Beth backed away from the window.

"Are you sure, miss?"

"Oh yes, quite sure. Thank you anyway." She walked back to the bar slowly.

"Going for a walk?"

Andrew's deep voice skimmed along her spine, sending delicious shivers down her back. She hoped her voice wouldn't show her fear. "Yes. Just needed a little fresh air."

"Found out the train wasn't coming until tomorrow, didn't you?"

Her head jerked up to stare at him. Beth knew she didn't have to say a word. The look on Andrew's face told her he knew the truth.

"Why don't I escort you back to your room?"

~

Beth sat, staring out her window the next morning. The high-pitched whistle of the train could be heard for miles. She wanted to be on that train, but instead she was stuck in this room, Andrew standing outside the sheriff's office with a perfect view of her room and Edward sitting in front of her door. Looking up and down the road, she wondered if she'd ever get another chance to escape.

There weren't many people on the street right now. Most she recognized from yesterday, but one stranger caught her eye. She shrunk back from the window, her hand on her chest.

It was the man from the train. She hoped he hadn't seen her.

~

Andrew kept an eye on Beth's window all morning. He wondered what made her back away from the window so quickly. If she planned on trying to escape again, he'd tie her up so tight it would take a week to remove all the knots.

He noticed the stranger a few seconds later. The man looked familiar, but he couldn't remember where he'd seen him.

"So how long you staying in town?"

The sheriff's question brought him back to why he was out on the street.

"We're leaving today, Sheriff, and I'm sorry about the bar. It couldn't be helped."

"I don't abide having anyone tear up my town. You Pinkerton men act like you're above the law."

Andrew knew better than to argue with him. "Do you know that man?"

The sheriff looked at the man Andrew mentioned. "He's new in town. He's not one of your men, is he?"

"No, sir." Andrew wasn't about to comment on the fact he looked familiar.

"I'll keep an eye on him just the same."

Andrew nodded before heading across the street. He needed to check on Elizabeth.

His long strides had him climbing up the stairs that led to their rented rooms quickly. Without knocking, he opened the door. He found Beth pacing the floor while she mumbled to herself.

He wished he could read her mind. He knew she wanted to escape, but he had to keep her safe. How would he do that when she fought him every step of the way?

Watching her pace, Andrew knew Beth would never listen to reason. If he did take her back, what would stop her from escaping her father the moment he turned his back? He knew she would be capable of it, so returning her home wasn't the answer.

Andrew rubbed his jaw. If keeping her at his side the entire time was the only way to keep her safe, then so be it.

He cleared his throat to let her know he was in the room.

She jumped at the sound. "What're you doing in here?"

"Making sure you're still in the room."

"And where would I go with that watchdog at the door?"

"You have your ways."

Beth glared at him. "As do you."

"I wouldn't have to watch your every move if I thought I could trust you, but I know better."

"That's because you want to force me to return home."

"It *is* for the best."

"Who says? How do you know Beau hadn't planned on getting to me at home? You honestly think my father can protect me from him?"

Andrew couldn't answer that one. He had promised her father that he would bring her home safe, but he'd been having the same thoughts ever since she said it the first time.

"For all I know, he could have someone following me." Her eyes cut to the window.

"Why did you move away from the window earlier?" He wondered if she was right. By the way she acted, he'd say yes.

She couldn't look him in the eye, so she turned toward the window. "So you were watching me."

"I'm worried about your safety."

"There's not a whole lot to see out that window." She sniffed. "I just got bored."

Andrew remained silent. He found that to work on her the best. She remained quiet but wouldn't look at him.

"So when do we leave?" she asked.

"Today."

"Now?"

"No. I have to meet with someone first."

She sighed.

"I promise it shouldn't take long. We ought to be out of here by lunchtime." Andrew headed toward the door. "I'll be back in a little while."

He closed the door behind him and looked at Edward.

"Keep an eye on her. I'll be back." Andrew headed down the stairs and walked around the front of the mercantile. Glancing in the window, he saw the stranger standing in front of the counter. Was the man here spying on Beth? Or was he just being paranoid?

The bell above the door tinkled as Andrew entered. He wasn't sure if Beth had backed away from the window because of this man, but decided it warranted further investigation.

Andrew wandered around the store, looking at the assorted merchandise. Canned goods were stored in one corner; bolts of cloth in another. A brand-new soda fountain stood next to the register, and so did the stranger.

As near as Andrew could tell, the man was writing something out.

"I need to send a telegram," the stranger said when he finished.

The store owner looked over the note. "What is this word here?"

"Train."

He wrote on the sheet, his pencil making scratching noises against the paper.

"And this one?"

"Lost."

"Okay." He made another note on the paper. "I want to read this back to you so I know I have it right."

The man looked around at the customers in the store.

Andrew slid out of his view.

"Okay."

"Followed her on train. Stop. She didn't make it to next stop. Stop. Lost her. Stop. Looking for train—"

"Looking for trail now," the stranger corrected.

He wrote the corrected words on the paper. "Your name?"

"He'll know who it's from."

"And where is it going?"

The stranger looked around before answering. "Jefferson City."

"All right." The store owner added up the letters and gave him a total.

The man paid it and walked out the door.

Andrew walked up to the counter. "Didn't know you had a telegraph here."

"Yep. Just got it a couple of weeks ago."

"I need to send a telegram too. To the Pinkerton Agency in New York." Andrew wrote a quick note asking for all agents in his area to meet with him in Bloomfield, the next town they would reach. Now that he had a lead, thanks to blind luck, he knew where to start looking for Beau Manning.

Once he finished paying for his telegram, he walked back over to the sheriff's office.

"You know that man I asked you about earlier? The young one with the mustache?"

"What about him?" The sheriff crossed his arms over his chest.

Moments like these made Andrew wish the badge he carried demanded respect. The sheriff stood there, staring down at Andrew like he was some sort of vermin that jumped off a stray dog.

"I believe he's trying to kidnap someone."

"Who?"

"The young lady I'm protecting."

"Oh."

"Look, sheriff, I don't care what you think of me or the people I work for, but that young lady is of the highest quality and deserves respect. A killer is on the loose and I believe that the man we are talking about works for that killer."

"And you think he's after the woman with you?"

"Yes."

The sheriff pulled his shotgun from the wall. "I can pull him in here and hold him for a while, but if he hasn't actually done anything yet, I can't keep him. You know that."

"Thank you, Sheriff." As long as the sheriff kept the man occupied long enough to let them leave without the man's knowledge, that's all Andrew cared about.

"I'll wait for your signal." Andrew wanted to meet with the Pinkerton agent who was supposed to show up in this town, but the man was due in yesterday. Something must have come up. He didn't have the time to wait any longer.

"Sheriff, if I could leave a note for the person I was supposed to meet with?"

"If it'll get you out of my nice, quiet town quicker, write your damn note and I'll make sure he gets it—if he ever shows and happens to come looking for me."

"Thank you, Sheriff."

~

Beau Manning crushed the telegram in his hand. Stupid man lost her. Miss Elizabeth Boudreaux had gotten on the train in New Orleans, but somehow hadn't stayed on board. How this happened didn't matter to him, but the fact she had gotten away did.

He thought he'd sent his best. Those who failed him suffered for that failure.

"Able?"

The young man in question sauntered up. "Yes?"

"I have a special job for you to do."

The young man grinned. "What do you want me to do, boss?"

CHAPTER 6

She wrung out the dirty handkerchief she'd used to wipe her face and placed it on a rock near the fire to dry.

At least they had water. Edward had packed the buckboard full of provisions before they had left the last town. It seemed that Andrew had made him his private lackey.

They hadn't been near any streams so she could clean off the grime properly. Something she really wished she could do.

Beth also wished for a soft bed and a hot bath. After a week of living out under the stars, she wanted to go home. Okay, maybe not home, but someplace that put a roof over her head and hot water at her disposal. Maybe have a normal conversation with someone other than her two companions. Andrew had kept most of his answers to one word and Edward did a lot of ducking his head and shrugging. She hadn't had a real conversation in a week.

Andrew continued to hang on to his anger because she refused to go home. At least she thought that most of the time. But there were moments when she caught him staring at her and she wasn't sure. Something about the looks he gave her when he thought she wasn't paying attention made her nervous. Beth would swear he looked like he wanted to devour her, but it was so fleeting, quickly hidden behind his shield of anger that she wondered if she had imagined it. So she kept her distance, speaking to Edward most of the time.

Edward was sweet, but so naive. When she did get him to talk it was like talking to the family dog. He would listen to her, tilt his head like he really did understand her, then start yipping on about something that had nothing to do with their conversation.

What happened to the adventure she'd dreamed about? She was dirty, smelly, and very bored. She could have gone home and saved herself from two of these three things right now.

Andrew told her they would stop in another town, but she wondered if he was telling her this to keep her quiet. After all, they'd already skirted a half a dozen small towns without stopping. She wouldn't have even known they were near them if she hadn't heard a couple of cryptic comments Andrew said to Edward.

Beth sat down at the fire, munching on a cold biscuit from their meal earlier. She also wished for a real meal, not hard tack and biscuits. The coffee Andrew served was so strong it could be cut with a knife and eaten. It reminded her of her father's. After a week she was actually getting used to it, but what she wouldn't do for a little sugar and cream.

Lying down, she closed her eyes as she imagined sweetened coffee with a wonderful home-cooked meal. A soft smile worked its way onto her face as she visualized a table piled with all her favorites.

"And what are you dreaming of?"

She opened one eye to find Andrew staring at her across the fire. The light danced across his face. The beard that had started to grow hid his chiseled features. As she observed him, butterflies started dancing in her stomach. Every time she found herself looking at him, she felt those butterflies take flight. "Nothing."

He continued to watch her. The fire between them snapped and crackled.

Beth felt like prey. If only she knew what he was thinking. His steady gaze made her heart beat faster. Her blood seemed to pound in her ears.

Silence stretched between them as she tried to still her wildly beating heart. How could she be so attracted to a man who held her captive? She shifted in her makeshift bed. He didn't look bothered by her nearness, but she was definitely affected by him. The heat she felt had nothing to do with the fire burning in front of her. Something she couldn't let him know. So she found her voice.

"I was thinking about how heavenly a bath and a home-cooked meal would be right now." Beth didn't even try to lie. Lying wouldn't work for her, especially now while she was too busy trying to act normal.

"I'm sorry your present accommodations don't agree with you. If you'd done what I asked and gone home..."

"Must you bring that up?" Why couldn't they have a normal conversation? Andrew always pushed her, making her angry. "I can't go home, which I have explained to you, and I'm tired of having this conversation every time we speak to each other. Can't you think of something else to talk about?"

"Like what?"

"I don't know. How far away are we from this town you keep talking about?" Beth watched the firelight flicker across his face. "And what is the name of it anyway?"

"Bloomfield." Andrew's eyes slid to her lips before he dropped his gaze and stirred the fire with a stick. "It's about a day's ride with the buckboard."

They were heading south, away from where she wanted to go. Beth needed to get away at Bloomfield, while she was still close enough to Wichita but she didn't know how.

~

Bloomfield was a lot larger than she expected.

She tried not to fidget while Andrew checked them into the hotel, but couldn't wait to settle into her room.

The first thing Beth did was order a bath, while Andrew and Edward took advantage of the public bathhouse down the street. She smiled as she slid into the hot water. He even allowed her to have the dresses she had worn on their ride here sent out to be cleaned and pressed. Beth was very grateful. Her last set of clean undergarments and her only fresh dress lay against the thick quilt that covered the bed.

She had volunteered to join them at the bathhouse, but Andrew shot her down cold. Beth leaned against the lip of the huge brass tub, feeling the heat of the water soak into her bones. Once the water cooled a little, she grabbed the soap and started to scrub herself. She swore she had twelve layers of dirt. By the color of the water when she finished washing her body, she was right.

After soaping up her hair, she stood up in the tub and poured clean water over herself to wash away the last bit of grime from her body.

Someone rapped sharply against the door. The woman who had the tub brought up warned her she couldn't have it very long. Other patrons wanted to use it too.

Beth quickly grabbed the bath linen and wrapped it around herself. "Come in."

The handle turned slowly.

Beth ignored it as she bent over to wring the water out of her hair.

"You meant it when you said you'd be back for the tub quickly." She straightened up and looked at the door. Where she thought she'd see the woman again stood a clean-shaven, freshly bathed Andrew.

Heat from a blush crept up her face as she stood there gawking at him. Common sense finally clicked in, making her dive behind the dressing screen.

"You shouldn't be in here," she squeaked.

Andrew cleared his throat several times before answering her. "I…ah…came to tell you when Edward comes back from his bath, we'll have dinner downstairs."

"Thank you."

"You're welcome."

She waited to hear the door close. Could he have left so silently she didn't hear him? There was only one way to find out.

Beth peeked from behind the screen.

Andrew stared at the screen like he wanted to bore holes into her hiding place. His eyes flicked over her face.

She felt trapped in his gaze. Her body heated up when his gaze roamed over her face to pause on one bare shoulder that stuck out of the screen. Wet hair tumbled from on top of her head.

Andrew's amber eyes darkened, almost smoldering as he watched her pulse leap in her neck.

"Um, Andrew, I'd like to get dressed."

"What? Oh." He cleared his throat again. "Of course. Um...I'll be next door."

The slammed door sent a strong vibration through the building, but it was nothing like the shiver that hummed through Beth. Andrew's intense look shook her to the core. She didn't remember ever having him look at her like that before.

Tremors of something she couldn't identify kept assailing her as she tried to dress. She fumbled with the buttons of her chemise that refused to cooperate and slide into the holes.

Another rap on the door made her jump. What if it was Andrew again?

"Madame? I came for the tub," said a soft, feminine voice.

"Come in. I'm done with it." She hoped the young woman entering her room wouldn't notice the color on her cheeks. She could feel the heat of a blush she couldn't stop.

"Thank you, ma'am."

"Um...before you cart that away, can I ask a favor?"

The young lady looked at her expectantly.

"Could you help me with my corset?" She had been able to loosen it while they were traveling so she could sleep, but now that it was off she couldn't get it on without help.

"Of course."

Beth grabbed the bedpost as the young lady violently pulled the strings in her corset. Good Lord, her mother never pulled them so tight. She couldn't breathe.

"Air," she wheezed.

"There, all nice and tight." The young woman looked at Beth as she turned blue in the face. "Oh dear!"

She quickly loosened the strings enough to let Beth catch her breath.

Hand on her chest, Beth sucked air into her lungs, at least as much as the corset would allow.

"Madame? Are you all right? I didn't mean to make it so tight, but most of the women who ask for my help beg me to get it as tight as possible. You just have such a narrow waist, I didn't realize how tight I made it." She looked around to make sure no one heard her.

Beth wanted to know who could be eavesdropping in her room.

"Most of these ladies are a bit thick in the middle, so I can never get the corset to close in the back," she said in a conspiratorial voice. "Is that the dress you're going to wear? I can help you finish getting dressed."

"Thank you." Beth grimaced at the faint wheeze escaping her as she talked. She sure hoped she didn't do that when she joined Andrew and Edward. She'd be too embarrassed to speak.

Fifteen minutes later she descended the stairs and walked toward the dining area. The sea of strangers in the dining room made her wonder if she should have waited in her room for him instead of down near the large double doors that framed the entrance to the room.

A warm hand grasped her elbow.

She jumped and swung toward the intruder. Her hand flew up to her throat.

"Calm down, Miss Elizabeth. It's only me," said Andrew.

Her fear gave way to a strange fluttering in her heart. Andrew's clean-shaven look affected her here as it had in her room. She knew it would take a while before she got used to it again.

"But I'm glad to see you on your guard." He recaptured her elbow. "Are you hungry?"

She nodded instead of speaking. Beth wasn't sure she could get any words out knowing her heart was in her throat.

Andrew led her to a quiet table in the corner of the room. Edward stood the moment he saw her.

"You look very lovely, ma'am."

"Thank you, Edward." Good, the wheeze had disappeared. "I must say the same about you," Beth continued. Edward's new suit fit him well. A crisp white shirt and brocade vest accented the dark brown suit he wore.

The tips of his ears turned pink from the scarlet blush that rose up his neck from her compliment.

Beth took the seat Andrew held out for her. He then took his seat. She wished she'd sat where he did. He could see the entire room, while she sat with her back to the crowd. She'd have to turn around if she wanted to see anyone. Not knowing who was behind her made her nervous.

Their meal came quickly, but Beth didn't really taste any of it. Her nerves were too taut to enjoy her meal. She felt like everyone was staring at her. Whispering about her behind her back. The hairs on the back of her neck stood up.

Andrew placed a hand on her arm. "Are you all right?"

She nodded, feeling like such a fool. Swallowing her fear, she continued to play with her food.

"Perhaps you'd like to go for a walk this evening, Miss Elizabeth? A little fresh air might do us both a bit of good."

Andrew stood and offered her his hand. He led her out of the dining room and away from the crush of people.

"Thank you."

Andrew remained silent, his boots clicking against the wood of the boardwalk.

"I don't know what happened in there."

"I do."

She looked up at his chiseled profile.

"You had that caged look on your face. You didn't like the fact you couldn't see what was going on around you, did you?"

She dropped her gaze to her shoes. "No."

They walked along in silence while Beth struggled to find the right words to explain what she felt. She felt the warmth of Andrew's hand as it closed around hers, giving her unspoken support.

"I don't like that feeling of helplessness. I kept waiting for something terrible to happen."

"But it didn't."

"But it could have."

Andrew chuckled. "I promise nothing will happen to you as long as you're with me."

Beth wanted to rail against him. She needed to control her own life, not stand by while someone took care of everything for her.

"Sure is a pretty night," Andrew commented. Tugging on her hand, he pulled her out onto the dry, packed road.

Stars twinkled above them. The moon, still hanging low and very large on the horizon, glowed in the night sky.

"Do you think man will ever go there?" she asked.

"To the moon?" Andrew paused for a minute. "Never really thought about it. Guess it could happen. Look at all the new advancements going on around us. Telephones, electricity, that phonograph that seems to crop up everywhere."

"Don't forget soda fountains. I've seen a lot of those coming out here." Beth smiled up at him. "I think we will do it one day."

One minute Andrew smiled down at her, the next he shoved her behind him before he drew out his weapon.

Beth peeked around him to see what caused this sudden change in Andrew.

There, just a few feet away, stood the man who had been on the train.

"I don't mean no harm, mister. Just going for a stroll out here."

"Why are you following her?" Andrew kept his weapon trained on the man.

"Following the little lady? Why, no, sir. I've never set eyes on her before."

"Then explain why you were in the last town we were in, and the telegram you sent to Jefferson City."

Dark shadows hid the man's face from them, but Beth could see him stiffen.

"What telegram?"

"Let's see." Andrew rubbed his chin. "Something like she got on the train in New Orleans, but somehow got off the train, and you were working on picking up the scent again."

"Look, I don't want no trouble with you." The man whipped out his pistol. The pearl handle flashed bright white in a beam of moonlight. "I just came for the little lady. Hand her over and there won't be any trouble."

"Now that's a problem." Andrew scratched his head. "You see, the lady is in my protective custody, so if you try to take her, there will be trouble."

"So you'll die protecting her."

"Yes."

Beth heard the deadly sound of a pistol hammer drawing back. "Fine by me." The man aimed.

One repeat from a gun thundered in the night air.

A dozen people swarmed around from all over the street to see what had happened.

Beth stared in horror as the man dropped his weapon, choked a little on the blood flowing from his mouth, then toppled over dead in the street.

Andrew looked shocked too.

He stared down at his gun. "I never got a chance to fire."

"But I did." A shadow pulled itself away from one of the dark alleys. "Name's Able. I've been sent here to help you and it looks like I was just in time."

CHAPTER 7

Andrew stared at him. The tall man must have had a bit of Native American in him with his long jet-black hair and obsidian eyes. Able looked familiar, but Andrew couldn't remember where from.

"Thank you," said Beth, who still hid behind Andrew.

"Welcome, ma'am." Able pulled a few papers out of a pocket and handed them to Andrew. "Got a message from the agency saying you were looking for men to help you track down Beau Manning. I didn't realize he had escaped."

Andrew looked over Able's forms. Everything seemed in order. Yet, something didn't feel right.

"Gotten any good leads?" asked Able as he pocketed his papers when Andrew handed them back.

"Had one, however, he's not a very good one anymore." Andrew pointedly looked at the dead man at his feet.

"Sorry. Guess I got a little trigger-happy. Saw him draw that gun and reacted automatically."

The sheriff huffed and puffed his way up to them, a napkin still stuffed in his neckline.

"Did we interrupt dinner?" asked Andrew.

"I don't cotton dead people on my streets, gentlemen. I hope you have a legitimate excuse." He pulled the napkin off as he adjusted his holster over his wide girth.

"Yes, sir." Andrew turned toward Beth. "This young lady is in my custody. This one here—" He pointed at the dead body. "—was trying to kidnap her. He drew a weapon and was shot for threatening her."

The sheriff knelt over the body. "The bullet hole is in the back. Unless you're one hell of a shot, you didn't do this."

"No, sir, he didn't. I did," said Able. "All I saw was that man pull a weapon. Guess I pulled mine just as fast. One minute he was standing there, threatening the lady and the next he just kinda slid to the ground. Didn't mean to kill him. It just happened."

The sheriff pushed his hat up on his head. "Well, you just happened to shoot the man right in the heart. That warrants a night in jail."

"Sheriff—" Able started to argue.

"Don't." The sheriff turned toward Andrew. "I'm going to let you go, so you can protect that lady properly. If it weren't for her, you'd be spending the night with him. But since I assume you know who is after her and why, I'm hoping you know the best way to protect her." The sheriff stood up and glared at Andrew. "Now, when are you leaving my town?"

"Sheriff, I explained that earlier." Andrew spread his hands out in front of him as he spoke. "I'm just not sure right now."

"You've been here one night, Mr. Pinkerton Man, and there's a dead man in my street. What's gonna happen tomorrow? I want you out of here by tomorrow night, or you and your companions will end up sleeping in my jail cell."

"Yes, sir." Andrew wanted to smile. The sheriff might be as tall as he was round, but he didn't back down from his duty. He liked the man already.

He turned, took Beth by the elbow, and escorted her back to the hotel.

~

Beth stared at the darkened ceiling above her head. Every time she closed her eyes she saw that man from the train pull the gun on them, except this time he shot Andrew and carried her away. She rolled over. Sleep wouldn't come easily for her tonight.

Well, now she had the adventure she longed for. It just wasn't what she'd expected. Her dreams were of some grand escapade where she would be in charge of her own fate, not some man with a gun. Maybe she should go running home to her family. At least she'd have familiar surroundings as she waited for Beau to come after her.

She rolled over again, climbed out of her bed and sat down on the window seat. Staring up at the stars, she wondered what would have happened if she had gone to her aunt's. Knowing her luck, she'd be Beau's captive once again.

Andrew was right. She shouldn't be out here. Tomorrow she'd tell him she'd go home.

~

"No."

"What do you mean, no?" Beth couldn't believe what Andrew had just said. "This is what you've been trying to convince me to do from the beginning."

She kept her voice calm. Making a scene in the dining room would bring too much unwarranted attention toward them.

"I know." Andrew ran a hand through his hair. "But after last night, I realized the safest place for you is with me. I know what Beau is capable of and I know the best way to protect you from him."

"I can't travel all over this godforsaken territory without a proper chaperone. What will people think?" She wasn't sure how Andrew felt about her but she needed to think about her future. No man would think of marrying her if he knew she ran around with two men unchaperoned. Not wanting to show her embarrassment, Beth broke eye contact as she picked up her coffee mug and took a sip. The sweetened flavor brought a smile to her lips, making her forget her anger for just a second.

"Beth, as far as society goes, you've already been compromised. You've been alone with two men, for over a week."

Her head snapped up as a stunned look of disbelief spread across her face.

"They can't honestly believe..." She set her coffee mug down, sloshing coffee over her hand and the tablecloth. Beth inhaled sharply as the hot liquid scalded her.

"Are you all right?" Andrew asked.

She nodded, lifting her damp fingers to her mouth.

"Haven't you noticed the way people stare at us? We're strangers in this town. It doesn't take much for idle tongues to wag. Sooner or later we'll go somewhere where they won't be afraid to throw it in our faces. No matter how innocent our trek across the wilderness has been, no one will believe us."

"Father will be furious," she said absently as she flexed her fingers.

"Your father is the least of my worries. First we must fix this problem of us traveling together unchaperoned." Andrew suddenly had an intensive gleam in his eye.

One she didn't like.

"I'll take care of everything."

"What are you going to do?"

"Stop those wagging tongues."

~

Andrew disappeared right after breakfast. The longer he was gone, the more Beth worried about how he planned on fixing her chaperone problem. Did he plan on kidnaping some poor helpless female to travel with them? Or hiring one?

Whatever his plan was, she was sure she wouldn't like it at all.

He showed up just as the town clock struck one o'clock. Without saying a word, he offered her his arm and escorted her down the street toward the church. Opening a side door, he gestured for her to precede him.

"What're we doing here?" she asked quietly.

"You'll see in a few minutes." He ushered her into the rectory.

The young minister popped out of his seat at the sight of her. "So this is your young lady."

Beth frowned as she looked at Andrew. *His young lady?*

"If you have all the paperwork signed, we can get started." The minister pushed his spectacles up his nose.

Her frown deepened. *Get what started?*

Andrew drew out a packet of paper and handed it to him. "Reverend Hailey, if we can have just a moment?"

"Of course, of course. I need to check something before we get started anyway."

Beth turned to Andrew expectantly. She couldn't figure out why he had taken her to a church.

"This was the only thing I could come up with."

"What?" Her eyes widened in disbelief. *He wouldn't.* "Marriage? You're mad as a March hare if you think I'm going to marry you."

"Beth." Andrew took her hands in his, demanding her attention. "I can't ask someone else to travel with us. Last night proved it. I can't send you home because the danger is far too great and I don't want to jeopardize your family. If we marry, we're free to travel together without making people talk. We'll blend in better."

"Oh? Is that all you're worried about? Blending in? And what will happen to this marriage once the danger has passed? You'll go on hunting down people and I'll be sent back home, right back where I started. No, Andrew. I made a promise to myself that I would only marry for love. What you are offering isn't love." She also knew they could just tell everyone they were married without actually having said vows.

"Marry me, Beth." Andrew pulled his hat off his head. "Let me protect you the way you need to be protected. Then after Beau is caught, if you want the marriage annulled, you can have that."

Beth looked into his eyes. The light green flecks really stood out, giving him an innocent quality. She couldn't believe her own ears when she heard herself ask, "Then this will be a marriage in name only?"

"If that's what you want."

Beth didn't know what she wanted. Barely a month ago she wanted to marry Andrew, but after her kidnapping she wasn't sure anymore. There were so many things she had learned about him recently that she didn't like. Then there were others that touched her heart. She should just walk away, but part of her wondered if it would be so bad for her to marry him for a little while.

She always wanted to know what it was like and, as a divorcée, she could keep her independence after she went back home. It was perfect, yet a part of her wanted more.

She bit her lip.

"As a married couple, people wouldn't think twice as we travel through their towns and Beau would never expect us to marry."

Beth walked over and looked out the window, keeping silent but weighing all her options. Since she had been with him, she had felt a lot safer than when she was traveling with Miss Rose. He had her best interests at heart. And if she could keep her heart safe, she just might be able to get some independence from her father.

But what if Andrew wanted to make the marriage real? That was the only stumbling block she saw at the moment. *Would that be so bad?* A shiver slid up her spine. Or would it be so good she wouldn't want it to end? Beth turned her mind away from those thoughts quickly. She turned to look at Andrew for just a moment before facing the window once more. Beth knew she could do a lot worse, and this just might work out in her favor.

"All right." She continued to look out the window, not wanting to see his reaction. She sensed him take a step toward her just as the minister came back in.

"Are we ready?"

Beth turned toward the two men. "Yes, sir, we are."

~

The gold band on her finger felt like it weighed a ton. Her plan to use this marriage didn't seem so easy now she had a ring on her finger. She was truly married. What would happen now? Andrew said their marriage was only on paper, but what if he changed his mind? What if she changed hers?

She turned the ring around on her finger, wondering how this would change the way they related to each other. Would Andrew continue to treat her like a stranger?

A swift knock made her hotel room door vibrate. Patting her hair, she crossed the room and opened the door.

"The gentleman down the hall sent these." The young woman held a huge bouquet of flowers.

The maid set down the riot of colors on the dresser as Beth continued to stare at it. It had every conceivable flower in it. *Whose garden did Andrew raid?*

"They're beautiful."

"These are Mrs. Whitall's prized flowers. She gets awards for them every year. Your young man paid her handsomely for the best ones she could find." The maid turned toward the door. "Oh, and there's a card too."

Beth stepped up to the flowers while the young woman walked out the door. She barely noticed the soft click of the door closing.

Beth closed her eyes and inhaled. The mixture of fragrances reminded her of her childhood when she, Andrew, Beau, and Trey used to steal into Mrs. Remmie's garden and pick her flowers. The woman would come running out of her house threatening to tell on them, but they never were punished.

She spied the small card tucked against the lip of the vase.

Beth,

Since I can't give you a proper honeymoon, I thought you'd like the flowers. They are as beautiful as you are.

Andrew

Her heart soared at the words before reality crashed down around her. This was a marriage in name only. Something she'd have to fight to remember.

CHAPTER 8

Beth blanched at all the attention she and Andrew received later that day. Just about everyone who passed them stopped to give them their congratulations.

"Good gravy, does everyone here know about our marriage?" she asked.

"Sure looks like it."

The sheriff headed in their direction.

Beth stiffened her spine at the sight of him. Was he coming to rail at Andrew or offer his congratulations?

"Understand you got married today."

"Yes, we did," said Andrew.

Beth tried not to look shocked when Andrew laced his fingers with hers.

"That doesn't change my ultimatum."

"I didn't expect it to." Andrew smiled at the sheriff. "We'll be leaving this evening, just like we promised."

The sheriff looked at Beth before commenting. "Tomorrow morning before the sun rises. You did just get married," he continued. "As long as you're gone before the rest of the town wakes up, I'll be happy."

"Thanks, Sheriff."

"Good enough." The sheriff turned to go. "Oh, by the way, I let your friend go this morning and had him followed. Looks like he left town. And you got a telegram."

"You get the telegrams now, Sheriff?"

"Only the ones going to people involved with dead men in my street," he replied. "It's in my office."

Andrew and Beth followed him across the street to his office. The small building held one jail cell and two desks. "You have a deputy?"

"Sure do, but he just got married so I gave him a few days off." The sheriff rifled through some papers on his desk. "That marriage thing must be spreading." It took a few minutes, but he finally pulled the small piece of paper from the pile. "Here's the telegram."

Andrew took the piece of paper the sheriff offered and read it. Several agents were in this area and would be contacting him as soon as they could. No names were listed, but that didn't surprise Andrew. Most of the time he never knew who his contact with the agency would be. They had already met one agent. It was just a matter of time before the rest showed up.

"Thank you, Sheriff."

"Just remember tomorrow morning before the sun rises."

Andrew nodded, then escorted Beth back out of the office.

"What if your friends don't show up by then?" asked Beth.

"I'll leave word where we'll be heading so they can catch up with us."

Andrew placed his hand on the small of her back, creating strange frissons of heat to spark throughout her body. She needed to concentrate on something other than the way she reacted to his slightest touch. "Do you really think you can recapture Beau?"

"It's not really whether or not I think I can, Beth. I have to. If I don't, no one will be safe."

"And what if you have to kill him?" Beth didn't want to voice her true fear. *What if Beau killed Andrew?*

"I'll face that when I have to."

~

They spent the afternoon like a newly married couple. Andrew gave her his undivided attention, making everyone they passed think they were in love. He remained a true gentleman too, never giving her a chance to question his motives.

He showed her the sights of the town and took her to Mrs. Whitall's house to show Beth the woman's prize-winning garden. He took her by the livery stable so she could see how well her horse was being treated. Andrew even took her to the mercantile to pick out a few new dresses.

Beth felt her resolve crumbling from his kindness and almost child-like joy at showing her the ins and outs of the town. He had gone out of his way to learn about this sleepy, little town just for her. This was the man she had fallen in love with.

He saw beauty in everything around him. As long as he behaved this way, she knew she'd have to keep a level head and constantly remind herself the marriage wasn't real. She knew she'd be hurt if she thought for a second it was.

The mercantile was the icing on the cake. He told her she could have whatever she wanted.

Her smile must have spoken volumes because Andrew stayed out of her way as she searched the store for exactly what she wanted. They had several dresses she knew would be better suited for traveling, so she purchased those, but she also wanted to get her husband a gift.

After all they did just get married. She studied all the male apparel the store had, but she didn't think a new hat would do the trick. Tack was nice, but not something a bride would give her husband. At least not this bride.

Beth wandered around, picking up different items that caught her attention, but nothing seemed right.

The clerk approached her. "Is there something you're looking for?"

"No. Yes. I want to buy something for my husband. Today is our wedding day, but I haven't seen anything that would make a good gift."

"Let me show you something." He took her to the counter and pulled out a drawer filled with pocket watches. "This is something he'll cherish for the rest of his life, plus I can have your names and wedding date engraved on it at no extra charge."

"How quickly can it be done?"

"Well, I don't know. We do have an engraver that comes through this town and he's due in soon, but I don't have a date for his arrival. It could be tomorrow or three weeks from now."

Beth looked at the different watches. One in particular kept jumping out at her. It was perfect. Relatively plain, the gold watch had a simple filigree etching around the edge.

"I'll take this one." Beth held up the one she wanted.

"Your names and wedding date?" He gave her a piece of paper.

She wrote down the information, as well as a small inscription she wanted to add. Beth also gave the young man her home address in case the engraver didn't show before they left. Her father might be furious once he saw the watch, but it wasn't something she could help.

"My husband is having all of our bills go to the hotel." She glanced around to see where Andrew had gone. "I don't want him to know what I bought. Is there a way to disguise this gift as something else when he gets the bill?"

The young clerk smiled. "Leave that to me, ma'am. He'll never be able to decipher what I sold you."

"Thank you." She gave him a grateful smile.

"That took long enough."

Beth jumped. Andrew was at her elbow before she could sign the bill. She prayed he hadn't heard anything.

"It isn't easy picking out a store-bought dress." She tried not to act nervous as she brushed a few strands of hair out of her eyes. "I needed something that would be very durable as we travel."

Eyeing the small bundle sitting on the counter he said. "I hope you picked out several."

"Of course." She scooped up her package, wishing she knew how the clerk would disguise the watch. If it showed up as a dress and she didn't give Andrew the right count, he'd get suspicious.

"Good. And you had everything billed to our room?"

"Just like you told me to." Anger laced her words. Andrew was treating her the same way her father treated her…just like she had no brain in her head at all. Then his words sunk in. “Our room?”

Andrew blushed. Something she had never seen before.

“Slip of the tongue.”

She just stared at him. He was the one who wanted a marriage of convenience. *Why would he make such a big mistake?*

Andrew didn't say anything else as he escorted her out of the mercantile. They headed back to their hotel.

“Dinner is in two hours. Perhaps you'd like to freshen up a little beforehand?”

She nodded, clutching her packages tighter.

He dropped her off at her room.

The scent of the roses caught her attention first. The flowers on the dresser beckoned to her. After closing her door, she crossed to the dresser to inhale the fragrances once again.

A soft smile played across her lips. Perhaps she should wear one of her social dresses. After all, it wasn't every day a woman got married. Using the speaking tube in her room she called down for the bathtub.

~

She entered the dining hall a little late, but seeing the stunned look on Andrew's face was worth every minute of her toilet.

He leaped out of his chair the moment he saw her, pulling one out for her to sit in. She smiled when she noticed that it allowed her to see the room.

She murmured her thanks as she took the seat he offered her. The deep blue dress she wore accented her fair coloring beautifully. Although the décolletage was a little lower than she would have liked, watching Andrews Adam's apple bob up and down made her realize she picked the right gown to wear this evening.

Andrew was flabbergasted.

There was some strange power in having a man confused like this.

“You look beautiful tonight, Miss Elizabeth.”

“Thank you, Andrew, but you shouldn't be so formal now we're married." She lowered her lashes. "Husbands and wives are supposed to be a little more familiar."

"You're right, Beth. It's just I didn't expect you to look so ravishing this evening. You're going to make it very hard for me to keep my promise if you dress like this all the time." He slid back into his seat.

She snapped open her fan, moving it up and down to cool her face. His comment made her feel warm all over.

"Where's Edward?" she asked.

"Edward won't be joining us tonight. He has some errands to run before we leave town."

Odd. Did Andrew give Edward errands to do to keep him away? Then she thought against it. Edward did run a lot of errands. Tonight should be no different. She had to remember this was a marriage of convenience. Andrew's kindness was only for those watching. Beth nodded as she opened her napkin and placed it on her lap.

Their waiter came over with a bottle of champagne. "Complements of the hotel." He popped the cork out and poured them both a glass. "Enjoy and congratulations."

Beth felt a blush creep up on her cheeks. She just wasn't used to this much attention.

"To us," said Andrew as he lifted his glass.

Beth lifted her glass, too. She assumed Andrew was putting on a show for the other diners. It wouldn't look good for the newlyweds to act like they hated each other. "And to the capture of Beau Manning."

They touched their glasses to their lips and drank down the bubbling brew.

Beth started to giggle.

"What's wrong?"

"Nothing. It's just I'm not use to champagne. It tickles my nose."

Andrew looked a little pained by her statement.

"Did I say something wrong?"

"No." He sat back in his chair. "Tonight I don't think you can say anything wrong."

She smiled at him. Moments like these made her realize why she'd wanted to marry Andrew. He made her blood race in her veins when she saw him. His handsome looks melted her heart.

A loud rumble filled the air.

She looked down at her offending stomach. Fine time for it to demand sustenance. Here she was warming up to the idea of Andrew as her husband and her stomach interfered.

"Sorry."

"Don't be," said Andrew. He signaled the waiter who stood near the door. Within minutes their meals were placed in front of them.

"I hope you don't mind." Andrew shook out his napkin before placing it on his lap. "But I asked the cook to prepare our meal earlier while you were changing. I thought you'd like to go for a stroll this evening before the sun sets."

She wondered where he wanted to take her. They had seen most of the town earlier. Slicing the beef on her plate, she speared it with a fork and brought it to her lips. Her mind kept wandering to how Andrew had been so nice today. The moment they said their vows the tension between them lifted. She felt safe.

Her eyes widened at the explosion of flavor in her mouth. The beef was so tender it practically melted as she chewed. A quick sip of champagne heightened the flavor.

"Good, isn't it? It's the local farm's prized beef."

She just nodded. The meat was so good she had already popped another piece in her mouth and followed it with a little more champagne. She could eat like this every evening.

~

Andrew watched Beth chase each of her bites with a sip of champagne. At this rate, she'd either pass out, or lose the very expensive meal she just consumed.

Fresh air would be the best thing for her.

Instead of waiting for desert, he stood, gripped Beth by the elbows and, as discretely as he could, steered her toward the door.

"Where are you taking me, Andrew?" Beth slurred just a little when she spoke. Her eyes opened wide and she hid her mouth with her hand. "I sound a little funny."

"For our walk." Andrew continued to propel her out of the dining room, hoping he could get her out before something happened.

"I don't really feel like walking right now."

"But it's a beautiful evening and I have something special I want to show you."

She sighed heavily, but continued to move with him.

Just as they neared the doorway one of the waiters entered, carrying a large tray of food.

Andrew didn't think, he just reacted, drawing Elizabeth to the right and swinging her around the outside of the man. They probably looked like they were dancing as they exited the room, but at least they averted disaster.

Beth giggled as they stepped out onto the boardwalk. "Wheee. That was fun!" She plopped down on a bench just outside the front door, her skirts billowing up in an unladylike fashion.

"I'm glad you're enjoying yourself." Andrew leaned against a post.

She took a deep breath. Pushing her hands against the seat, Beth forced herself up on her feet again.

Andrew straightened.

"Well, are you going to show me this wonderful thing you've been going on about?"

He lifted one brow. He had only mentioned why he wanted to go walking to get her out of the dining room before she embarrassed herself.

"Of course." Taking her small hand in his, he placed her hand in the crook of his arm and guided Beth off the boardwalk. Slowly he led her down the road to the church. The minister's wife had spoken of the grotto to him earlier. The wife of the owner of the hotel had mentioned it too. The two women had said it was the most romantic place at sunset.

Andrew looked down at Beth and wondered if she'd even remember this tomorrow. She didn't act drunk, but he could tell by the awkward way she bounced against him as they walked she'd had more than she should have.

"You feeling okay?" he asked.

"Oh, yes." She swayed into him. "You know, you are very handsome."

Andrew smiled, knowing the alcohol loosened her tongue. "And you're very beautiful."

She blushed and ducked her head.

"Come now, I'm sure you've heard that before."

"Only from my father." She hesitated for a moment. "And you."

"Then you need to hear it more often." Andrew vowed to make sure she did hear it too. Every day for the rest of his life if he could.

He spotted a small copse of trees next to the church and pointed. "That is where we're going."

"I'll race you."

Before he had a chance to react, Beth slipped her hand from his arm and ran toward the small wooded area. He could hear her laughter floating back toward him.

"Maybe I should ply her with champagne all the time," he muttered to himself. Picking up his pace he hurried toward the area into which she had just disappeared.

A small creek wandered through the area. Its trickling and tinkling soothed his mind.

Beth sat on a large rock next to the babbling brook, resting her back against a large oak tree.

Just as he stepped up to her the sun dipped below the trees, bathing her in a golden light.

His heart stopped for just a second as he gazed at her. This was an image he would carry with him for the rest of his life. Light kissed her soft features, caressing her flawless face the way he wanted to.

The sun dipped lower, the hue turning to a deeper golden, then orange, before red highlighted her lips and her hair.

He took one step toward her, knowing if he wasn't careful, he'd forget all about protecting her. In fact, she just might need to be protected from him.

Andrew had just leaned down to take her hand again when he heard a solid *thunk* against the tree. Not worrying about Beth's feelings at the moment, he grabbed her arm and pulled her onto the grass, rolling so she was under him.

"What in the blue blazes are you doing?" she shrieked as she struggled to get up.

"Keeping you from getting shot."

CHAPTER 9

Andrew reached for his gun.

"A shot?" Her urge to struggle fled as fear took over.

"Yeah, you know, like in bullets flying through the air? Someone is shooting at us." She started shaking all over. "Beth, I need you to be strong right now. It's probably just some kids shooting at targets nearby and a shot went astray, but I want to be sure. You need to get to the church and find the minister if I'm wrong."

"Andrew..."

"I'll be fine, sweetheart. I'll probably catch up to you before you even get to the door."

She nodded, staring up at him.

Andrew felt the quick hot press of her lips against his.

"For luck." She eased out from under him, ready to run to the church when she felt safe enough to do so. Beth glanced over at Andrew as he pulled himself up into a crouched position and eased his way toward where he thought the shot came from.

Taking several deep breaths, she tried to calm herself. She watched the surrounding trees, making sure no one would suddenly attack her. Quickly, she started working her way in the direction of the church. The edge of the grotto shielded her from anyone outside. Her throat became dry when she realized she had a lot of ground to cover before she would reach the safety of the minister's house. There was still just enough light for her to be spotted if she tried to dash across the lawn.

What if whoever shot at them had already attacked Andrew and was waiting for her to come out?

She looked around, but couldn't see anyone out there. In fact, it was a little too quiet for her liking. Beth chastised herself. Expecting the worst didn't help anything. She had to calm down and get to the minister. Just as her bravado strengthened enough for her to take a step out into the clearing, a hand touched her shoulder.

A scream wrenched itself out of her throat. She didn't want to die this way. Blindly, she struck out, feeling her fist connect with skin.

"Ow. You sure pack a mean wallop, Beth."

"Andrew?" She stopped herself before she hit him again. "Don't sneak up on me like that! You scared me half to death."

"I'll remember that." Andrew rubbed his jaw. "That was powerful. Who taught you to hit like that?"

"Alexandra." Beth flexed her fingers.

He gave her a look of disbelief as he crossed his arms over his chest.

"What did you think she taught me when I learned her martial arts? How to beat a man senseless with my fan?" Beth placed one hand on her hip. "Don't forget who were the ones kidnapped by Beau Manning."

Beth and Alexandra were kidnapped by Beau because Alexandra's harebrained scheme didn't work, even though it was the only thing they had come up with to capture Beau the last time.

"And don't forget who was the one who rescued me."

Alexandra had been the one who'd loosened the ropes that secured the two women to a pole and convinced Beth to sneak off while Beau was preoccupied with taunting Andrew and Trey.

"Never did figure out why she didn't run too," Andrew muttered.

"She knew we both couldn't escape. Beau might let me go, but he'd shoot her if she tried to get away. Alexandra trusted you and Trey to free her."

"But not to free you?"

"She was actually trying to make it easier for you. One less distraction for you and Trey to deal with." Beth smiled, noticing his ears were turning red. "You feeling a little threatened?"

"What makes you say that?"

"No reason." His ears turned red every time he was angry, but didn't want someone to know it, but Beth didn't think voicing this childhood insight would be a good idea, so she changed the subject. "Did you see anything?"

"No. Whoever it was either took off after the first shot, or it was a stray. But I didn't see anyone doing any practice shooting nearby, so I don't think it was an accident."

"You have that many enemies?"

"Just being a Pinkerton man gives me a lot. I've dragged husbands from their wives and families. Killed men who were fathers."

"Were you ever in this town?"

"No, but maybe someone who knows me has moved here." Andrew put his arm around her. "I don't know about you, but I've had enough excitement for one night."

Beth nodded. "Thank you for bringing me here."

"You like being shot at?"

"Well, I could've done without that part of the evening, but I have really enjoyed our time together." She walked alongside him. "Today was like a faerie tale. We weren't arguing."

"You didn't plead with me to let you go to your aunt's house," Andrew added.

"The wedding was nice."

"About that—"

Beth placed her fingers on his lips. "Let's just leave that alone for now. I've had a wonderful day."

"I have too."

Andrew said it so softly she wasn't sure if she heard it or wished he said it.

They walked back to the hotel hand in hand, just like newlyweds should. All the while, Andrew scanned the buildings and alleys they passed. Beth felt the tension in him, his protectiveness of her taking over.

She wondered what the rest of the night would bring her. Andrew told her the marriage would be one of convenience. Did that mean he really didn't care for her? Or was he trying to be honorable?

She wished she knew what he was thinking.

A slight movement in a darkened doorway caught her attention. One quick glance stopped her dead in her tracks. *Did Andrew see it?*

"What's the matter?"

He couldn't have. Andrew would've reacted if he had.

Beth started walking again. Grasping Andrew's arm, she pulled him alongside her. "Nothing. I think I'm still a little nervous about what happened today."

"You were shot at." He looked back the way they came before gazing at her.

"Twice now, if you're counting. Thank goodness both times they were a bad shot." She looked up into his eyes. The fading twilight highlighted the angles in his face. Dark shadows ran across his cheekbones, making his features harsh. She sighed. She couldn't lie. "I just saw something out of the corner of my eye, but I could've conjured it up after our little adventure in the grotto."

"What did you see?"

"A gun barrel."

Andrew started to pull away.

Beth wouldn't let go. "If you think you're going to go after what I think I might have seen, I have a question for you. What're you looking for?"

"I don't know, but that has never stopped me before." Andrew brushed a stray hair off her face. "Normally, the guilty party acts guilty. They run from me, knowing I'm chasing them and don't even stop to think of how I would know what they look like, unless they run. Most don't use their brains."

"Well, use yours this time. I could've imagined it. If I didn't, the person probably has already moved and we'll see them again if they work for Beau like we suspect."

"We?"

"Stop." She gave him a serious look. "Beau will hire people he can trust and who are intelligent enough not to do something stupid."

"True. He hates it when people make mistakes." Andrew started walking again. "Then I guess you're stuck with your escort."

She gave him a soft smile.

The hotel had quieted down. Most had already retired to their rooms for the night.

As they walked up the stairs to Beth's room, she felt the butterflies in her stomach take flight. The question of how they would spend their first night as a married couple would be answered in just a few moments.

"Beth…um…I don't want you staying alone." Andrew hurried his words so she wouldn't interrupt him. "I promised you a marriage of convenience and you can have that. I promise not to force myself upon you, but I worry about what you might have seen earlier. What if the man from the train had an accomplice and they try something while you're sleeping?"

Beth's heart did a little flip. Was this just an excuse to get into her room? Yet she knew that Andrew did look at things logically.

"You wouldn't…um." She blushed. How could she ask him this question?

"I won't touch you unless it's your decision."

Her eyes widened. She'd have to make the first move? She bit her lip. Could she make the first move if she really wanted to? Beth knew Andrew waited for an answer. "All right, but how will we handle the sleeping arrangements?"

"I'll sleep on the floor."

She wanted to argue, but the thought of sharing a bed with him frightened her.

Andrew didn't give her a chance. He dashed into his room, gathered what he needed, and stood beside her before she could really react.

With a shaky hand she inserted her key into the lock and opened her door.

"Let me go first." Andrew slipped into her room. After looking around, he came back to the door and held it open for her. "It's safe."

Beth stepped into her room, which suddenly felt three times smaller with Andrew's presence. The door closed with a thud, making her heart pound even harder. Here she was, on her wedding night, with her husband and he was really going to sleep on the floor!

She gaped at him as he laid the quilt from his bed on the floor. Placing a pillow for his head on the quilt, he lay down and made himself comfortable.

Beth slipped behind the screen and changed into her nightgown. She thought about staying dressed, but knew that wouldn't be practical or comfortable. Plus, Andrew would think she didn't trust him if she did that.

Peeking out from behind the curtain, she made sure he wasn't looking in her direction before darting to her bed. In a flash, she had the covers up to her neck.

"Good night, Beth."

"Good night, Andrew." She hastily blew out the lamp next to her bed and laid down.

She knew sleep would be a long time coming this night.

~

Beth woke up cranky. They had traveled to another town so Andrew could keep the sheriff happy, but it had been hard on Beth. She hadn't slept well since. Her nights were restless, but when she did sleep, she dreamed. They were so erotic she was sure the blush from thinking about it went from the edge of her hair to the tips of her toes.

She stole a peek at Andrew's bed and found it vacant. A sigh of relief escaped her as she stretched before sitting up. He had taken to sleeping in the same room since their wedding. He still spent the night on the floor, but too close for comfort as far as Beth was concerned. At least she didn't have to face him right away this morning.

She quickly went about her toilet, hoping to be dressed before he came back. Getting into her undergarments caused no problems, but her corset was another matter. There was no way she could get the corset tight enough without help.

A swift knock on the door made her jump. *What if it's Andrew?*

"Ma'am, I've come to make the bed."

Beth opened the door a crack. "Can you help me with something first?"

"Of course."

The door opened wider so the young woman could enter.

"I need help with this." Beth clutched her corset against her chest.

The young woman closed the door and smiled. "We'll have you dressed in no time."

~

Andrew heard the voices coming from Beth's room just as he got ready to knock on the door.

"You're not gripping hard enough." He didn't recognize the voice.

"Well, if you didn't jerk so hard I wouldn't keep letting go." He knew that one was Beth's. What was she doing in there?

Easing the door open quietly, he stared at the scene in front of him. His wife had her fists locked around one of the bedposts while some strange woman pulled at her back.

"What is going on here?"

They turned to look at him, bright stains of red splashing across their cheeks. Beth stood there in her underwear, while the young woman held tightly to some ribbons. That's when it dawned on him.

He felt heat fill his own cheeks as he stammered and backed out the door. "I'm so sorry, my dear. I didn't realize…um…I'll be…I mean, Edward and I will be waiting for you downstairs." And he beat a hasty retreat.

"That's the new husband, huh?" The young woman went back to her task.

"Yes." Beth's breath hitched as the strings around her rib cage tightened painfully. "Guess he's not used to seeing a woman getting into her corset."

"Probably not. Though by the looks of him, he's probably helped quite a few out of them." The young woman patted her back. "All done."

"Thank you," Beth said between gritted teeth.

"You'll have the slimmest waist I've seen. Just give yourself a minute to get used to the tightness and I promise you'll feel fine. Every lady I've helped has hated me when I left after tightening their strings the first time, but by the end of the day, they all wanted to take me home with them." She closed the door behind her as she left.

Beth still had a death grip on the bedpost. If she had relaxed her hold on it while the young woman was in the room, she just might have scratched her eyes out. *How dare she say that Andrew had been with a lot of women.* What did the woman know about her husband anyway?

Releasing her hold, she straightened up and took a couple of breaths. The woman was right. She could breathe quite easily. Crossing to her bed, Beth shook out her day dress before putting it on. But why did the maid have to voice the fear Beth had refused to acknowledge before.

Andrew was a handsome man. Of course he would've had his share of women. *Was that why he wanted a marriage of convenience? Did he have a woman in every town he visited and had plans of going back to them after this was all over?*

Although Alex had told her that Andrew had feelings for her she never really felt that when they were together. He was a gentleman all the time. Even when they found a few moments alone. He never tried to steal a kiss or declare his love for her.

The truth was Andrew had only married her now so he could protect her from Beau. That was why he seemed so adamant about not touching her unless she wanted him to. He planned on going back to his old life, and if she allowed him to sleep with her, she'd just be another notch on his bedpost.

Beth straightened her shoulders. Not if she could help it.

CHAPTER 10

Andrew picked at his food. He couldn't believe how stupid he'd acted when he'd realized what was going on. *Stammering, for God's sake.* He'd acted like a green little schoolboy.

Edward sat across the table from him, eating his meal in silence.

He probably wondered why Andrew had been so sullen, but what could he tell the boy? 'Sorry. Just saw my wife getting into her corset and it startled me.'

Nope. He'd never admit that one. Andrew was supposed to be a man of the world. After all, he was a Pinkerton agent. Little did everyone know how badly he was treated in the towns he went to, or how little time he had when he did visit them. Most of the time he was hunting someone. Socializing was out of the question. He knew most of the midwest states like the back of his hand and he could count how many cotillions he had attended on the same hand.

He looked up just as she came through the door. His chair scraped against the wooden floor as he stood up.

Edward followed suit.

"Good morning, Edward. I hope you slept well last night." Beth bestowed a smile that stunned the poor thing.

"Good morning, Andrew." She didn't even look him in the eye.

"Good morning, Beth." So what had put her in the tiff she was in? The fact he walked in on her? What did she suspect? He was her husband, and something like that was bound to happen. "Look, I'm sorry about earlier."

"That's quite all right. I'm sure you've seen that kind of thing before." Beth took the seat beside him.

Andrew sat back down. *Seen that kind of a thing before.* What did she think he was? *A Casanova? Of course!* That's why she was giving him such a cold shoulder. She was jealous. He couldn't stop the smile that creased his lips.

A spark of hope lit in his heart.

Beth ordered her breakfast and a coffee from the waiter.

Now he had to figure out how to get her to tell him she was jealous and why. He could tell from her posture she wouldn't dare do it here.

~

Beth tried to ignore the intense look Andrew was giving her, but she couldn't. Why was he looking at her like that anyway? And with that smile?

She took a sip of her coffee. Keeping her distance was the key. If she did that, then his devastating smiles wouldn't affect her.

Her breakfast arrived quickly. Beth ignored Andrew and turned her attention to the steaming-hot pancakes slathered with butter. In order to continue ignoring him, she gazed out the window as she chewed.

Well, wasn't that odd. There was a woman staring in the window. Beth took another bite of her pancakes.

Good Lord, the woman was waving at her.

Beth heard a chair scrape against the hardwood floor before she realized that Andrew was standing up.

"Excuse me for a minute." He slipped out of the room.

The woman in the window turned toward the right, then disappeared from view.

Andrew did come back pretty quickly. Unfortunately, he brought the woman she'd seen in the window with him. It wouldn't have been so bad if she was a little bit homely, but this woman was beautiful. The men's clothing she wore did nothing to hide her petite, shapely frame. To top it off, she had blonde hair that shone like gold.

"Sally Mason, I'd like you to meet Beth Leroux and Edward Cross."

"Nice to meet you." Sally took a chair from another table, turned it around, and sat down. Her soft honey velvet voice turned a few heads. "Aren't too many Lerouxs in the world. You related to Andrew?"

"I guess you could say that." Beth didn't know what to think of this woman. Her manly actions contradicted the feminine look about her, yet the men around them all made sure they got a good look.

"You guess? You either are or aren't."

Beth blinked at the woman's straightforwardness. Her papa wouldn't like this woman one bit.

"Beth is new to the Leroux name. We just got married."

"Married?" Sally laughed hard.

"It's true," said Andrew.

Sally stopped laughing. "You actually found someone who would put up with your shit? Sorry, ma'am."

Beth just stared at her. She knew she probably looked like an idiot, but she couldn't help herself. This woman flabbergasted her. Under different circumstances Beth decided she would really like Sally.

"Although I definitely look like one, I forget how to act like a lady most of the time."

"Why are you here, Sally?" Andrew interrupted.

"Heard you were looking for Beau Manning and thought I could help." The waiter appeared at her side. "Coffee, thanks."

Once the waiter left, she spoke again. "I've been hearing rumors about some big man gathering some of the true lowlifes near Kansas City. Don't know if it's your man, but figured the information could help you."

"Anything you can give me would be a great help."

The waiter returned and Sally thanked the man for her cup. Inhaling the heady aroma, she smiled. "Don't get coffee this good too often. Most of the time it's like rotgut."

"I thought that was bad alcohol," said Edward.

"Son, when you've been dealing with some of the people we've dealt with long enough, rotgut covers just about everything." She took a deep swallow. "Good coffee."

"So what can you tell me?" asked Andrew.

"There's a new man taking over the Smith gang."

"Never heard of them." Andrew took a sip of his coffee.

"They ain't that big. Mostly petty theft, horses, an occasional purse, cheating at cards, that type of thing. They tried to rob a couple of stage coaches about a year back but failed so miserably they stuck to what they could do." She took another drink of her coffee. "Anyway, about two months ago they started hitting bigger things and were successful at it. They robbed two banks. Held some rich girl for ransom and hit a Wells Fargo stagecoach for several thousand dollars.

"That's when the rumors started that they had a new leader who knew what to do. A lot of the petty thieves started drifting toward the town they were working out of. The robberies got bigger too. The last one was a train about three days ago. It carried the government payroll for the forts out west. The moment they made off with all that, they went on the Most Wanted list. The bosses want them caught. I'm thinking this could be tied up with your escapee. He was a mastermind at this type of thing."

Andrew nodded. "That would be right up Beau's alley. But you're not sure it's him."

"No. All I know about the guy is he's very charismatic. No one can really give a description of the man in charge."

"That fits too." Beth spoke up. She remembered what happened with Trey Dalton. "My friend and her husband had problems with Beau…they just didn't know it. Remember, Andrew? Trey blamed you for a lot of the things Beau was actually responsible for. Beau was very good at covering his tracks."

"Especially if he didn't want to be discovered." Andrew rubbed his chin. "I'll help you with this since it does sound like him, Sally, but it would sure ease my mind if I knew for sure it was Beau behind it all."

"Someone has already been sent to find out the man's identity. I should hear something soon, I hope." Sally finished the last of her coffee. "I'll be staying in town for a few days."

"The sheriff here has already told me I must be out of here by tomorrow. He doesn't cotton to Pinkerton men."

Beth glanced at Andrew. She was surprised he was going to do as the sheriff asked.

"Really? Wonder how he feels about Pinkerton women?"

"Sally, don't be causing no trouble."

"Now, Andrew, would I do that?" She acted offended.

"Yes."

"You know me too well." She laughed. "I'll catch up with you later. First I need to check into my room and then call on the sheriff."

"Sally."

"I'll behave." She stood up. "Beth, Edward, it was nice meeting you. We'll have time to talk a little more later."

Beth watched Sally saunter out the door.

"She works for the Pinkerton Agency too?" asked Edward.

"Yes. She's one of our best. Most men never suspect a woman to work for the agency." Andrew stood as well. "I'm going to check on our horses. You two stay here at the hotel until I get back."

~

Beth wanted to walk around a little. Being cooped up in her room was making her stir crazy. She thought about going to Edward's room and asking him to escort her outside, but decided it wasn't such a good idea. Andrew would be angry if they went against his wishes and he was horrible when he was angry.

Maybe if she wrote a note to her family. She sat down at the desk in her room and pulled out a piece of paper. What would she tell them anyway?

Dear Mom and Dad, I've been kidnapped by Andrew Leroux. We got married. Will explain everything later.

Without realizing it, she started to write to Alexandra. Of all the people she knew, Alex would understand what she was going through.

Several hours later she stifled a yawn. It felt good explaining everything she'd been through to Alexandra. At least it made her look at her situation in a better light. She folded the thick paper and put it in an envelope. She scratched out Alex's name and the town where she lived. Now Beth felt like taking a nap. She caught herself dozing at the table where she sat.

A soft rap against her door startled her awake.

"Beth?"

It was Andrew.

She got up from the desk and opened the door.

"The minister and his wife have invited us to dinner this evening. They found out we were newlyweds and want to offer their congratulations. I told them we'd be there around five."

"What time is it now?"

"Two." Andrew searched her face. "Are you feeling all right? You look a little tired."

"I was just thinking about a nap." She yawned.

"Why don't you go ahead and take one? I'll come back by in an hour to make sure you're awake. Will that give you enough time to get ready?"

"Yes, if you help me with my corset now and send that young woman up to help me dress for dinner this evening."

Andrew hesitated for a second before stepping into the room. Beth was already asleep on her feet or she wouldn't ask him for help. She hadn't gotten much sleep last night, but then neither did he. "I'll make sure she comes up when you need her."

Beth presented her back to Andrew to help her with all of the buttons on the back of her dress. He wondered how women were able to dress themselves. Once the buttons were opened, he undid the strings to her corset, then stepped back.

"Better?"

"Much. It's hard to sleep with this thing on." She curled up on her bed. "One hour should be enough."

She was asleep before her head hit the pillow.

Andrew watched her for a few minutes. Her features were so soft now. Keeping his distance was getting harder, and knowing they were married made it damn near impossible. The urge to lie down beside her pushed at him, and seeing her look so sweet in repose made that urge irresistible.

But he couldn't. He had a job to do and a promise to keep.

CHAPTER 11

Beth came down the stairs in a new, store-bought dress. At first, she'd thought of wearing one of her older ones because some were designed for evening wear, then decided against it. How many of these ladies had dresses like that? She hadn't noticed a lot of silk on anyone, except of course, for the ladies who worked in the saloon.

She smoothed the gingham material before rounding the corner to the parlor where Andrew waited for her.

Her forehead puckered into a frown when she saw Andrew talking to some strange woman. *Another Pinkerton agent? Were they all women? Pretty women?*

As she walked closer, her frustration grew. The woman was not only pretty, but wore a pale mauve silk dress that accented her beauty perfectly. Suddenly, Beth felt as frumpy as a cow, but before she could turn around and leave Andrew spotted her. She had to approach them. Holding her head high, as her mama had taught her to do, Beth stepped toward them, hoping she showed more grace and poise than she felt.

Andrew stood up, offered his hand to the vision in mauve and helped her to her feet.

Now or never. She steeled her spine and walked over to them.

"Beth, you look lovely in that dress. It's perfect for supper with the minister and his wife." It was Sally in the silk confection. "And the flowers are a nice touch."

"And you." Beth glanced down at her hand. In her shock she had completely forgotten about the flowers. "I didn't even recognize you. That is a lovely gown."

"I do clean up real nice, don't I? I'm joining the sheriff for supper this evening. Thought I'd dress for the occasion." Sally picked up her parasol. "Well, guess I'll mosey on over to the sheriff's office and see if he's ready."

"Shouldn't you wait for him to come and get you?" asked Beth.

"I never wait for any man. Andrew knows that. The sheriff should too. Besides, I can't wait to see his face when I show up in this." She laughed. "He wasn't sure I even owned a dress. This ought to prove I do."

Once Sally left, Beth felt the heat of Andrew's gaze. Looking up at him, she caught herself staring at the little green flecks in his clear amber eyes.

"You ready to go?" The rumble of his voice startled her back to reality.

"Yes."

He escorted her to the little white house behind the church. The minister and his wife stood outside on the porch waiting for them.

"Mr. and Mrs. Leroux, thank you so much for coming to supper. Please come in." The minister ushered them into the house.

"Thank you for inviting us, Minister," said Beth. She couldn't remember the man's name.

"Please, call me Mike. This is my lovely wife, Deborah."

"How do you do." Deborah took Beth's hand in hers. "Supper is almost ready, but we're waiting for another guest."

"Yes," said Mike. "We try to keep in touch with our flock. So those who don't invite us to supper, we invite here. They should be along any minute. Then we can sit down to eat."

Deborah glanced out the window. "Dear, our other guests have arrived."

"Good, good." Mike stepped out on the porch with Deborah right behind him.

"Do you think they're like this all the time?" asked Beth softly. She placed the bouquet of flowers in a vase on the table. Deborah had some flowers already in it, but there was plenty of room for hers as well.

"Sure seems like it." Andrew frowned when he saw who the other guest was.

Beth glanced out the window and her heart sank. The sheriff and Sally stood there talking to the minister and his wife. She felt like mooing. For some reason, every time she saw Sally this evening Beth kept seeing herself as a cow. A sigh escaped her.

Andrew leaned closer to her. "I promise not to pick a fight with the sheriff." He must have misinterpreted her sigh, which was a good thing, because she didn't want to explain the real reason she sighed.

The sheriff stepped one foot in the door and stopped dead in his tracks. "Mike, you didn't say you would be entertaining other guests."

"I know, Matthew. If I had, you would've demanded to know who it would be and refused to come, and that would've defeated the whole reason for this supper." Mike pushed past Matt to step between him and Andrew. "You know news travels fast in this town and it's been filled with the Pinkerton agent, the shootout and how you were forcing the man who stopped the outlaw out of town right after he got married."

"I invited the two of you here to give you a chance to talk like civilized people. In my house. You're not on duty, Sheriff. Neither are you, Mr. Leroux. You are on the same side of the law, even if you don't approve of the way the Pinkerton Agency does things, Matthew. But you won't look past that shiny badge of yours to realize that Andrew Leroux needs your help."

"We thought having you here for supper would be neutral ground for you and hope you'll talk. Help each other," added Deborah. "So if the ladies will help me, we'll get the food on the table."

Beth followed behind Deborah like a cow in tow. Sally, thank goodness, walked behind Beth. She didn't think she could handle having Sally walk in front of her. She'd have to stare at that pretty, form-fitting dress if she had.

Supper was placed on the table in no time. Everyone took his or her seat. Mike said grace, and then they started to load their plates without a word. They ate in silence too. It was so thick Beth was sure she could cut it with a knife.

"So, Beth…It is all right if I call you Beth, isn't it?" asked Deborah.

She nodded as she chewed her food.

"Where are you from?"

"Jennings. It's a small town near New Orleans."

"Is that where you met Mr. Leroux?"

"Deborah," Mike admonished.

Deborah gave her husband a level stare. "No one else is talking, and I'm tired of hearing the silverware clanking against the plates."

"It's all right," said Beth. "Andrew and I grew up together."

"That right, Leroux?" asked Sally. "And here I thought you came out a grown man."

"We grew up in the same town." Andrew glared at Sally who seemed to enjoy watching him squirm.

"What was he like as a little boy?" asked Sally.

"Papa called him and his friends trouble. Andrew liked putting frogs down girls' dresses." Beth sipped at the tall glass of water in front of her.

"I only did that because Trey and Beau dared me."

Just the mention of Beau's name quieted everyone down.

"What's the matter?" asked Deborah.

"Beau is the one I'm looking for." Andrew set his fork down on his plate. "Beau Manning was arrested several months ago for many crimes including kidnapping Beth and a friend of hers, murder, and attempted murder. He escaped about two months ago, vowing to get even with everyone involved in his capture. I believe he is out in this area now."

"We've heard rumors of a new man working near here, gathering up a small army and wreaking havoc across two states," added Sally.

"That's why I'm here, Sheriff. Pinkerton agents are gathering together to capture this man. I don't know how many there will be, but I've been notified everyone in this area will be at my disposal to go after Beau."

"I haven't heard of a Beau Manning." Matt sat back in his chair.

"He's been known to go by several aliases. The last one he used was Beaumont." Andrew leaned his elbows on the table. "He's very charismatic. Stands about six foot two. Blond hair, blue eyes, and a Southern gentleman accent."

"He hasn't passed through my town. I think I'd remember someone like that. But I have noticed we've had a lot more drifters passing through. Bar fights have increased with these strangers too." The sheriff scratched his chin. "What sort of men you think he's gathering?"

"The worst. Smart, ruthless, and ones that'll do whatever he asks."

"Yep. That fits a lot of them. Not too many have been very talkative when I've thrown them in jail for the night. A few tried to get out of spending the night by saying they were just passing through to Jefferson City, and if I let them go, they'd head on out right then and there." Matthew watched Andrew's face. "Some I let go. Others I made stay."

"Any threaten to come back?"

"One or two, but I figured it was just the whiskey talking."

"Don't be so sure," said Andrew. "If Beau is doing what I think he plans, everything in a two-hundred-mile radius of his hideout he'll figure will be his for the taking."

"Over my dead body." Matt crossed his arms of his chest.

"That's probably what he's hoping for." Andrew paused for a moment. "As Beaumont, he caused trouble for a lot of the southeast states. Although based in New Orleans, he had a long reach. He's also very good at covering his tracks. A lot of men willingly took the fall for him. He drove me crazy." Andrew ran his hand through his hair. "I'd corner Beaumont, only to find out that the man I caught wasn't Beaumont at all but one of his generals. We played this game of cat and mouse for years."

"How ever did you catch him?" asked Deborah.

"Our friend Trey." He looked over at Beth. "Trey was getting married to a woman Beau Manning fancied for himself. Because of his desire to have the woman, he became sloppy."

Beth wondered why he glazed over the details of Beau's capture.

"He won't get sloppy like that again." Andrew waited.

The clock on the mantel ticked the minutes by.

"I'll need a picture of what he looks like, and you'll have to keep me up to date on what you learned."

"Thank you, Matthew." Andrew smiled. "I'll make sure you have that before we leave tomorrow."

"You're leaving?" Mike glanced from Andrew to Matt.

"Yes. The sheriff told just about the whole town he wanted me out of here, so some might get suspicious if I were to suddenly stay here and the sheriff seemed all right with it."

"I could throw you in jail." Matt smiled. "Just to make it look good."

"No, thank you." Andrew laughed. "I can't look for Beau from a jail cell anyway."

"Well, what about your wife? You don't plan on taking her with you, do you?" asked Deborah.

"Yes, I do." He looked at Beth, noticing she'd held her breath while she waited to see what he'd say. She would probably hightail it to her aunt's if he let her out of his sight for one minute. "The safest place she could be would be with me. Beau won't come after me until he's good and ready."

~

The cool evening air danced across Beth's skin as they headed back to the hotel.

"How can you be so sure Beau won't come after us right away?" Beth couldn't understand why Andrew was so adamant about that.

Just about everyone at supper had tried to convince him to leave Beth there while he went after Beau, but he kept telling them no. In fact, the only person who didn't say anything about Andrew's decision was Sally.

Andrew patted the hand she had laid across his arm. "You remember this past summer? When Trey and Alexandra were planning their wedding? Beau did everything he could to break them up before they married. It wasn't until he thought he could get away with it that he so boldly kidnapped Alexandra from her own house. He'll do the same thing this time."

"But he did kidnap Alexandra before that. She just got away."

"I honestly don't think that was his idea. Remember, she didn't know who kidnapped her right away and probably wouldn't have figured it out if she hadn't seen Beau at the hideout. I think since she was out on her own that one time, one of his generals decided to take advantage of it. They'd been watching the house for weeks by then."

"True. She saw him through the cracks in the ceiling of the cellar they stuck her in. Beau didn't even know she had seen him." Beth walked along beside him quietly for a few moments. "So you think they would've kept her there until Beau could do away with Trey? Then he'd act like he was the one who saved her?"

"And she'd be so grateful she would've probably ended up married to him, which was what he wanted. Plus he would've inherited Trey's land."

"And that's what he really wanted. I remember his little speech when he had us tied up. He was going to force Alex to marry him so he could get his hands on Trey's lands. And if he got tired of her, he could kill her off and still control what he thought he deserved." Beth shuddered.

"That's why I want you to go with me. If he knew you were here by yourself, he'd come after you. Use you as a pawn to draw me in."

"He can't possibly know I'm here. I'm sure I'd be safe at my aunt's house." She stopped walking. "Then you wouldn't have to worry about me."

"I'd worry about you more if you weren't with me." Andrew touched her cheek. "Not knowing if you were safe would scare the hell out of me, Beth. I wouldn't be able to do my job."

"So I have to travel with you?"

"Yes. But at least you'll have some female companionship now." Andrew took her hand and started walking again. "Sally has agreed to travel with us."

Oh, wonderful. Just what Beth wanted. Another woman traveling with them and one who had a lot more in common than she did with Andrew. Could it get any worse?

CHAPTER 12

Beth sat in the wagon next to Edward, while Andrew and Sally scouted ahead. Glumly, she looked about, wondering how she'd gotten herself into this mess. She was married to a man who wouldn't touch her. Not that she really wanted him to. It was just the principle of the thing.

Plus, she also found herself surrounded by people who thought they knew best. She felt like a trapped animal. A cow to be exact, and until Sally went on to other things, she'd probably continue to feel that way.

Sally had once again donned her pants and cowboy hat, while Beth sat primly on the wagon bench, yearning for the freedom she had been denied.

It just wasn't fair.

"Do you know where we're going?" she asked Edward.

"No, Mrs. Leroux."

That sounded so strange. *Mrs. Leroux*. She didn't really feel married. But then she hadn't really been a wife that long, and it was in name only. Beth stared at the small gold ring on her left hand. Sunlight glinted off of it. A few words spoken and a ring on her finger had changed her life. How much was the question.

~

"Sure don't understand you, Leroux." Sally tipped her hat back on her head. "Thought you'd never get married."

"Things change."

"True. Still, you're a loner. How is that wife going to fit into your way of life?"

Andrew didn't answer her. It was none of her business anyway.

Luckily, Sally changed the subject. "Where did you tell Matthew to contact us?"

"I told him we're going to head for Jefferson City first, then on to Kansas City. I also want to follow the railroad and stop in some of the smaller towns. Maybe we'll hear something."

"This Manning fellow wouldn't go to a big city like that, would he?"

"He wasn't that far from New Orleans with his last gang. Maybe a day's travel."

"What makes you think he's in one of those two cities?"

"A dead man and Beth." Andrew pulled his hat up and wiped his brow. "I overheard a potential kidnapper send a telegram to Jefferson City and I'm pretty sure he worked for Beau. Plus Beth received a telegram from a sick aunt in Wichita asking her to come visit. The next biggest town is Kansas City."

"You think he sent the telegram to Beth?"

"I don't know what to think, but it's one of the reasons I don't want her out of my sight."

"Okay, I get Jefferson City, but not Kansas City. Sounds like wishful thinking. Lots of people have aunts, sick and healthy." Sally paced her horse with his. "It could have been a real aunt that sent that telegram."

"Beth got on the train in New Orleans and almost immediately she got off it because she was afraid. She noticed a man watching her and decided to follow her instincts and duck off the train rather than try to ignore him. He ended up dead at my feet when he tried to kidnap her again a couple days ago. He was the same man who sent the telegram."

"She's got good instincts." Sally looked over at him. "Did you recognize him?"

"No. If he worked for Beau, he was new. And he had to be a flunky. He made too many stupid mistakes."

"The last one was being on the wrong end of your gun."

"I didn't shoot him."

Sally looked up at him in surprise.

"Another agent. Met him three days ago. He's out scouting to see what he can learn."

"He must be pretty fast to outshoot you."

Andrew shrugged. "I'm just glad he's on our side."

Sally nodded.

"Anyway, we're going to Loose Creek and spend the night. Then we'll head for Jefferson City."

"Loose Creek, I understand. It's nice and small, but Jefferson City? I wouldn't call that small." She leaned forward and rubbed her horse's neck. "You honestly think you'll find Beau there?"

"I don't know what we'll find but I have to go and look."

"And what about your wife?" Sally looked back at the small wagon. "It'll be hard to protect her in a city that size."

"She'll do what I tell her."

Sally snorted. "Sure can tell you haven't been married very long."

"And what is that supposed to mean?"

"Nothing." She smiled at him. "Nothing at all."

Sally slowed her horse down so the wagon could catch up. Beth sat primly on the bench, a downcast look etched across her features. "Mrs. Leroux, I thought you'd like to go for a ride. You know, stretch your legs a little."

"I'd love that." Beth turned to Edward. "Stop the wagon, please."

"But we're already way behind Andrew, ma'am."

"So a few more minutes won't hurt. I promise to have the horse saddled in five minutes." Beth leaped down from the wagon and headed back to the extra horse tied to the back of the buckboard.

Crooning to it softly, she rubbed its neck, allowing the horse to get used to her scent before she placed the blanket, saddle and tack needed to ride. She swung up in the saddle quickly, adjusted her bonnet, and took off. It felt good to feel the wind on her face. The past few hours had been awful. Sitting in the wagon, she realized how out of place she was. She was nothing more than an extra piece of baggage that slowed down Andrew and Sally. If it weren't for her, they'd probably would've already caught up with Beau.

Andrew keeping her at his side just didn't make sense. Wouldn't she be safer someplace where Beau would never expect her to be? Her thoughts kept going over that fact.

"You're sure deep in thought."

She almost fell out of the saddle at the sound of Sally's voice.

"Didn't mean to startle you."

"You didn't. I mean, it's okay." Beth didn't know what to say to her.

"Sure is pretty out here."

Beth looked around. Nothing but wide-open spaces. The vast openness should've had a calming effect. Yet she found her eyes kept straying ahead to Andrew. He might be able to ignore her, but she couldn't do the same thing. He dominated her thoughts, blocking out the relaxation she should have felt out here in the wilderness.

"You miss your home?" Sally asked.

"Not really." She did miss her family, but liked being out on her own. If you call being watched over like a hawk on your own.

"Um-hum." Sally rode beside her.

"How do you know Andrew?" Beth didn't realize she had said the question out loud until she heard her own voice.

"Met him several years ago. I was engaged to be married to a nice man, or so I thought. Turned out he was wanted in several states for murder. He liked to marry rich debutantes, and then after a year or so, he'd kill them off and inherit their money and property."

"Didn't their families get upset?" asked Beth.

"He was smarter than that and only dated women who had no family. You know, the last survivor of the family, so no questions were ever asked. Until he married a young woman who left a letter telling her friends what she feared. When she turned up dead, someone contacted the Pinkerton Agency and Andrew was put on the case. I was lucky. He caught up with my fiancé before we were married."

"Then how did you become an agent too?"

"I helped Andrew set my fiancé up. Once he was caught, I found I rather liked the adventure so signed up. Now don't get me wrong...it's not all that glamorous. There's a lot of danger involved, but I have a knack for it."

"You're a debutante?" Beth couldn't believe it.

"Couldn't tell by looking at me, huh? This—" She gestured at her clothing. "—throws people off. One day I can be a school marm, the next some high society lady, the next just a poor ol' cowpolk."

"When do you get to be you?"

"I don't. Not anymore." Sally paused. "Once you get into this way of life, it's hard to get out. You can never retire because you never know when someone is going to come looking for you for killing a loved one."

"Do you miss your old life?"

"No. I wasn't much on the high society type of life. It bored me."

Beth felt the same way about her life back home. Helping her father out in the store every day was monotonous. All she ever did was sweep the floor, help customers, and add up figures at the end of the day. She wanted more out of life than that.

"So what brought you out here?"

Beth smiled. "Oh, I'm sure Andrew has told you already."

"That man can be quite tight-lipped when he wants to be. He didn't explain everything." Sally pushed her hat back on her head. "You know how men can be."

Beth nodded. She looked over at Sally. How much could she trust the woman? Did she want to tell her that she and Andrew only married so people wouldn't talk?

"I was on my way to visit my aunt when I ran into Andrew on the train."

"That's it?" Sally laughed. "You're even more tight-lipped than he is."

"Why's that?" asked a deep husky voice.

Andrew.

Sally gave him a brilliant smile before she headed back to the wagon, leaving Andrew and Beth alone.

"You could've told me you wanted to ride."

"How? You never came back to check on me." Beth tugged on her bonnet. It had seen better days, but it was the only thing she had to cover her face from the unyielding rays of the sun.

"I'm sorry about that." He brought his horse even with hers as they rode along. "We'll be in Loose Creek in a couple of hours. Would you like to ride with me?"

"Yes." She smiled. *Anything except riding in that wagon.*

~

Beth looked out the window of the hotel room and watched the sun set. Her ride with Andrew had been wonderful. No terse words or angry retorts. In fact, the last few days had been that way. It was as if Andrew had turned over a new leaf.

She wasn't quite sure what to make of it. Andrew always had a reason when he did something. Not knowing the reason he was being nice bothered her. *What if it was all a ploy?* His way of keeping her from her aunt's?

Beth had to admit, though, she liked the way he was treating her these days. Their constant bickering had really worked on her nerves, keeping her constantly on edge.

Sally was still downstairs finishing a cup of coffee. She had mentioned something about trying to pick up a little gossip from the local folk.

Beth sighed. Something she was doing a lot lately. Just as she was about to turn from the window she noticed movement below. The young woman who walked briskly across the dirt-packed road was Sally. A few moments later, Beth saw someone following her. Beth held her breath. She'd know that gait anywhere. Andrew.

Why was Andrew following Sally?

Seconds ticked by as she debated about what she should do. Then she grabbed her wrap and headed down the stairs.

Twilight had already passed when Beth made it outside. So had several precious moments. *Where did they go?* She saw them head toward the mercantile. Since lights were still on there she assumed the store was still open. Maybe they were inside stocking up on supplies, except that was Edward's duty. *Unless Andrew needed something he didn't trust Edward to get.*

Beth shook her head. Here she was trying to second-guess Andrew. She stepped onto the dirt road and dashed across the street to the safety of the boardwalk there. Keeping her pace slow and even, hoping a lone woman out after dark wouldn't attract too much attention, she walked down toward the mercantile. Just as she reached the doors, the lights went out.

Oh, great. Now what?

She walked past the now-darkened store. Her heels banged against the wood as she moved. Hairs on the back of her neck stood up. A quick glance behind told her no one was following her. Walking a little quicker, she reached the end of the boardwalk and stepped down.

Sounds from a nearby alley caught her ear. Probably the people from the store. Not everyone lived above their workplace. Her nerves tightened when she realized the sounds in the alley were getting closer. She couldn't be caught like this. A darkened corner beckoned.

Seconds ticked by. The less noise she made the better. Deciding to remove her shoes, she hopped on one foot as she tried to make her way to the boardwalk and pull her ankle-length boots off at the same time. Damn all the laces on her shoes. She ended up wrenching them off her feet, not caring if she did any damage in order to be quieter.

Beth tiptoed up against the wall, her mangled boots in her hands. Just as the noises cleared the alleyway, she ducked back into the shadows. Her heart beat loudly in her chest. Why didn't she stay in her room like she was supposed to?

Three men emerged from the alley. Big men. Carrying rifles as large as they were. What were they going to do with those? They moved toward the hotel as one.

Oh, dear. Beth prayed they were just going for a bite to eat.

One of the three moved out in front of the other two and yelled into the night, "We know you got a Pinkerton man in there. Send him out and everyone else will be left alone."

But Andrew wasn't in there.

She stepped forward, knowing she had to tell these men Andrew wasn't there. Protecting the people in the hotel was her only thought.

Hairs on the back of her neck rose again when she sensed movement behind her. She wasn't alone. Before she could scream, a hand snaked its way across her mouth while another wrapped itself around her waist and pulled her back into the darkness.

CHAPTER 13

Her whole body shook. Tears sprang up in her eyes. She didn't want to die now.

"What the hell are you doing out here?" a deep masculine voice growled.

"Andrew." Beth felt tears spill down her cheeks, but these were from relief.

Andrew must have felt them on his hand because his whole manner changed. "Are you all right?" He released her mouth as he cradled her against him.

"Yes." She hiccupped. "Considering I thought I was going to die a few seconds ago. What are you doing hiding in this doorway?"

"I just asked you the same question."

"I came looking for you." Thank goodness she couldn't see his face because she felt his body stiffen.

"That was a very stupid thing to do." Andrew eased his grip around her waist. "But I'm glad you did. Knowing you, you would've blundered out of the hotel to tell them I wasn't there and they would've captured you."

"Who are they?"

"I don't know." Andrew stopped whispering when the door to the hotel opened.

The proprietor stepped out on the street. "We don't have a Pinkerton man here. Go home."

One of the men leveled his gun and shot the dirt just inches from the proprietor's feet.

"We know he's staying here. If you want to live you'll turn him over right now."

Another shot rang in the night. The rifle flew out of the shooter's hand.

"Boys, this here is a nice, quiet town and I aim to keep it that way. You can either go home like Sam suggested, or you can talk to Old Bessy here." Beth noticed the shiny shield on the sheriff as he patted his gun. "Bessy hasn't had a chance to talk in a long while, and I know she's just itching to get to know you boys a lot better. So what's it gonna be?"

The three men grumbled among themselves.

Beth felt her breath catch in her throat as she watched one of the other men bring his rifle up and leveled it at the sheriff's chest.

The repeat of Old Bessy filled the night.

The man screamed as a bullet tore through his shoulder, rendering his shooting arm useless.

"Two down and one to go," said the sheriff.

"We're leaving, but you make sure that Pinkerton man knows we were here. We ain't finished with him yet," one of the men said with a defiant tone.

"I'll be sure to do that." The sheriff stood in the middle of the street, Old Bessy trained on the three men as they made their way out of town.

"Okay, everyone. Show's over. Go on home now." The sheriff waited for the street to clear before he headed over toward Andrew and Beth.

"Leroux, you really got to get a better group of friends."

Beth wondered how the sheriff knew they were hiding there as Andrew led her out into the street.

"Who you hunting?" asked the sheriff.

"Beau Manning."

"Never heard of him." The sheriff draped Old Bessy over one arm as he offered his hand.

"He's from New Orleans." Andrew took the hand and shook it. "How did you know I was in town? I thought I kept a low profile."

"Obviously not low enough," the sheriff said as he glanced back down the street. "Is Manning that Beaumont you were after when you came through here a while ago?"

"Yep. He escaped a couple of months back."

"Watch your back. Those men didn't come here to dance with you."

"No. But I'm sure they're not too happy with you either."

"I can take care of myself. You know that."

"Thanks, Dan."

"I'll take that thanks when you leave town tomorrow. Don't want my people frightened because of you."

"Promise. We'll be out by daybreak."

"Good."

Andrew led Beth back to the hotel in silence.

"Well, I must say that was the strangest conversation I ever heard."

Andrew laughed. "That's pretty normal for Dan."

Once they were in their room, he spun her around. "You never told me why you were out there this evening."

"Yes, I did."

"Why?"

A faint blush stained her cheeks. "Because I saw Sally leave the hotel and you seemed to be hot on her heels."

"Jealous?"

"Of course not. I...I just wanted to know what you two were up to. That's all."

"You are jealous."

Her blush got deeper. She could feel the heat of it all the way to her hairline. "What did happen to Sally anyway?"

"I don't know." Andrew released the grip he had on her. "I didn't realize she left before me. I thought she was in the dining room with you."

"But she stayed downstairs to finish her coffee when we finished dinner. Didn't she join you?"

"No. I went next door to speak to the sheriff when you left."

Beth bit her lip.

"What?" asked Andrew.

"Well, I haven't seen Sally come back." Beth placed a hand on his arm. "What if she's hurt?"

Andrew smiled bitterly. Just like his wife. Beth always saw the good in everyone. She was wondering about Sally's health while he questioned her loyalty. It was a little too strange that Sally happened to be out of the hotel when he would have needed her most. Luckily, the sheriff was an old friend and not afraid of his shadow or in the pocket of some politician.

"Maybe you just missed her when you came out here looking for me."

She felt the blush return. Just the mention of them sharing a room made the butterflies in her stomach take flight. Andrew didn't allow her to argue over the room situation earlier. A married couple shared a room and they had to keep up appearances.

The heat of his arm under her hand sent tingles up and down her spine.

"Why don't we go to see if Edward knows where she is."

Beth nodded and followed him into the hall.

Edward popped his head out the door of his room next to theirs when Andrew knocked.

"Everything all right?"

"Sally around?" asked Andrew.

"Yep. Heard her banging around in her room a minute ago."

"Good." Andrew turned back to their room and pushed the door open for Beth to go in. "Go and get Sally. We need to talk."

A few minutes later, they heard a knock on their door.

Andrew opened it and found Edward and Sally standing there. "Come in."

Sally sauntered into the room and sat on the bed that dominated the room. Beth stood by the armoire. Edward took the chair by the small desk.

"It seems an awful lot of people know where we are and I don't like it."

"What happened?" asked Sally.

"Didn't you hear the commotion outside?" asked Edward. "Three men as big as mountains came looking for Andrew."

"I went to visit some friends and just got back," Sally explained.

Andrew shot her a strange glare.

"I do have friends, Andrew. They might be few and far between because of the type of work we do, but I try to see them when I can."

"Dan's wife."

"Yes." Sally smiled. "She and I have corresponded when she knew where I was staying. I didn't think it'd be right for me to be in town and not stop by."

"We're leaving in the morning. I promised Dan we'd be out of here by the crack of dawn." Andrew ran a hand through his hair. "But from this point on, I think we should know where each other is going. Beth ended up out there in the thick of it because she didn't know where either of us were."

Sally nodded. "So what did these men look like?"

"Big. One was blond, the other two brunet," said Andrew. "I noticed one of them had a scar across one cheek."

Beth looked at him in surprise. It had been too dark for her to notice a scar.

"All about the same height?"

"Yeah. They didn't strike me as the most intelligent men, but they definitely worked as a team. Dan disabled two of them and all three took off."

"That sounds like the Butler boys." Sally pulled one leg up under her. "Triplets and three of the meanest men around."

"Are they from around here?"

"A couple of towns over. So close enough."

"How did they know I was here?" Andrew questioned.

"Did they ask for you by name?"

"No," Edward piped up. "They just knew a Pinkerton man was in town."

"Could they have found out about your telegram?" asked Beth. "Maybe they overheard someone mention talking about a Pinkerton man gathering agents in the area and they just figured out that person could be here. After all, you did let the last sheriff know we were headed toward Kansas City."

Andrew looked at his wife. Sometimes he forgot just how smart she was. Beth had an excellent point.

"All right. They could've made a lucky guess. But if we continue to run into people calling me out in every town we stop in, we won't be able to stay in any after a while."

Another knock on the door startled them all. Andrew drew his gun before answering the door.

A pair of frightened eyes stared back at the gun.

"A—a telegram ca—came for you." The young boy thrust the envelope at him before dashing down the stairs at a breakneck speed.

Andrew chuckled silently. He didn't mean to frighten the poor kid, but after this evening, he didn't want to take any chances.

He tore into the envelope and pulled out the message.

"Headquarters has contacted several agents. Three are on their way here now. According to this, they should catch up with us just about the time we reach Jefferson City. I know two of the three men." Andrew looked up from the piece of paper and glanced at Sally. "Ever heard of James Pool?"

"Can't say I have, but I'd have to see him first. I could've met him while he was using an alias."

"Well, let's all get some sleep. Daybreak will get here real quick."

Sally nodded before rising and heading for the door.

"Sure am glad nothing happened to you out there tonight." Edward pushed against the arms of the chair he sat in and stood as well. "Never felt my heart pound so hard in my life."

"Edward." Andrew put his arm around the young man and guided him toward the door. "That is something you'll have to get used to if you want to do this. Remember how we met?"

Edward ducked his head in shame. "Yeah, not one of my more brilliant moves."

Andrew couldn't argue with that. "But what a unique way to meet new friends."

"Sure. You can always get a friend when you point a gun at them." Edward smiled. "But not too many will stick around once you let that gun down."

"But I did."

"Yes, you did."

"And I dragged you into a very dangerous situation."

"No." Edward looked up into Andrew's face. "I would've followed you if you hadn't taken me along. But I think you knew that."

"I did suspect it, but I also didn't think I'd be hunted the way I've been. This might get to be too dangerous."

"You can't get rid of me now. I'm not afraid."

"You're one of the bravest men I've met. You did approach me with a gun, but were smart enough to know what you tried to do was wrong."

"But—" Edward said to him.

"But you're not seasoned enough to keep yourself from getting killed."

"Who says? I should've been killed with my ma and pa, but I escaped. They died six months ago, and I've been on my own since. I'm not as green as you think."

"Edward, let me put it to you this way. I couldn't live with myself if you got killed because of me." Andrew had heard the hurt in the young man's voice. "Promise me, if we get into a situation where you have a chance to get away, you will, even if you're the only one who does. Someone must carry on in case we don't stop Beau Manning, and I'm counting on you to do it."

"Yes, sir." There was that hero worship look in his eyes again. "But I know you won't fail."

Andrew watched Edward walk to his room. He wished he had the confidence Edward did.

Once the boy's door closed, Andrew closed his own and turned toward Beth. Her eyes looked even larger in her face. All her color had drained too. Poor thing was scared to death.

She stood rooted to the floor, looking like she was ready to faint.

"Beth, nothing will happen to you."

"But what about you? You're willing to die."

"No, Beth." He stepped up to her and brushed his knuckles against her cheek. "I don't want to die, but I'll do whatever it takes to stop Beau."

Beth searched his face before wrapping herself around him and holding him close. She mumbled something he couldn't hear.

"It's getting late." Although he loved the feel of her body pressed against his, they needed to get to bed.

She bobbed her head when she stepped back.

"We need to get some sleep." He really didn't want to spend another night on the floor, but how could he convince her to share the bed? How could he ignore her soft presence if they did share it?

She nodded at him woodenly. "You..." She cleared her throat. "Don't sleep on the floor."

"Are you sure?

She nodded again.

He wanted to laugh. Her head bobbed up and down like a marionette puppet.

He kept eye contact with her as he took off his vest. She swallowed hard as he undid the cuffs of his shirt.

"Shouldn't you get dressed for bed?"

"I—Yes." She darted to her trunk and pulled out a gown before she looked back at him, holding it in front of her like a shield.

"The dressing screen is over there." He pointed behind her.

Beth glanced over at the screen before looking at him again. Without saying a word, she slipped behind it.

Andrew pulled his shirt off.

A soft thump forced him to look over where Beth was. Her dress was now draped over the screen. He could imagine what she looked like standing there in her petticoat and chemise.

His saddlebags sat against the wall. Perhaps if he put on a pair of long johns, she wouldn't feel so skittish. He grabbed his only pair. After shedding his pants he stepped into the long johns, pulled them up and buttoned them closed.

Her petticoats now hung on top of her dress. He saw a flash of white as she lifted the nightgown over her head and allowed it to drop over her body.

Andrew drew back the covers and sat down. Then he waited. And waited.

"Beth, are you finished dressing?"

"Yes." Her voice came hesitantly from behind the screen.

"Then come on out and let's go to bed." Andrew knew that didn't sound right. "Would you like me to turn the lantern down?"

She stepped from behind the screen. Her long white cotton gown swept the floor. The fear in her eyes softened a little when she realized he wasn't lying naked in the bed.

"Come to bed now, darling. I promise not to bite." He patted the side of the bed he had turned down for her.

Beth stood there staring at him. He could see she was at war with herself through her eyes.

She must have made some sort of decision because she padded slowly to the bed. Sitting down on the edge, after a slight hesitation, she swung her legs into the bed, then pulled the covers up to her chin.

Andrew leaned toward the lantern. After blowing it out, he turned on his side, away from her, and settled down in the bed.

"Good night, Beth."

He felt her shift in the bed as she settled down too. Andrew also thought he heard a sigh of relief when she whispered good night back to him.

CHAPTER 14

Sleep took a long time to come to him. Andrew could hear Beth's soft breathing as she fell into a deep slumber. The subtle fragrance she wore teased his senses, making him want something he shouldn't. He finally fell into a fitful sleep, but it was the soft slide of a leg across his that jerked him back awake.

In her sleep, Beth had abandoned the edge of the bed she had clung to and had sought out his body heat. Now she was draped across him like a piece of silk, one thigh on top of his two. Just the feel of her weight on him had him as hard as a rock. It was downright painful too.

He was going to push her off and hope she would just curl up against him, but his hand contacted the bare flesh of her knee and froze.

Oh, God.

He couldn't move his hand off her leg. Gently, he slid his hand up her thigh. Andrew never realized how long her legs were; her skin soft as rose petals. His breathing became constricted when he realized her gown was hiked up to her hip.

Yet, he couldn't stop himself from exploring. The curve of her buttock, the flair of her hip, the smoothness of her leg. He prayed she didn't wake during this or he'd have a hard time explaining why he was taking such liberties with her body. Especially when he'd promised he wouldn't.

~

It felt like soft butterfly kisses against her skin. Beth smiled and snuggled against the warmth that surrounded her. Her consciousness floated slowly up to wakefulness. The soft sliding sensation up and down her leg and hip lulled her into a languid feeling. Like a cat that found the perfect spot in the sun, she wanted to purr her contentment.

The warmth she propped her head on was a lot harder than her pillow should be. She lifted her head to try to find a more comfortable spot. Beth blinked, then froze, realizing what she rested her head on.

And what caused the butterfly kisses on her leg.

Her first thought was to leap off the bed as quickly as she could, but what if Andrew was asleep. He could be caressing her unconsciously and she had to admit that it did feel good against her skin.

The beat of his heart picked up when she slid her hand up his chest to place it under her cheek. Did she cause that?

Andrew's hand still rested on her hip. Delicious tingles from that contact shot up and down her body.

She slid her leg down his a little and felt the beat of his heart quicken again. Beth slid her leg up, stopping when she felt the solid length of him beneath her thigh.

Heat from him seared her through his long johns. If he affected her this much with clothes on, she wondered what it would feel like if it were skin against skin.

A strange fluttering sensation started in the pit of her belly, spiraling upward, making every nerve snap alive. She wanted more. Of what she wasn't sure, but the emotions she felt were wonderful and she didn't want them to end.

Her hand slid from under her cheek, down across Andrew's chest and came to rest on his lower abdomen. Just a few more inches and she would be touching the heat that fascinated her so.

Andrew couldn't breathe. If her hand inched any closer he would explode.

Was she awake? No. She couldn't be. Beth would never touch him this way if she were.

He felt her hand flex against his abdomen and sweat beads broke out across his brow.

"Fire!"

He heard the words shouted from out in the hallway but didn't pay any attention to them. More voices sent out the cry.

"The hotel is on fire!"

"Shit!"

Beth's head popped up when he spoke.

Time stood still as they stared at each other.

Andrew wanted to forget the rest of the world and make Beth his in every essence of the word, but reality had come crashing in on them.

"We've got to get out of here." He sat up in the bed when Beth did the same. Andrew grabbed his pants and threw them on. Beth grabbed the dress she had worn earlier that day and pulled it on over her nightgown.

Taking her hand, he led her out into the smoke-filled hallway. Banging on Edward's door, then Sally's, he waited for them to open. Edward came out, hopping on one foot as he tried to get his boots on.

"Make sure the women make it downstairs. I'm going to see what I can do to help." Andrew didn't wait for an answer. He raced down the hall to where the smoke was the heaviest.

Guests ran past him, trying to escape the hotel as quickly as they could.

The black smoke curled up from under one of the doors.

"That's a linen closet," the proprietor said from behind him.

"Can we get water up here?" Andrew asked. "We need to stop this as quickly as possible."

"I've already sent for the fire department. Some of the guests have gone down to get water from the well. You need to get out of here, sir."

"No." Andrew shook his head. "I want to help."

Two of the guests appeared with buckets. More stood along the back steps to start a water chain. Buckets of water were thrown against the door to make sure it wouldn't catch before anyone dared to open it.

Andrew wrapped a wet towel around his hand and twisted the handle. Heat seared at his face when he eased the door open. Water buckets found their way into his hand. Each emptied into the burning inferno before being sent back down for more. Slowly, the fire lessened. The entire room had been gutted before they were able to put the fire out, but the fire had not spread any farther.

The fire department came on the scene as the last of the flames sputtered and winked out. The chief entered the charred room and stirred the ashes as well as checked the walls and ceiling to make sure the fire was completely out.

"That was some fast thinking there, Joe. You could've lost this whole place if you'd waited for us."

"My guests were a great help." He looked at Andrew. "I don't think we would've gotten it under control so quickly if this fellow here hadn't come by to help."

Soot covered Andrew's face, making his white teeth glow when he smiled. "Didn't want to have to sleep out in the road tonight."

"We're going to have to close this floor off until we can be sure there won't be any flare-ups," said the chief. "Do you have enough rooms to put your guests elsewhere?"

"If I ask some of the guests to double up until we can get this cleaned up I should. I have quite a few who are moving on today. They might not even want to go back to bed. It's only a couple of hours 'til morning." The proprietor ran his fingers through his sooty hair. "I'd like to know what started it. If one of the maids was careless with a lamp, I'm going to have to let her go."

"We'll check into it, but I don't see any lamps in here," said the chief. "But I do smell kerosene. Is this where you normally store it?"

"No. We keep that out in the shed, away from the hotel. Same thing with the lamps. I can show you if you'd like."

"Let's go." The chief spoke to another fireman, giving him his duties before he followed the proprietor down the stairs and out into the night.

Andrew trailed behind.

"This is where I keep it. All locked up." Joe stopped talking when he saw the door swinging in the slight morning breeze. "That door was locked when I went to bed."

Andrew had seen enough. Someone had deliberately set that fire, and considering what had transpired earlier that evening, he'd say they were trying to get him and his small party. It was definitely time to move on.

He continued walking and went around front. Beth rushed to his side when she spotted him.

"Are you all right?"

"Yes." He gave her a smile. "The fire has been put out, but the whole floor is closed. The smoke will take a little longer to go away."

"Is traveling with you going to always be this exciting?" The look she gave him sent a flame of desire straight to his groin.

"What happened here is more frightening than exciting, so I hope it isn't a constant thing. Although the way things have been going, I have a feeling it could get worse." He reached up and cupped her cheek smearing soot where he touched her.

"However, there was another fire started this evening that can't be put out with a little water," he grumbled softly as he stroked her cheek and throat. "And I hope to turn that fire into a blazing inferno the first chance I get."

CHAPTER 15

Beth thought she was going to fall asleep in the seat. The last week had been one big push to get to Jefferson City. Andrew had kept his distance as they traveled across the territory between Loose Creek and Jefferson City, but his heated glances let her know the physical distance was so he could remain a gentleman in front of their friends.

Her heart started to pound in her chest at the sight of the city. Would Andrew want to pick up where they had left off that night in the hotel? And could she go through with it? She had been caught up in the heat of the moment, but that moment had passed. Would it be right for them to truly be man and wife if he was going to leave her once Beau was captured?

She shook those thoughts off when she saw Edward riding toward them. Edward had ridden ahead to reserve hotel rooms for them. Beth hoped this place was big enough they'd blend into the crowd. Maybe, for once, they wouldn't be threatened by someone after Andrew's scalp.

"We have three rooms, but I had to get them in two different hotels."

"Is there something going on here?" asked Andrew.

"It's because of the trains. They say a lot of people wire ahead to get their rooms, so those that wait until they come into town don't get the best of choices."

Andrew climbed down from his horse and tethered it to the wagon before climbing in with Beth. He shook out the reins and started the horses moving.

They came into the city and traveled down Main Street. Edward inclined his head toward the hotel Andrew and Beth would be staying at before he led Sally to their hotel.

"Stay here for a minute." Andrew got down and entered the hotel.

A few minutes later, he came back out, followed by two porters who would take their things up to their room.

After they had unloaded Beth's trunk, Andrew drove the wagon to the livery stable. This time he didn't flash his Pinkerton credits around, but paid cash.

"We're registered under the name of Mr. and Mrs. Drew Smith," he told her as they walked back to the hotel.

"Do I have a first name?"

"Yes." Andrew patted the hand she had resting on his arm. "Your real one. Thought it would be easier for you."

"Thank you." The hotel loomed in front of them. Beth felt the butterflies take flight in her stomach again.

The lobby was filled with travelers from all over the country, many coming out west to make a new life for themselves. Andrew retrieved the key to their room and led her up two flights of stairs. Opening the door, he ushered her into the room they'd be staying in.

It was small but clean. The freshly made bed beckoned to Beth. What she'd do to be able to curl up for a couple of hours.

Andrew must have read her thoughts because he suggested the same thing.

"I need to check in with the police department here, then look around a bit. You can have a couple of hours to rest if you like."

She knew she could accompany him if she wanted, but she would hinder him if she did. So she smiled and nodded. "A little rest is just what I need."

Andrew looked relieved. "Then I'll wake you when I return." He hesitated for a few seconds before he left the room.

Beth wondered why.

~

Andrew closed the door behind him. Taking a deep breath, he headed toward the stairs to the lobby. For a moment there he thought about staying with her. His body wanted to finish what they had started a week ago, but this was not the time. They'd have plenty of time to pick up where they left off this evening, after a nice dinner and maybe a walk.

The street bustled with people. Most were travelers. He could tell by the way they gawked at their surroundings. Many had probably never expected this. According to the papers back East, the West was a wild frontier, not dotted with major cities along the way.

He stopped in at the police station, letting them know who he was and why he was in town before walking to one of the many saloons. Andrew discreetly looked for the men who were supposed to meet him, but had no luck. After visiting all the saloons on the main street where the hotel was, he headed over to the mercantile to meet up with Edward.

"Heard anything?"

"No, sir," answered Edward. "It seems pretty quiet around here. A couple of people have mumbled something about a pack of ruffians coming through here, but that was over a month ago."

"That's what I heard too, but don't let down your guard. We can't trust anyone right now."

Edward nodded.

"And keep an eye out for those three mountains as you call them. They could be lurking about too."

Edward nodded, grinning hard.

"What?"

"It's just they'd be hard to miss. You really think they'd show up here?"

"With the way things have been going?" Andrew wanted to laugh at that one. "It would be nice to stay in one town where no one tried to kill us."

"True, but from the stories I read that's normally how you know you're following the right leads."

Andrew had to admit Edward was right. Beau seemed to know where they were headed and was trying to stop them before they got there.

Somehow he had to get one step ahead of Beau's thinking so the attempts on their lives would stop, but how? Andrew knew all the attacks had to be from him. Maybe they should head north for a while before swinging to Kansas City, or maybe south. He had to throw him off somehow.

Andrew pulled his hat off and scratched his head. They were in a big enough city right now to shake anyone following them.

He continued to think on the matter as he headed back to the hotel. Each time someone had called him out, they always asked for the Pinkerton man. So he assumed they weren't sure who they were chasing. But Beau would expect him to follow, so why not call him by name? Unless Beau hoped Andrew hadn't tied the attacks to him. It didn't matter. Andrew felt like he was playing right into Beau's hands by doing exactly as Beau predicted.

That was going to stop here. He had arranged to have everyone meet him within the next few days. Once they all knew their jobs, they wouldn't be in contact with one another until they located Beau's hideout.

He hurried up the wooden steps to the hotel. A crowd of people blocked him from the stairs.

"Poor thing."

"Heard she fell down the stairs. Broke her neck." The voices of the crowd floated around him.

"Anyone know who she is?"

"No. Heard tell she and her husband just checked in today."

Andrew felt his heart stop. *Dear God, was Beth lying at the bottom of the stairs?* He had to know, so he elbowed his way through to the front, swallowing hard when he spotted a patch of blue gingham. Beth had just bought a dress that color.

"That poor man."

"Who?"

"The one sitting over there. It's his wife, you know."

Andrew didn't know who spoke, but his heart soared at their words. Beth was all right. He felt for the man, though. His own few seconds of fear had affected him strongly.

The woman lying at the bottom of the stairs was an older woman with a touch of gray at her temples. He thought about staying to see if he could help, but he also had a strong desire to take Beth into his arms to prove she was okay. In the end, his desire to see her safe outweighed his sense of duty.

He eased his way around the crowd and bounded up the stairs. Using his key, he opened the door and smiled when he saw Beth still curled up on their bed, sound asleep.

Andrew didn't question the joy that welled in him when he found her resting peacefully. Just knowing she was safe was enough.

She must have heard the soft snick of the door as it closed because Beth rolled toward him and opened her eyes.

"Rest well?"

"Yes. Thank you." She stretched and yawned.

Andrew felt his body respond as her chemise molded to her skin. God, she was beautiful. Every day he spent with Beth, her beauty grew. What surprised him the most was how much he noticed her inner beauty. He'd never had the time to notice things like this before, but with Beth he found himself catching all the little nuances. The way her smile would light up her eyes, or the infectious sound of her laughter. No other woman affected him the way Beth did.

He also didn't like the direction his thoughts were headed.

"Dinner is still an hour away, if you'd like to rest a little longer," he said.

Beth shook her head. Pulling herself into a sitting position, she ran her fingers through her tangled hair. "A bath is what I'd like. After traveling all that time I feel like I have about ten layers of dirt on me."

"Of course. I'll see to it." Andrew left the room and went down to the front desk.

The dead woman had been moved, but people were still milling about the lobby, talking about the tragedy. Andrew waited patiently by the desk.

Finally, a clerk stepped up to where he leaned against the counter.

"I'd like to order a bath brought up to my room."

"Yes, sir." The young man wrote down his room number and promised to have it upstairs as soon as possible.

Andrew went upstairs long enough to let Beth know her bath was on the way before asking her to meet him in the lobby when she was ready. If he stayed in the room while she bathed, they wouldn't make it to dinner; neither would he make any of his meetings. Instead he would make love to her until neither could take it anymore.

Heading across the street, Andrew walked into the small saloon there and ordered a whiskey. Commandeering the table closest to the window, he gulped his drink while he stared up at their window. Perhaps he should've stayed because his imagination was creating the most erotic images in his mind. Reality might not have been this hard on him. Ordering another drink, he watched as the curtain in their room swayed a little. A hint of color peeked out.

It took two more whiskeys before he had enough courage to go back to the hotel and wait in the lobby for her. Her appearance was well worth the wait. Beth's brown hair was swept up off her kissable neck with little ringlets cascading down from where it had been pinned up in the back. She wore a russet-colored dress that hugged her curves to perfection. Concentrating this evening would be difficult.

Beth stopped in front of him, fidgeting with her gloves.

Andrew stood up and took her hand. "You look ravishing, my dear."

Her cheeks pinkened. "Thank you."

"Would you like to go for a walk? Dinner won't be served for another half hour." Andrew offered her his arm.

"I'd like that." She rested her hand in the crook of his arm and they stepped out onto the boardwalk.

"Let's head toward the mercantile. Edward should be there with some information for me."

The tinkling of the bell sounded their entrance. Andrew looked around and spotted Edward toward the back of the store, playing chess with an older gentleman.

"I didn't know he could play," whispered Beth.

Andrew shook his head. This was another facet of the boy he hadn't known about either.

They stood and watched silently as the two men moved their men around the board. The older man moved his queen, sat back and said, " Check." Edward moved his bishop, looked the man in the eye and said, "Checkmate."

The man sat up straight and stared at the board. "Damn, boy, you're right. It's been so long since anyone beat me. Congratulations." The man offered his hand.

Edward stood up and took the man's hand. "I'm sure I was just lucky."

"Three times in a row? Don't think so. Play again?"

"Thank you, but maybe some other time." He shook the man's hand again before walking over to where Beth and Andrew stood. "Sally had to leave town. Some sort of emergency. She'll try to be back before we move out, and if not, she'll try to catch up with us as soon as she can."

"Did she say why she had to leave?" Edward's overall change amazed Andrew. When he first met Edward, the boy had no manners and couldn't string a proper sentence together to save his life. Now Edward hid his uneducated background. Andrew knew he was trying hard to be just like him. It made him proud to know the boy.

"Nope. Only said it was business and for us not to worry." Edward shoved his hands in his pockets. "Been here since she left."

Andrew wondered what would have pulled her away. If it was that urgent, why didn't she come looking for him. He didn't like this at all.

~

Andrew sat back in his chair and sipped his wine. Dinner had been superb, but so was the company. He looked over at Beth, who sat primly in her chair.

She picked at imaginary lint on the sleeve of her dress, but kept a smile on her face. He reached over to pat her hand. "You can retire if you'd like."

"No." She shook her head. "As my mama always says, 'In for a penny, in for a pound.'"

"I'm pretty sure your mama didn't have this in mind when she said that to you." Andrew looked at her face for any signs of backing down.

"Probably not, but I'm just as involved in this as you are. It's too late to back out." Beth smiled at him. "You said it yourself. No one should be kept in the dark about each other's whereabouts and this falls into that category. I'm going with you. If you won't take me, I'll follow you."

Andrew thought about what she said for a few seconds. It would probably be safer for her if he could leave her in the room. His hesitancy wasn't the smartest thing he could've done.

"And Drew Smith, if you think for one second I'm going to quietly go back to our room you're sadly mistaken." Her eyes snapped with the anger that coiled up inside her.

"Have I ever told you how pretty you look when you're angry?" Andrew sat back in his chair and smiled. He had missed this. Pride welled up in him as well. She remembered their fake name even in her anger.

"Really? If you think I'm pretty now, just wait a few moments and I'll be downright stunning." Beth sat straighter in her chair.

"I didn't say you weren't coming with me. You've already proven you can get in just as much trouble with me as without me." Andrew picked up his wine glass. "I just wish we could disguise your looks a little. With everything going on lately, I don't trust anyone."

"Too bad I'm not Sally, huh? I could dress up as a man and no one would even look at me."

This time Andrew sat up. "That's it!"

"What's it?"

"We'll dress you up as a boy." Andrew turned toward Edward. "You have some spare clothes she can borrow? You're a little closer to her build than I am."

"I'm sure I can come up with something." Edward stood and pushed his chair back.

Once Edward left, Andrew took Beth's arm and half-led, half-dragged her back to their room.

"I won't go parading around in men's clothing. My father would kill me," Beth snapped.

"Your father isn't here right now." Andrew paced the room. "Let's see. We'll need a hat, jacket, shirt, pants, and boots."

"Why can't I wear my own shoes?"

Andrew looked at her feet, encased in the high-heel boot that was the latest fashion.

"Okay, so they're not exactly men's shoes, but I did bring my riding boots. They're pretty plain and have a low heel on them." Beth opened her trunk. After digging around a little she pulled the boots up for Andrew to inspect.

"Those might work. All anyone will see is the toes of them anyway." He glanced toward her trunk. "You don't happen to have a hat in there do you?"

"No."

"Well, we'll see what Edward brings. You'll have to get out of your dress and those petticoats."

Beth grumbled as she slipped behind the screen. This might not be the way she had envisioned it, but Andrew felt it was a lot better to try to pass her off as a boy, than to show up in one of the saloons as the lady she was. Her presence there would spread like wildfire.

Her dress plopped against the screen.

"And what if someone figures out I'm not a boy?"

"I'm sure someone will realize you're female, but probably won't say anything. As long as you stay quiet and out of the way they'll remain focused on me instead."

She opened her mouth to retort, but a knock at the door stopped her.

Andrew opened the door to let Edward in.

"I brought everything I could think of." He laid everything on the bed and backed toward the door. "Only thing I didn't have was a hat, but Sally had a spare one. I didn't think she'd mind if we borrowed it for just a little while."

"Thanks." Andrew gathered the clothes and headed for the screen. "We'll meet you downstairs as soon as she's ready."

Twenty minutes later Beth mumbled to herself as she followed Andrew and Edward out into the street. This was crazy.

Her hat, pulled down low to cover as much as her face as possible, was tight. She had only been wearing it for maybe ten minutes, and she was already starting to get a headache. The brown pants she had on, like the cream-colored shirt, were too big. Andrew ended up tying a bit of rope around her waist to keep the darn things from sliding off her when she walked. It sure wouldn't have looked good for her to lose them in public, since she had nothing on underneath. Her pantaloons would've been too obvious.

The coat was the worst, big, dusty and brittle. She knew she'd be chafed by the end of the evening. Maybe staying at the hotel was a good idea.

Andrew's stride didn't give her a chance to change her mind though. She practically had to run to keep up with him and Edward, which was no easy feat. Her boots had been rejected when Andrew saw them peeking from under her new outfit. They looked far too feminine. Edward had run to the mercantile and grabbed the smallest pair of men's he could find.

The boots were still a little too big. Extra socks would keep them on, but she felt like she was walking with two sheep tied to her feet because of them. Every time she tried to run, she feared one of the boots would go flying off her foot and hit some innocent bystander.

Andrew slowed his pace a little. He must have noticed her struggling to keep up. If not, they must be nearing their destination.

Beth had never been inside a saloon before. After getting a good look at it, she was glad she'd disguised herself. If she had gone in there in her normal attire, she would've been the talk of the town.

Brushing her hand across the back of her neck, she made sure her hair was tucked neatly up inside the hat. Then she slouched her shoulders, pulling the coat tighter round her. She hoped she looked nonchalant, instead of how she felt – terrified.

The noise seemed loud from the outside, but once they stepped through the threshold, Beth changed her mind. Deafening was the word. Booming voices carried from across the room as different people demanded more alcohol.

She kept her head down and followed Andrew as he wove his way around the tables. Focusing on the floor, Beth didn't realize Andrew had stopped. She bumped into him, knocking her hat askew because her head had dipped down too low. If Andrew hadn't spun around and jammed her hat back on her head everyone would have known she was a woman.

"Be more careful," he said softly before he yelled at her in a harsh voice. "Boy! Watch where you're going."

She nodded silently, and followed at a safer distance.

They entered a private room off the main saloon, normally used for special guests. Andrew had paid a lot to use it without having a lot of questions asked.

One of the saloon girls strutted in, bringing a bottle of whiskey and six shot glasses.

"Gentlemen, I'm here for your pleasure." She batted her eyes at Andrew. "Whatever you want, you can have."

Beth sure was glad she didn't have a gun just then or she just might have blown a hole in the pretty lady's skimpy outfit.

CHAPTER 16

Maybe gouging her eyes out might be better. Beth fumed as she watched the woman fawn all over her husband. Then it dawned on her. She was jealous.

She sat down quickly. She didn't want to think about why she was jealous. There could be only one reason and she refused to admit that.

She didn't want to have to rely on a man. She wanted her independence. Yet here she was, dressed like a man. Why? Not for any sort of adventure, but because she didn't want to be left alone.

Andrew smeared a little soot on her face so she would look like she had a five o'clock shadow. Personally, she just felt dirty and this woman prancing around in such a skimpy outfit didn't help matters.

Andrew thanked the woman, then sent her out of the room. He lined the six glasses up and filled them.

"Gentlemen, drink up."

Beth looked up at him, but he wasn't looking at her. She turned her head toward the door and realized their visitors had arrived.

For just a second, her heart skipped a beat. They stood in the shadowy hallway, their silhouettes revealing three huge men. Her heart started to beat normally again as each stepped into the room. Once she saw their faces she knew they weren't the mountains who'd threatened them earlier.

Andrew gestured for the men to sit.

The first man picked up his drink and downed it in one gulp. "Leroux, good to see you."

"Same here, Tom." He acknowledged each man with a nod of his head. "Thanks for coming."

"What's this about?" asked Tom.

"You remember the Beaumont case?"

They nodded.

"He's escaped." Andrew stood up and started to pace. "I've been following his trail and believe he's hiding out somewhere near Kansas City."

"So what do you need our help for?"

"He's intelligent, ingenious, and dangerous. I need you to help me locate his hideout and bring him to justice. This is something I can't do alone."

"I've been hearing rumors of a new gang working in that area. They're deadly too. So far one family was wiped out when they wouldn't surrender their crop. Some old man who knew more than he should have, and two sheriffs." Tom scratched his head. "No one is willing to do anything."

"They're afraid," said another man.

"You Jim?" asked Andrew.

The man nodded.

"What have you learned?"

"Mostly the same things Tom has mentioned. They've also been robbing a few trains, mostly the ones with gold or weapons on board. They did hit a passenger train a few weeks back. Taunted the passengers by making the men and women strip down to their underwear, then took all their jewelry, money, and their clothes. The more I've heard about the incident, the more I think they were just out having fun. Kinda like their boss gave them permission to go and shoot up the train for themselves. Several women were taken. All young. We have agents searching for those ladies, but haven't heard if they've been successful in finding them."

"Can you get me the names of the agents working on that?"

Jim nodded. "I was on my way out there to help when I received the telegram to meet you here. Once I make contact, I'll let them know what you're working on and how they might tie together."

"Thanks."

So what do you want us to do?" asked Bob, the third man.

~

Beth found the rest of the meeting pretty boring. Andrew explained what had happened to them in the past few weeks, and the theory he'd come up with. He gave them a sketchy itinerary of where they'd be over the next few weeks in case anyone needed to get in touch with him. Then he went into detail of what he wanted them to do.

After two hours, the meeting finally came to an end.

She was able to stifle the first yawn, but the second one slipped out before she realized it.

Jim stood up and shook Andrew's hand.

"Maybe you ought to get the lady back to her hotel before she falls asleep on you, Leroux," said Tom as he stood up.

Everyone turned to look at Beth.

"I told you this wouldn't work." She knew better than to deny it.

"Actually the disguise worked fine. It's your hands."

Beth looked down at her hands. She'd forgotten she had removed the beaten up leather gloves because they had made her hands sweat.

"Guess they're a little too small and soft to pass as a man's?" Beth looked up at Tom.

"Yes, ma'am."

She gave Andrew a sheepish grin as she pulled the gloves back on.

"The disguise will see you safely back to your hotel. That's the important thing."

The door banged open again.

"Another round, gentlemen?" asked their barmaid.

"Thank you, but no," said Andrew.

The three men filed out of the room while the barmaid picked up the glasses. Andrew grabbed the bottle, stuck the cork in the neck, and slid it into his duster coat pocket.

"Perhaps you'd like to stay and keep me company," she purred at Andrew.

"Maybe later, honey. Right now I have to attend to business." He smiled at the woman as if she were the center of the universe.

Beth's hackles went up. Just as she was about to smack the woman into next Tuesday, Andrew roughly ushered her out of the room. Edward followed them.

The night air was filled with bawdy voices and off-tune pianos. It smelled of manure and something else Beth really didn't want to identify.

She shook off Andrew's hold on her arm. "So am I the business you have to take care of? I can walk back to the hotel on my own if you have more pressing matters to take care of."

"Jealous?"

Beth stopped walking. Andrew realized what she'd been trying hard to deny. She *was* jealous.

"I'm going to head to my hotel now," mumbled Edward as he veered off to the right.

She forced her limbs to move, walking in front of Andrew. There was no way she'd admit it out loud to him.

They didn't speak any more during the walk to the hotel. Beth kept her pace just fast enough that Andrew stayed a little behind. She wasn't sure if he did on purpose or not, but she was glad he did. She didn't know what she'd say to him if he tried to talk to her.

She continued her pace through the lobby and up the stairs to their room.

The door squeaked as it closed behind Andrew.

"You know, sooner or later, we're going to have to talk about this."

"We'll talk about it later, then." Beth ducked behind the screen.

"Avoiding it won't help matters."

She disagreed.

"Beth."

She saw his hand wrap around the screen she hid behind and paled.

"If you don't come out from behind this screen, I'm going to shove this thing out the window."

Hiding wouldn't do her any good if he did that so she stepped from behind the screen to face him. Head held high she looked him straight in the eye. "What makes you think I'm jealous?"

"You wanted to rip that woman's eyes out."

"I did not!" Beth couldn't keep any eye contact with Andrew.

"Then what caused the anger I sensed in you? I only felt it when she was in the room talking to me."

"Don't be silly." Beth walked over to her trunk and grabbed her nightgown. "I was just afraid the longer she stayed in the room, the quicker she'd figure out I was a woman."

"I'm pretty sure she did that from the beginning, Beth, and I'm sure she's seen it before. A lot of women will disguise themselves when traveling alone and no one can blame them."

Beth darted back behind the screen.

"I also think she acted sweet on me because she knew it upset you."

She poked her head back out. "She had designs on you, Mr. Leroux. I recognized the look."

"Designs?" Andrew gave her a wicked smile.

Beth didn't like that smile at all. It made her think he actually liked the idea. She ducked back behind the screen and started to undress.

Undoing the buttons of Edward's shirt, she thought about how she could face Andrew now. Should she act like she wasn't jealous? Would Andrew know better since he had already accused her of it?

The shirt slid down her arms.

Perhaps if she didn't bring it up, he'd leave it alone. She undid the buttons of the denims she wore.

She scratched her brow. Andrew didn't ignore things. If he wanted to know something, he'd go after it the way a dog goes after a bone.

She slid the jeans down as far as she could before remembering she had to remove the boots and socks. Hopping around on one foot she tried to pull one boot off.

A loud thump accented her success. The second boot, however, was another story. The socks on her feet made the hardwood floor slippery, causing her to lose her balance several times.

"Women's shoes don't cause this much trouble," she mumbled.

"Did you say something?" asked Andrew.

"No." She continued to struggle with the other boot, hopping around in circles while fuming at the offending shoe.

A huge gust of wind and a loud bam stopped her dead in her tracks.

The screen had fallen, taking her nightgown and Edward's shirt along with it and leaving her naked from the knees up. A bright crimson blush filled her face and neck.

~

Andrew watched the screen fall toward him. For just a second he considered catching it and righting it, but it fell too fast for him to get a hand on it. The moment he saw her standing there, he lost any thought flitting through his head.

She was beautiful. Shadows dipped and stretched across her body, hiding and revealing the softness he had only fantasized about before.

His mouth went dry.

A soft plop filled the room. The other boot had fallen.

He couldn't move. Andrew had never been at a loss for words before. Instinctively, he took a step toward her.

Beth's eyes grew as large as saucers. Scurrying for her nightgown, she grabbed the bottom and tried to pull it free from the fallen screen.

"Beth." Andrew hesitantly touched her wrist. He didn't know how she would react to him right now.

A single tear slipped down her cheek.

"Don't be afraid." He pulled the gown loose and helped her into it. The soft cotton warmed in his hands as he slid it over her head.

Beth let out a shaky breath when the hem of her gown glided down her legs.

The hesitant smile she gave him slipped in past his defenses. Her trust in him made him feel ten feet tall.

Taking her hand once more, he gently drew her to the bed, sat down and pulled her into his arms. A sigh escaped him when she rested her head against his shoulder and curled up against him. At least her fear hadn't made her bolt from his arms.

His body tingled where she lay against him. The parts of his body she didn't touch screamed in agony. They wanted to feel her warmth too.

As her breathing deepened, he wondered how this had happened. This wasn't the way he had planned on spending the evening with Beth. He wanted to lose himself in her. Hear her scream in ecstasy from their lovemaking. Instead he'd settled for holding her in his arms the way he had dreamed of many times.

She snuggled against him as she slipped deeper into slumber.

Andrew kissed the top of her head, settled back against the headboard, and closed his eyes. Sleep might be a long time coming, but he'd enjoy this while he could.

CHAPTER 17

Beth snuggled deeper into the warmth that surrounded her. It felt like heaven. Something soft tickled her nose. She didn't want to move a muscle so she tried blowing at it to see if that would move whatever was making her nose itch.

When she finally realized the blowing wouldn't work, she tried to brush it away, but it popped back up to annoy her some more. This time she slapped at it.

"Ouch."

She jerked up into a sitting position. The first rays of the sun streaked into their room.

"Not the way I want to be wakened up in the morning." Andrew gave her a lopsided grin as he rubbed his chest. His shirt had been unbuttoned somehow during the night.

Beth blushed. *No wonder it wouldn't go away.* It was his chest hair that tickled her nose, and what did she do? Beat at it. Her blush deepened when she realized Andrews's thighs cradled her. Her hip leaned against something long and hard. It didn't take much for her to figure out what that was.

How was she going to get out of this awkward situation? She looked up into Andrew's eyes and wished she hadn't. His intense gaze trapped hers. Her heart started to beat a little faster.

Andrew's fingers traced the edge of her jaw. His feather-like caress felt like velvet against her skin. When he cupped her face, she turned into it, realizing she craved his heat. All thoughts of escaping flew from her mind when his mouth touched hers. One, soft, gentle brush of his lips made her ache for more.

Her face tilted up toward his in a silent plea. A sigh escaped her when he complied. His tongue swept into her mouth, sending tingles through her body. Of their own accord, her arms crept up around his neck to pull him closer. The sensations from their kiss started to build in her. Then, suddenly, the kiss ended.

Andrew rested his forehead against hers.

"As much as I'd like to do this all day, we have a lot to do." He brushed his lips against hers again.

"We do?" She wanted to find out where their heated kisses would take them.

"Yes." He eased her away from him. "Go get dressed, sweetheart."

She nodded, scrambling out of bed before she did something foolish, like throw herself at him.

Andrew righted the screen for her as she picked out what she would wear today. Once she stepped behind it, she started to dress and tried to gather her thoughts. Making love to Andrew should be the last thing on her mind.

Hadn't she already convinced herself that was a marriage of convenience? That this would give her the freedom she sought? Then why did she feel so depressed when he backed away from her? Why did she want to be with him even though she knew that could jeopardize everything?

She didn't like these jumbled feelings she had. Maybe once they made love she'd get it out of her system and they could go back to the way they used to behave around each other. At least when she felt animosity toward him, she knew where she stood. Right now, she just felt lost.

Holding her corset against her stomach, she thought about what she wanted. It was time for her to go after it.

"Andrew? Can you help me?" Butterflies flew about inside her stomach, but she wasn't going to back down. If she had to seduce him, then she would. Anything to get their relationship on better footing.

"What can I help you with?"

She stepped out from behind the screen and smiled when she noticed his face looked a little pale. "I need help with my corset."

"I'll get one of the maids." He almost bolted for the door.

"It would be faster if you just help me."

"I'm not sure I can get those strings tight enough." He hedged toward the door again.

"All right, but it will delay us considerably."

Andrew looked at the corset, then at the door.

"Fine. But don't start complaining when you realize what a bad job I did." He stepped up to her, making a motion for her to turn her back to him, and began lacing the satin strings.

"What are you doing?" Beth tried to grab her corset back. He was the man with a woman in every town. Didn't he know how to string a corset?

"Helping you."

"How? It has to be around my waist first." She pulled the corset from him and wrapped it around her. Presenting her back to him she spoke. "Now lace it."

Andrew grumbled something as he ran the ribbon through the eyelets once again.

"No. Don't tighten them yet. Let me make sure it's in place." She didn't realize she had turned toward him as she tugged the front of the corset up, causing her breasts to almost swell out of the top.

An odd sound made her look up. Andrew's mouth hung open as he stared at her breasts.

She dipped her head down to hide the smile spreading across her face. Placing one arm just below the cups, she walked over to the bedpost and grabbed it with her other arm.

"Now I need you to start tightening it."

Andrew hooked his fingers though the ribbons and tugged hard.

A loud *woof* escaped her. "Try tightening all the strings a little at a time."

"Right." Andrew pulled on the bottom strings, then worked his way up to tighten it up, trying not to think of how soft her skin was against his fingers.

"Now tie it. Then go back, starting at the bottom, tighten them again."

He swallowed hard. The only way he knew he'd get out of this unscathed would be if the floor suddenly opened up and swallowed him, if a large rock were to fall from the ceiling, or if his hands fell off. Since he knew none of these things would happen he just prayed he could remain a gentleman and escort her to breakfast quickly.

~

He didn't think he'd ever finish with Beth's corset. Although only minutes had passed, it had felt like hours. Her subtle scent surrounded him, and when he wasn't guarding his vision, he would catch himself staring over her shoulders at her breasts. Each time he tied that ribbon to keep the corset from coming loose, his fingers brushed against her satin skin. It was enough to test a saint, and was driving him insane.

Andrew sipped his coffee as he watched Beth do the same. Even now, with her sitting so demurely across from him, he could still feel the softness of her skin and smell that soft rose scent she had started to wear during their journey.

She looked up at him and smiled.

He wondered what she was thinking. Did she know how helping her earlier had affected him?

"So, what do we have to do today?" she asked.

"Edward is supposed to meet us for breakfast and fill us in on anything new he has heard. Then I need to send a telegram."

"But earlier you made it sound like we had a lot to do." Beth looked at him through her lashes.

Andrew made a fist under the table. Didn't she know how that affected him? Their close physical contact was weakening his resolve not to touch her until she asked him to. He'd used a busy schedule as an excuse to get them out of their bedroom. "We do, but first I need to talk to Edward before I follow through with any of my other plans."

"Oh." She took a sip of her coffee, still watching him.

A shadow crossed over him. Looking up, he saw Edward standing in front of him. Relief swamped him.

"Sally's back," Edward said as he took a chair. "She should be joining us in a few minutes."

"She tell you why she took off the way she did?"

"Nope. But she did say she'd explain it to us all when she got here."

The waiter came over and took Edward's coffee order.

Andrew let him know they would wait a few more minutes before ordering breakfast because they were waiting for one more guest.

"Have you heard anything new?"

"Not sure. I've heard a few rumblings about someone looking for a few hands to help out on a ranch. Thought it was normal until I heard someone else say any decent man wouldn't work on that particular ranch." Edward paused as he thanked the waiter for his coffee. "The ranch is south of here. McCord's Way is what it's called."

"I've heard that name. Good-sized ranch," said Andrew.

"Yes, but Mr. McCord passed on a few months ago and someone else is running it," said a new voice.

"Sally!" exclaimed Beth. "Where have you been?"

She slid into the vacant chair. "One of my operatives sent me a telegram. I had to meet him last night. It was our only chance."

"Why didn't you tell anyone?" Andrew asked.

"I know you asked each of us to let you know where we were, but the message was urgent, and I didn't want to leave a note with the details. I was afraid my operative was in trouble."

Andrew sat back. "So what did you learn?"

"He's working on that ranch as a cook. When he described the new owner, he sounded just like the man you're after."

The waiter brought her a cup of coffee.

"Now that's the kind of service I like. Didn't even have to ask for it." Sally wrapped her fingers around the cup. "The owner is going by the name of Monty McCord. The distant nephew of the late owner. Tall, blond, has a scar on his right cheek. It's new. It's said his horse threw him, but my operative said it looked like a bullet winged him. He had a handlebar mustache when he first showed up, but has shaved that off now."

"There are a lot of blond men with handlebar mustaches." Andrew gave her a disgusted look before he sipped his cooling coffee.

"True, but this particular one talks like a Southern gentleman. The accent hints at somewhere near New Orleans. And he's quite fond of the ladies. There are at least a half dozen that drop by the ranch with one excuse or another."

"What makes you think this is Beau?"

"The young ladies normally use the excuse of bringing food for Monty. Pralines, since they are his favorite."

Beth reached over and touched Andrew's arm. "Beau loved pralines."

"I know, but it could just be a coincidence too."

"True, but something strange is going on. Mr. McCord is hiring a lot of men…more than he could ever use on his ranch. They're there for about a month, then move on before the next batch shows up. Most are the worst of society. There are a few who look more destitute than criminal, but they normally don't stay past a few days."

"Foul play?"

"My operative doesn't think so." Sally took a sip of her coffee. "Bad for morale if those who didn't fit in ended up dead."

Andrew rolled the information around in his head. *It did sound like Beau.* He'd done the same thing before.

"How did your operative get in? Beau has always ferreted these people out in the past," asked Andrew.

"He was following another lead when he found out about the ranch needing a cook. He thought the job would give him a chance to stick around the area."

"So he wasn't following Beau?"

"No. In fact, he'd been sent to check up on the sheriff in a small town near the ranch. The man fit the description of a wanted man. When he realized what he had fallen into, he contacted me." Sally set her cup down. "He's going to stay where he is instead of investigating the sheriff right now. Beau is a much bigger threat."

Andrew had to agree with that.

"So what do we do now?" asked Beth.

"It looks like we're going to head to McCord's Way and capture Beau."

CHAPTER 18

Beth thought Andrew was out of his mind. "How? You planning on taking him down with just the four of us?"

"No." Andrew gave her a calculated smile. "I plan on contacting everyone in this region and getting lots of help. But Beau Manning will be in my custody within a day of reaching that ranch."

Beth sat back in her chair. She couldn't believe his arrogance.

"Edward, I need you to contact those men we spoke to last night. Let them know I want to have another meeting. Sally, get in touch with everyone you know around here and see if I can meet with them. I want to leave by daybreak."

Sally nodded before getting up. Edward did the same.

"Drew, how can you possibly believe he'll be that easy to catch?" Beth didn't want to make a scene in public, but she couldn't keep quiet about this.

"He won't be expecting us."

"So you're just going to march in there and arrest him? He'll kill you." The words slipped out before she could stop them.

"Miss Elizabeth, I have a job to do. And I will do that job in my own way. Your fear for my safety, although very sweet, won't change a thing." He stood up. "Now, we have some things to do."

"You are the most arrogant, pompous fool I've had the misfortune to marry." She stood as well, seething with anger. "Beau Manning isn't stupid enough to stand by and wait for you to come for him. You think he'll be there when you show up? That man probably has twice the number of spies you do. He probably knows our every move and will be waiting for you to do something this crazy."

"You're probably right, but like I said, that's not going to stop me from trying. I've been chasing him for too long to let him slip through my fingers."

Beth knew she couldn't convince him otherwise right now.

With his teeth clenched, he gave her an intimidating stare.

She lifted her chin and stared back.

A hint of a smile flashed before he gestured for her to precede him out of the dining room.

Beth kept her eyes ahead, too angry to look around. A familiar face hovered in her peripheral vision, but when she turned to look, the face was gone.

The soft click of Andrew's boots echoed her angry stomps down the steps. She had never been one to throw a temper tantrum and she wouldn't start now, but the thought did cross her mind. Stopping, she took a deep breath to calm herself down. Unfortunately, Andrew didn't anticipate her stopping in the middle of the street and plowed into the back of her.

She felt her balance go, pinwheeled her arms to try to regain it, and smacked Andrew in the face in the process.

A strong arm wrapped around her middle just as the ground started rushing up toward her face.

"You are trying my patience, Miss Elizabeth."

"I'm trying your patience? You're the biggest fool who won't see reason. If anyone's patience is running thin, it's mine."

Andrew's eyes darkened as he let her go. "Do you know how beautiful you are when you're angry?"

Gaping at him, she blinked. A few seconds later, she snapped her jaw shut. He wasn't going to get her to change her feelings about this with sweet talk.

"Thank you." As inane as it sounded, she refused to let him defuse her anger. She spun around and started walking, realizing she had no clue where they were headed.

Andrew cleared his throat.

"Yes?"

"The mercantile is this way."

She did an about-face, strode past him and walked into the store.

While Andrew spoke to the clerk, she wandered around the store. The elderly gentleman that had played chess with Edward was there again. She stopped to watch as he beat his latest opponent.

"You play?" he asked her.

"Oh, no. My father tried to teach me as a child, but I was never very good at it. Checkers is more my game."

"Then checkers it is." He moved the chess pieces to the side before opening a small wooden box and pulling out his checkers.

Beth arranged her pieces on the board.

"Ladies first."

She smiled as she slid her first piece forward.

Then the gentleman moved his.

They played in silence for several moves. A small crowd started to gather around them.

Just as Beth moved one piece to the top of the board he asked, "What's your name, child?"

Automatically she said, "King me," then blushed. "I'm sorry, it's Elizabeth."

"Well, Elizabeth, you play very well."

She glanced over at the small pile of checkers she had removed with her jumps.

"My papa was a good teacher." She watched in dismay as the gentleman jumped two of her pieces. "And may I ask your name?"

"Jacob."

"Well, sir, you're as good a checkers player as you are a chess player." She slid a piece forward, blocking him off from several other pieces that were vulnerable.

"Don't have much to do since I retired." He smiled as he took another of her checkers from the board.

"What did you do before you retired?" Beth asked as she studied the board.

"I was the mayor here."

She looked up. "It's your turn."

Returning her gaze to the board, Beth noticed if she moved one checker to the right she could take two of his men during her next move, but that would leave several of hers open. She leaned her chin into the hand of the arm she propped on the table. She slid a checker closer to the ones she would leave open, hoping to set up a block before she went after the opening she saw in his game. "That must've been a very hard job to do."

"Sometimes, yes." He made his move. "But as long as the roughnecks stayed out, it was pretty quiet around here. Not like it is now."

"Oh?" Her checker scratched across the board as she slid it toward the move she'd spotted earlier.

"Too many vagrants wandering through this city now. Can't trust the lot of them."

Beth held her breath as he made his move.

"Been more crimes committed in the last three months than we saw all last year."

"That's horrible." She picked up her piece and proceeded to jump three of his men, leaving only one on the board.

He laughed when he realized he'd lost.

Andrew stepped up to her side.

"Drew, I'd like you to meet Jacob. He's the retired mayor of this fair city." The she turned to Jacob. "Jacob, this is my husband, Drew."

"It's a pleasure to meet you, sir." Andrew offered his hand.

"So you're the lucky fellow married to this young lady." Jacob shook his hand.

"Yes, sir."

"Where you two headed next?"

"Heard there were some jobs available at McCord's Way."

"You don't want to be going there, young fellow. Not a safe place for a family."

"Why?"

"Because families aren't welcome there."

Beth thought he sounded a bit cryptic. Pretending she didn't know better, she asked, "But I thought ranches were the best places for families to find a job."

"Where you two from?"

Beth looked at Andrew since she had no clue where he said they were from.

"Uh-huh," said Jacob. He stood up and cornered Andrew. "Who are you, and before you tell me Drew, think about your next words. I am the retired mayor and still have a lot of pull in this city."

"And can get me thrown in jail?" Andrew crossed his arms over his chest. "Are you threatening me?"

"Just consider it good advice. I know you don't want this young lady to have to fend for herself while you are dealing with the sheriff." Jacob gestured toward Beth. "A city like this isn't a safe place for a young woman alone."

Beth held her breath as the two men stared at each other. She knew Andrew hated to be backed into a corner.

"I'm a Pinkerton agent."

Relief washed over her.

"Figured as much. Heard about your little meeting last night." Jacob sat back down.

Beth gripped Andrew's arm. *If Jacob had heard about it, how many others knew as well?*

Andrew patted her hand.

"Don't worry, I had to ask to get any information. I knew that young kid who played chess with me was with you and he made curious with all his questions about this town. They weren't your normal what-can-I-do-while-I'm-here type of questions," said Jacob.

"I'll have to teach him to be a little more subtle in his questions," commented Andrew.

"Now, don't blame the boy. He actually was very subtle. I've just been dealing with people asking the wrong type of questions for too long."

Beth relaxed a little after hearing Jacob's explanation. She still wasn't sure if she liked the reason. It would mean anyone with a suspicious nature would probably wonder about them if they asked too many questions. Was that how those other people found out about them?

"You still going out to the McCord Ranch?"

"Yes," said Andrew. "I believe the man I'm looking for is there."

"And what about this little lady? You taking her too?"

"I'm traveling with friends that can keep her safe while I investigate the ranch."

"You aren't going to leave me behind."

Jacob laughed. "It looks like you got your hands full. Come by my house for dinner tonight and I'll tell you what I know about the McCord place."

"Thank you, sir. We'd love to."

"How many should I expect for dinner?"

"Four."

"Good. Cook doesn't like it when I spring these surprise dinners on her, but she gets downright irritable when she doesn't know how many to cook for."

~

Jacob's house looked warm and inviting to Beth. Of course, the silent walk to his place made her edgy. It felt like some sort of silent communication was going on among Andrew, Edward, and Sally, and they were excluding her from it. Something she didn't appreciate.

Light spilled out into the night, illuminating the porch and part of the front yard. Beth smiled when they stepped through the gate next to the white picket fence. She had found out that Jacob's wife had passed several years before. Since then Cook had taken care of him.

She hoped the small bouquet she had clutched against her would be enough of a gift. Her parents had taught her you never show up for dinner without a gift. It was unmannerly and unneighborly. Flowers were her favorite gift to get, so she normally gave them too.

Jacob opened the door as the four of them started up the steps. "Come in. Make yourselves at home. Cook! Our guests are here."

Beth imagined a little old woman with a round figure and a sour expression. She was taken back a little by the elegant, middle-aged woman who entered the room. Cook's ready smile relaxed Beth in an instant.

"By the look on your face, I see Jacob didn't prepare you for me. My name is Mary Cook."

"Elizabeth Smith. It's a pleasure to meet you." She looked down at the flowers in her hand. "Oh, these are for you."

"Thank you." Cook took the offered bouquet and inhaled the sweet fragrance. "I love flowers."

Beth thought she said it a little loudly. When she saw Cook steal a glance at Jacob to see if he heard her, she understood why. Cook was sweet on him.

"Let me get these in water." Cook hesitated for a second. "Would you like to help me?"

"Sure." Beth followed her into the kitchen.

Cook opened one cupboard after another until she found a jar big enough to hold the flowers.

"So...Jacob tells me you're from New Orleans."

"From Jennings. It's a little bit south of the city."

"You and your husband planning to move out west then?"

"No." What could she tell this woman? That they were trying to catch a killer? "My aunt lives near Wichita. We thought it would be nice to visit her."

"You're a bit north to be heading to Wichita."

"Well, we decided to do a little traveling too." Beth picked up one of the flowers and twirled it in her hand. "We're also looking for someone."

"Ah...Jacob mentioned something like that."

Beth blushed, knowing she'd just been caught in a lie. "What else did Jacob tell you?"

"Enough. He's worried for your safety. He plans on convincing your husband to let you stay here while he takes care of his business."

Beth mulled this over in her mind. If Andrew did leave her behind, she could leave without him being able to stop her. But she knew better than that. Andrew would think the same thing.

"I doubt Drew will change his mind," said Beth.

"Your husband would rather put you in danger than leave you here?"

"Not exactly. He just feels he's the best one to protect me and he can't do that if I'm not with him."

"Why?"

"Because." Beth sighed. "The man we're after wants to kill me."

The jar clattered against the table.

Beth put out her hand to steady it. "It's okay."

Cook looked up at her. "How can you say that?"

She hadn't really been able to talk about what was really happening to her with anyone and she felt the need to unburden herself to this kind woman.

"Is there someplace we can talk?"

"Of course." Cook led her out on the back porch.

The night air was filled with pleasant fragrances and the croak of bullfrogs.

"Several months ago, a friend and I were kidnaped by the man we are after. He was captured and swore revenge. I never thought much of it. After all he was behind bars. Unfortunately, he escaped." Beth wrapped her fingers around the balustrade. "I wasn't aware of this when my aunt sent me a telegram asking me to come for a visit."

"And Drew came after you."

She nodded. "When he caught up with me, he wanted to take me home, but circumstances have made that impossible."

"So you travel with him under the guise of marriage?"

"No. We're really married." Beth heard the catch in her voice. Although she really didn't know this woman, she did care about what Cook thought. "Drew knew traveling together would make people talk."

"Then this is a marriage of convenience."

Beth nodded, forgetting that Cook probably couldn't see her head move that well in the dark. "And the problem has escalated to a point he's afraid to send me home. I could just draw the trouble to my parent's house."

"Exactly," said a deep voice behind them.

Only one man had a deep voice that sexy. Andrew.

CHAPTER 19

She felt about three inches tall. The first time she confided in anyone she got caught. It was a good thing she hadn't had a chance to reveal much more or Andrew would've gotten an earful.

"Beth."

"You were eavesdropping."

Andrew hesitated for a second. "You're right."

"I'll go in and see about dinner. It should be just about ready." Cook skirted around Andrew and entered the kitchen. The screen door banged against the frame after she entered the house.

The silence between them was deafening, until it reached a point Beth couldn't handle anymore. "Why?"

"You disappeared."

"Afraid I had ran away?"

"I was worried about you." Andrew ran his fingers through his hair. "Look, I didn't mean to overhear your conversation, but you know you aren't supposed to talk about it to anyone."

"No one is supposed to know the truth," she spat out. "But I needed to talk to someone. You won't listen to me, I can't talk to Sally about it, and Edward would just get all embarrassed and find a way to change the subject. Just how long am I supposed to keep this bottled up inside me before I explode?"

"Beth, I—"

"Don't. I know the rules and I broke them. So what're you going to do? Tie me up now? Gag me so I can't say another word to anyone?"

"I never meant to hurt you."

Beth looked at him. It was hard to see his face with the light of the kitchen behind him.

She didn't want his apology now. Not when she had all this anger inside her. When she tried to brush past him, he grabbed her arm, halting her escape.

"Beth."

"You didn't hurt me," she lied. "You had a job to do. I understand that."

Andrew didn't let go. Instead, he pulled her closer. As his head dipped closer to hers, she turned her face away. "Dinner is ready. We should get back inside."

"Not until I do this." Placing his hands on her face, he leaned in again, this time brushing his lips against hers. "Your make me crazy, yet when I'm not near you I miss you. I don't want anything to happen to you."

His lips brushed hers again.

"Why?" She could feel his breath on her lips. It sent heat though her blood.

"What a question." His thumb brushed away a stray tear that had slid down her cheek. His lips touched hers again, causing sweet sensations to spiral through her. She leaned into him for support as he deepened the kiss. His tongue stroked the softness, asking for entrance. With a sigh, she opened her mouth to him. Wave after wave of desire rolled through her. Where their bodies touched she burned.

"All right, you two lovebirds. Dinner is ready. Cook asked me to come and get you." Jacob stood just inside the door, grinning hard.

They bolted apart. Nothing like getting caught to cool the fires. Beth knew her cheeks were flaming. She wondered if Andrew felt the same way.

He offered her his arm, then led her back inside to the noise and the safety of the crowd.

~

"Tell me what you've heard so far," said Jacob as he filled everyone's wineglass again.

"The original owner of McCord's Way passed on a few months ago. A distant cousin is now running it," said Andrew.

"Matthew McCord disappeared about three months ago. No one really knows what happened to the man," corrected Jacob as he put the wine bottle on the table. "I've heard he was heading into town for monthly supplies, which he purchased, but he never made it back to the ranch. Search parties looked for him for weeks."

"No body?"

Jacob shook his head. "If he was killed, the killer is very good. The wagon, horses, everything disappeared. Many wonder if he just high-tailed it west."

"But is that something this McCord would do?"

"No. He might've been single, but that ranch was his life."

"He normally took in those who were traveling west, sold them supplies and such," added Cook.

"When did the distant cousin show up?" Andrew gazed at Jacob intently. He needed to know the information.

"I'd say about two months ago. He seemed nice enough."

"You've met him?" asked Beth.

"Yes. Came into town about a month back. Tall man, good looking too. All the single women were smitten with them."

"Blond? About six-two?"

"He had a thick mustache too." Jacob sat back in his chair. "I'd put him in his thirties. Brown eyes, I think. I just remember a bit of harshness that made me uneasy."

"Did he play chess with you?"

"Everyone plays chess with me." He smiled at Beth. "Or checkers."

"Did he win?"

"No, and not too happy about it either. He was like a thundercloud one minute, then suddenly as nice as can be the next." Jacob paused. "That's when I saw the killer eyes."

"Come now, Jacob."

"Cook, you didn't see that look. Once a man has killed his share of people, his eyes get a look…a flat fathomless look."

"Soulless," Beth whispered.

"Yes." He looked at her. "You've seen that look before."

"I've seen that man before."

"That one look made me wonder what really happened to Matthew. Although I've found nothing, I have learned a lot about the man who claims to be his cousin. The cousin who really died about six months ago in some freak accident."

"It's got to be Beau."

"Let me warn you now. He keeps that place locked up tighter than Fort Knox. You won't be able to slip in undetected."

"Then you tried."

"No, but someone I trusted did. He found sentries about every two or three hundred feet surrounding the ranch. They brought him in front of this Beau you keep saying is the McCord cousin, hands tied behind his back and forced him to kneel." Jacob took a sip of his drink. "My friend didn't think he would make it back alive, but Beau believed him when he said he was on his way here and had wandered off course. Either that, or he knew the man was there to gather information and we'd be on alert if he didn't return. We left the McCord ranch alone after that."

"But you make sure anyone who's come from that ranch is spoken to, don't you?"

Jacob just smiled.

"No wonder you're in the mercantile all day long," murmured Edward.

Andrew gave him a quizzical look.

"Everyone plays chess or checkers, especially those who are trying to blend in after being at the McCord ranch."

"You catch on quick, boy."

"And what have you learned?"

"That he's training some sort of militia. Don't know what for yet, but each day brings me closer to the answer."

"Are you sure?" asked Sally.

"He's been buying a lot of guns since he took over. And that doesn't count how many trains have been relieved of government-issue firearms recently."

Sally turned toward Andrew. "That would explain why he only keeps the new recruits for the ranch there for a month. Once he's sure of their loyalty, he moves them to a safe place to train."

"And his real hideout," added Beth.

"But what is his goal? What does he want that army to do?" asked Andrew. He rubbed the back of his neck, trying to come up with Beau's strategy.

"Personally? I'd say he wants to take over." Beth felt Andrew's gaze rivet on her the moment the words left her mouth. "Well, think about it. He hated the war because of all he lost…all the South lost."

"He didn't give a damn about the South," snorted Andrew.

"True, but we know his mind is twisted. It's no longer the war that is his problem. He probably paints himself as a war hero, but since the South lost, life has been hard for everyone who struggles to survive. His family lost everything." Beth paused for just a second to take a sip of her wine. "Remember what he said to Trey? He went to war expecting everyone to fawn all over him, but he was ignored. He came back expecting to be treated like a war hero, but came back to nothing. His money, his prestige, everything was gone."

"Then Trey came back from France, unchanged because he didn't go to war, with money lining his pockets."

"Exactly," said Beth. "He hated Trey for that."

"What're you getting at?" asked Edward.

"Beau went to war, thinking his way of life was right and the South would win. He came back, thinking he'd be held in high esteem because he fought for the cause. But that wasn't what happened. Most of the South was too busy trying to recoup their losses. They had taxes to pay for the years during the secession.

"Now America is growing, and the war is nothing more than history. Those he fought against, in principle and physically, are gaining the land and honor he covets. What would you do in his place?"

"Try to stop it." Edward paused for a moment. "You know what you're saying? Do you really think he'll try to take on the government to bring the South back to the time before the war?"

Beth chewed on her lip as she thought. Beau only cared about himself. She honestly didn't think he would do this for the glory of the South.

"I think he wants ultimate power. He doesn't just want to enslave certain people, but everyone he views as below himself." Trying to verbalize her thoughts wasn't easy. "Which is everyone else now.

"He is searching for the most loyal men he can find…those who won't question his orders. Once he's sure of their trustworthiness, he moves them somewhere else. To me, it sounds like he's preparing for war. He thinks no one will expect this because he's doing it so discreetly." Beth looked at Andrew. "I also think he won't come right out and attack the government, but will infiltrate each town around him, then continue that tactic until he has control over most of the West."

"If what you say could be true then he's already started to do this," said Jacob.

"I'd think so."

"But this is all conjecture," said Sally. "You could be wrong."

"I know that, Sally," said Beth. "But I grew up with Beau, Drew, and Trey. I also know what he did to torture Trey all because Beau thought he had been wronged. He killed Trey's parents because he envied the love they had for Trey. He felt Trey didn't deserve it. He tried to kill Trey's aunt and wife because Beau was jealous of the love between them. He sabotaged Trey's plantation, hoping to make him waste his money until it was all gone because Trey had money when others didn't."

"Put that on a grander scale," interjected Andrew. "He never got the hero's welcome he thought he deserved when he got home from the war. Starting another war, and being the victor, would be the perfect way for him to get the recognition he feels he so rightly deserves and create a country where he rules in the process."

"As a dictator."

Andrew and Beth nodded.

Silence filled the room as everyone thought about the implications.

"We have got to stop this man," said Edward.

"I know," said Andrew. "Believe me, I know."

~

Andrew and Beth walked back to their hotel room in silence.

She wondered if Andrew thought she'd been too forward during their conversation with Jacob. At home her father had never allowed her to voice her opinion. It was very refreshing to have everyone listen to her theories and even agree with them.

"What if I'm wrong?" she blurted out.

"Huh?" Andrew seemed to be lost in his own thoughts. "Wrong about what?"

"About Beau. Him taking over the country, I mean."

"I don't think you're wrong, Beth. His mind does work the way you pointed out."

"You really think so?"

"Yes, I do." Andrew put his arm around her shoulders. "Beau is a very complex man. He is demented enough to think he could take over this country and set himself up as some sort of hero. He'd also have total control, which is what he has wanted all along."

"Then why didn't he do this before? The war would've given him the perfect opportunity to do this."

"True, but he was much younger then. Even if he had this planned all along, I'm sure he wanted it to be done subtly. If the South had won, he would've come back as a hero, his way of life would've been preserved, and it would've satisfied him for a while."

Beth remained silent, wondering what had really turned Beau mad.

"There's the hotel." Andrew steered her toward the brightly lit building. "Let's get some rest."

They passed through the doorway and started to head up the stairs to their room when the clerk on duty stopped them. "Mr. Smith? A telegram came for you today."

Andrew took the envelope and thanked the young man. Fishing in his pocket, he withdrew a penny and placed it in his hand.

Once they were in their room, Andrew went over to the desk and lit the lamp. After breaking the seal on the envelope he scanned the contents of the telegram.

His deep laugh filled the room as he reread what it said.

Curiosity piqued, Beth waited for him to tell her.

"I think you better read this," said Andrew, still laughing.

She took the telegram and started to read. What she read made her heart stop.

> *Received telegram from New Orleans stop William Boudreaux's daughter has been kidnapped stop He fears the worst stop He wants to hire you to find her and do whatever it takes to keep her safe and bring her home stop*
>
> *HQ*

Beth didn't see what was so funny about this telegram.

"Your father said he feared the worst has happened to you and asked me to do what it takes to keep you safe. I wonder what he'll think our marriage is a smart way to keep you safe."

CHAPTER 20

"This is not a laughing matter," snapped Beth. How dare he take this lightly. "My father has heard from Miss Rose. For all we know, he could be on his way here by now."

"I suspect that's true, Beth. But where would he start? He only knows where Miss Rose saw you last. Your kidnappers could've traveled anywhere once they had you."

"Andrew Leroux, you're the kidnapper!"

"But your father doesn't know that. All he knows is that you've disappeared, and he fears for your safety. So much so he's asking for my help."

Beth felt the sharp pang his last words brought. Her father must be very worried if he humbled himself enough to contact Andrew. She knew how her father felt about him. "So what are you going to do?"

"Exactly what he's asked me to do. Keep you safe."

"I don't think he'll like your method."

"Probably not." Andrew undid the buttons to his coat before shrugging it off.

Beth walked over to her trunk and pulled out a nightgown. Awkward silence hung between them. She looked over at his stiff back, wondering what she should say to him.

"I'm not going to change my mind about taking you to the McCord ranch."

What was he, a mind reader? Beth bit back an angry retort and headed behind the screen.

She didn't want to go anyway. Maybe she could escape and head straight to her aunt's. Angrily she reached behind her and unbuttoned the back of her dress.

"Are you all right back there?"

Beth stopped. "Yes. Why?"

"The grunting and groaning coming from behind the screen," answered Andrew.

Beth wanted to be appalled, but having one elbow up in the air while the other pointed to the ground as her hands fought to reach the buttons that ran down the middle of her back she couldn't. She looked ridiculous, and probably sounded it too.

"I'm trying to undo the back of my dress, thank you very much."

"Do you need help?"

His voice slid down her spine. Have him help her? While she was angry at him? She swallowed hard. "That might not be a good idea."

"Why?"

"Because it's not proper." *And far too dangerous.* She might not be able to keep her anger.

"But I'm your husband."

Beth stopped breathing. He was right. Her heart beat harder against her chest. She wasn't sure she could handle him touching her like that right now. But how could she convince him she didn't need the help when she did? The buttons on this dress were a lot smaller than her day dress, and she had allowed him to help her this morning.

Why was she suddenly so frightened? Isn't this what she wanted? Didn't she try to seduce him when she got dressed earlier?

She must have waited too long to answer him because the screen scraped across the floor as he pulled it away from her.

Wide brown eyes stared into sexy amber ones. She noticed how his eye color deepened when he took in her state of undress Her shoulders were bare when her arms were at her side. The front of her dress gapped open to show a bit of the top of her camisole and corset. She couldn't continue to look at him like that, so she quickly presented her back to him. Hoping he'd undo the buttons, then move away.

His fingers gently brushed against her skin, sending goose bumps up and down her spine. *Oh, this isn't good.*

She could feel the back of her gown tighten, then loosen as he undid the buttons. The cool evening breeze caressed her hot skin.

He released the last of the buttons, but instead of stepping back, he pushed her dress forward, then down her shoulders, the slide of his hands leaving a wave of sensations she didn't know how to react to.

The heat of his breath danced along the back of her neck. She had to lean against him for support. Beth didn't think she could stand on her own. His hands skimmed up over the tops of her breasts before slipping behind her. She barely noticed the gentle tugs as he loosened the strings of her corset.

Beth didn't feel the corset as it slid down her body. All she could feel was the warmth of Andrew's hands as he cupped her breasts. Soft kisses against her neck made her arch it to give him better access as his thumbs gently rubbed against her rosy peaks. A strange sensation started to pool in the lower part of her body. Languid heat spread through her veins.

She felt the softness of the bed against her back, but had no clue how she got there. All she could do was feel the magic of his caresses. The cool night air kissed an exposed nipple before Andrew drew it into his mouth. It beaded under the ministrations of his tongue.

She arched against him, silently telling him she wanted more. While his mouth suckled and tugged on one tight nipple, a free hand teased and gently plucked at the other. Her hands held him there at her breasts. She prayed he'd never stop, and that the wonderful sensations coursing through her body would never end.

A cry escaped her when he lifted his head, followed by a sigh of relief when he turned his attention and his mouth to the other peak. Mama had never told her it would be like this.

She felt his hands slide along her stomach, stopping at the ribbon that held her pantaloons together. With a few quick tugs he continued his path, unobstructed by clothing. Her whole body arched up off the bed as his fingers slid down toward the center of her. They wove their way through her curls, softly caressing as they went. Beth swore her whole body would explode as his fingers brushed against a small nub there. Instead of bursting into a thousand pieces, the feeling became more intense.

Her hands took on a life of their own, reaching for him, pulling at his clothing. She didn't know how she did it, but she rid him of his vest and shirt, at least most of it. Languishing in the feel of his skin against hers.

~

Andrew knew Beth could be a passionate woman, but he'd never expected the little firebrand he had in his bed. He wanted to take his time with her, knowing he needed to introduce her to the ways of love, but she didn't want to wait.

He slid up her body and captured her lips with his so he could remove his shirt and hopefully slow down the pace. His erection rested in the juncture of her thighs. The same thighs she had just wrapped around him. A shudder racked him as he tried to maintain control.

His tongue plunged into her mouth, drinking in its sweet nectar. It was like a drug for him. He could never get enough. Devoid of shirt and vest, he pulled what was left of her camisole off her. He couldn't stop himself from pressing into her softness, or wrapping a hand around her derrière to bring her closer, and let her feel what she did to him. He heard her gasp as he pressed into her. "Don't be afraid."

She looked up at him in awe. "Did I do that to you?"

"Yes." He wanted to laugh with relief. Instead of being afraid, she was curious. His breath hissed through his teeth when he felt her hand slip under his pants. When her small slender fingers wrapped around his shaft he thought he would explode.

"Beth." He rolled onto his back, taking her with him. The image she made straddling him was an image forever burned in his mind.

Andrew made quick work of the fastenings on his pants while Beth continued to stroke him. Sitting up, he took the red bud of one nipple into his mouth as he started to stroke her. He knew she was ready when she started to rock against his hand.

Without breaking contact, he rolled her back onto the mattress and straddled her. It took some maneuvering, but he was able to remove his pants while still giving her pleasure.

Slowly, he lowered his weight onto her, stopping when his tip slid against her opening. He wanted this to be right, and prayed he wouldn't mess everything up.

"Beth." He wanted to warn her about the pain that might come at first. He wanted to ease into her slowly, if he could take the torture, to soften the pain as much as he could. He never expected her to arch up against him, drawing him in before he could utter a sound. Her barrier broke as he slid deeper inside.

"Beth." He remained still, to allow her a chance to grow accustomed to his size. Instead of trying to soothe her with words, he rained kisses against her eyes and throat. His hand searched for the nub he knew would help wash away the pain for her and started to rub. Her muscles started to tighten the moment he started his ministrations.

He pulled out a little.

"Andrew."

Then slid back in. "Yes."

Her heart started to beat a little faster.

He pulled out a little farther, then slid back inside her, going just a little deeper than before.

She arched against him, giving him access to a rosy tip. He pulled out and buried himself even deeper as he suckled her.

His movements picked up as he felt her muscles tightening against him. Any control he had, shattered when she wrapped her legs around him again, urging him on.

~

Her whole body tightened like a coil, reaching for something she didn't know was out there. Andrew moved above her, making her body sing with anticipation. One moment she didn't think she could stand it anymore, then the next she felt like she was diving off a cliff. Colors exploded behind her eyelids. Tears ran down her cheeks. She knew she had just experienced something most never experience in their lifetimes. Something special.

~

Andrew's body tensed a few seconds after hers before he relaxed against her. He buried his face in the pillow that cradled her head while he tried to catch his breath.

"That was amazing."

He lifted his head to look in her eyes. "That was only the beginning."

"You mean there's more?"

"I mean–" He pressed a kiss to her temple, then started to nibble his way down to her throat. "—it gets better."

"How?"

He gave her a wicked smile. Still buried deep inside her, he could feel himself starting to pulse to life already. "Would you like me to show you?"

"Now?"

He captured a nipple in his mouth.

"Now," she sighed.

~

The next morning came too early for Beth. She snuggled deeper in the covers, wishing the sun hadn't risen so quickly.

"You can't stay in bed all morning."

A smile worked its way onto her lips at the sound of Andrew's voice. After the night they had spent together, she was sure she could convince him to stay in bed with her if she tried hard enough.

Stretching, she felt a quick twinge of pain.

"How are you feeling this morning?" Andrew brushed a stray piece of hair from her face.

"Wonderful," she sighed, resting her head against his bare chest.

He shifted a little, making Beth aware of his naked state.

Of course she was just as bare, and a little embarrassed now.

Andrew cupped her chin and planted a soft kiss against her lips. "If we stay in this bed much longer, we won't be leaving it for a while."

"And that is a bad thing?" she asked. A soft blush crept up to her face, belying her bold words.

He laughed as he rolled her onto her back. "No. But I know Edward will come up here if we don't show ourselves soon, and I'd hate to be interrupted."

He placed a kiss on her abdomen before standing up and offering her his hand.

They dressed in silence. Andrew helped her into her corset and dress, making sure any evidence of their night together was well hidden beneath her gown.

He noticed her brow furrow as she slipped her shoes on. "Are you all right?"

"Yes, just a little sore." She stood up and took his hand. "Can you tell?"

"Tell what?" He paused for a second. "Oh no, my love, unless of course you keep blushing like that. Although it's very becoming, it will make people wonder what causes you to blush so easily."

"Right." She straightened her features, trying to give an aloof look.

"Now you look like you've just sucked on a lemon." He couldn't keep the chuckle out of his voice. "Just relax and be yourself."

She nodded and followed him down to the dining area.

Edward was waiting for them. "Jacob sent a message to my room and said we needed to meet with him right away."

"Did he say why?"

"No. Only that we meet him at his house as soon as possible."

They hurried over to Jacob's house, finding Sally already there.

"We came as quickly as we could."

"A body came in this morning from the McCord place. He had

Pinkerton papers on him." Jacob pulled on his coat as he filled them in on what he had learned.

Andrew paled. *Had Sally's man gotten caught?*

"Our mortician is keeping it quiet for now. I'm hoping you'll be able to identify the body before the rest of the city learns of the murder."

Jacob walked down the steps of his porch, followed by Andrew, Beth, Sally, and Edward.

Beth couldn't help but notice how the men surrounded her and Sally, and feared they expected trouble.

The walk was short, for which Beth was very grateful. Her body was tender, and she found muscles she didn't know she had hurting when she walked.

Quietly, they walked into the unmarked building. Its cool interior filled her with a sense of dread. There was a dead man in here. A shiver raced down her spine.

Jacob asked them to wait while he went to get the mortician. He came back into the room a few minutes later with a tall, gaunt man.

Beth gaped when she saw him.

"Preacher."

"Drew."

"You two know each other?" asked Jacob.

"We've had dealings before," was all Andrew said.

Beth remembered the man from when Beau had kidnapped her and Alexandra. He was the one who was supposed to marry Alex and Beau once Trey was killed. This man also worked for the Pinkerton Agency and had been there when they captured Beau, but since Andrew didn't give this information out, she wouldn't either.

"So, who you got?"

"Not sure. Been beaten to death in the face. Found a note pinned to his chest that had your name on it." Preacher turned away. "Come. I'll show you."

He took two steps before he spoke again. "Just Andrew and Jacob. The ladies need to stay here."

Beth sagged against the straight-back chair that rested against the wall. Sally and Edward did the same. They sat in silence while they waited.

~

Andrew crumpled the note in his hand. *Damn, Beau.*

"Who is this man?" asked the preacher.

"Jim Pool. I just recruited him and two others a couple of nights ago." Andrew started to pace. "How the hell did he find out so fast?"

"Anything is possible with Beau, but I'd say you have a spy among you."

"I would too, but which one? Sally works for the agency too." Andrew didn't voice his own suspicions about her. If the preacher had heard anything, he would tell him, and Andrew would rather it be that way. "Beth is one of the people he's after, so I can't see her working for him." And after last night he prayed it wasn't her. He'd never be able to turn her in.

"Edward is just a kid, but even after a shaky start, I feel I can trust him." Edward had come up with some amazing information, but he also had plenty of opportunity to get rid of Andrew and had never done anything to make him suspicious.

"You've been with these people all the time?" asked Jacob.

"Beth, yes. The other two, no."

"What about the other two you hired? Could any of them been spies?" asked Jacob.

Andrew looked at him. How could he explain the code the Pinkerton agents lived by? "Possibly, but I doubt it. Beau would have to have offered an awful lot of money for them to turn their back on the only life they understood."

"Why?"

"Because they know that anyone who turns their back on the agency will be hunted down."

"Unless they believed this Beau could follow through with his plans," said the preacher.

Andrew looked at the preacher. The man didn't say much, but when he did, it always made Andrew think. The scary part was he was right. If someone believed Beau could pull this off, he wouldn't worry about the repercussions of getting caught.

So now the question was, who knew enough about Beau to turn his back on the agency? With each question, one name kept popping up in his head. *Sally.*

CHAPTER 21

Andrew entered the room silently. All three stood up the moment they spotted him.

"Well?"

"We're going to the McCord ranch now," he said. "Edward, get the wagon ready. Sally, go with him and help him out. I've got a few things to do before we leave."

Edward nodded and headed out the door.

"How much time do we have?" asked Sally.

"Not much, why?"

"I have a few things to do too. I'll be quick about it."

Andrew watched her leave.

"Andrew?"

He took Beth's hand. "I want you to stay with Jacob, Beth. This is going to be very dangerous."

"No. I'm going with you."

"You'll just get in the way."

She gave him a stricken look before she turned her back on him.

"Look." He touched her shoulder. "Worrying about you getting hurt will be too big a distraction for me. I'd feel better if you stayed here."

"Forget it, Andrew." She shrugged his hand off her shoulder. "Go ahead and leave me here. I sure don't want to be a bother to you."

"Beth, we both know what Beau is capable of."

She didn't let him finish. "Yes, we do. For all we know, he could be waiting for you to do just this so he can grab me. You go ahead and do what you think you must. I'll just wait here like a sitting duck for Beau or one of his men to show up."

"Why must you be so exasperating? I'm trying to protect you and you're determined to prove me wrong." Andrew gripped her shoulders in anger. "Jacob can get the entire police department to keep an eye on you here. I can't promise you I can keep you safe while we're at McCord's Way."

"I don't want to be safe. I want to be with you." Her own frustration forced the words out of her mouth before she could stop them.

Andrew stared at her in shock.

Beth closed her eyes, not wanting to see the rest of his reaction. She could just imagine him getting some cocky smile, then saying something inane like, 'Don't worry your pretty little head about it.'

But she didn't hear those words spoken, or anything even remotely close. Andrew didn't utter a word, just wrapped his arms around her and kissed her soundly.

It was the feather-like pressure against her lips she noticed first. Then the viselike grip he had on her body…not that it hurt, but she knew every part of her body was molded to his and they weren't exactly in the privacy of their own room.

She forgot all about that as he deepened the kiss. As his tongue started to dance with hers, she didn't care where they were. All she could feel were the sensations sliding up and down her body, following the trails of his hands as he moved them over her.

He was right. She was wanton. She didn't care about what other people thought about her. All she wanted to do was feel.

A throat clearing itself broke them apart.

Andrew cupped her face. "You know I'd take you with me if I thought it was safe."

She nodded. Speaking was out of the question right now.

"I'll keep her safe," said Jacob as he joined them.

"I'll be back as quickly as I can." Andrew kissed her once more. "Be good."

Beth crossed her arms over her bosom. She knew exactly what he meant by that statement and wasn't happy about it.

Andrew looked at her for a few more seconds before taking his leave.

~

Andrew pushed his horse hard until they drew close to the ranch. He hoped Beth did as he had asked and stayed with Jacob. With any luck, this would all be over quickly and he could be back before she got into any mischief.

Sally and Edward rode with him, neither asking why Beth didn't join them. Something he was grateful for because he didn't want to answer the same question that had been gnawing at him since they left. After all the danger she had already been in because of him, was it safe to leave her behind now? If Beau wanted her would he find a way to get her, no matter how much protection Andrew gave her?

Stopping his horse, he slid to the ground and signaled for the rest to do the same. It was just the three of them since he hadn't had a chance to contact any of the agents in the area. His first thought had been to just ride through the front entrance. It would be the last thing Beau would expect him to do.

"We need to create a diversion," he said softly when Sally and Edward had tethered their horses and joined him.

"What type of diversion?" asked Edward.

"A small fire over there." Sally pointed to an older barn near the edge of the ranch. "It's close enough to attract attention, but will allow us to hide after we start the blaze.

"That's a good idea," said Andrew. "Edward, can you do that?"

"Yes, sir."

"Sally, you'll need to be lookout while he does."

She nodded.

"Once the fire has been spotted, I'll go in and try to find Beau. Join me as soon as you can." Andrew worked his way to the front entrance of the compound while he waited for the smoke.

It took a few minutes, but before long, he heard the shouts go up and watched as men ran from everywhere, all heading toward the fire.

Once he was sure he could sneak in undetected, he raced to the first building, then proceeded to maneuver from one to another, working his way toward the main house.

His brow furrowed when he noticed a lack of activity around it. Beau should be out on the porch by now, shouting orders and acting like the God he thought he was. So why wasn't he outside?

Andrew didn't like the feel of this. He went around back, and found it as vacant as the front. Slipping inside, he cautiously moved from one room to the next, checking for anything that moved.

"Nothing." He walked into the library on the first floor. The room had papers piled everywhere. Most were overdue bills. He found a few scraps of paper with a name or an address, but nothing else. He opened drawers and found them empty.

Taking the stairs two at a time to the second floor, Andrew checked each of the bedrooms. All deserted. The largest had the armoire wide open, drawers hanging open, now void of whatever they had held just hours ago.

"Damn it." The soft click of a gun hammer made him turn around. In his disgust at being outsmarted again by Beau, he'd forgotten to check to make sure no stragglers snuck up behind him.

~

Beth returned Jacob's smile for the twentieth time in the last fifteen minutes. She was going to go crazy if she had to sit here all day.

Jacob worked out in his garden, pruning his flowers, while he held Beth captive on the porch.

She sighed. Maybe captive wasn't the right word, but that was how she felt. Every time she shifted in her seat, he was right there at her side, asking if she needed anything. She needed the one thing he wouldn't give her—privacy.

Jacob walked up onto the back porch, carrying a large bouquet of flowers. "Let's put these in some water, then have some lemonade. Cook makes the best around."

Beth nodded as she stood. At least she could get up out of the chair. She followed Jacob inside, knowing he'd be back outside looking for her if she didn't.

He chatted about his garden as he poured them each a glass of lemonade.

The cold liquid felt good as it slid down her throat. Somehow nodding at the appropriate times, she didn't really listen to what Jacob said. Instead, she worried about Andrew. Not knowing if he was all right had her stomach in knots. So much, she hadn't been able to eat anything all morning.

Cook came by about lunchtime carrying a basket under her arm.

"There're some men in town asking about you," she said to Beth.

"Really?" Had her father tracked her down this quickly? Andrew swore he wouldn't know where to start, but maybe he came looking for Andrew.

"They were asking about the lady who rode in with a Pinkerton agent."

Fingers of dread snaked up her. She wanted to ask what they looked like, but couldn't find her voice.

"Did anyone tell them she was still here?" asked Jacob.

"No one knew he was an agent, except us and a few of the police. Everyone just shook their head and said no."

"Just the same, I think we need to make preparations." Jacob stood up and walked into his pantry. When he returned, he held a rifle in his hands. "Cook, take Elizabeth down to the cellar and stay there until I tell you to come back up. I think I'll go sit on the porch for a little while."

Beth stared at Jacob with wide eyes.

Cook nodded and led her down the stairs. She closed the door before she lit the lamp Jacob kept in the cellar.

"You know this is just a precaution. I'm sure those men don't mean you any harm, but Jacob takes his job seriously and he aims to protect you."

Beth nodded, fear stealing her voice for a moment.

"Why don't you have a seat over there?" Cook said. "I'm going to check on something first."

Just as Beth settled into the seat she heard Cook whisper her name. She crept over to where Cook stood and found her looking through a small peephole in the wood just about eye level. Beth blinked several times before she could focus on what she saw.

"Mirrors," Cook answered her unasked question. "Jacob fancies himself a scientist at times. Came up with this idea of placing small mirrors so anyone down here could see the front yard with ease. He was like a child the day he installed it."

"I bet." Beth looked back at the woman. "It's ingenious."

"That's Jacob," Cook gestured toward the small hole. "Do you recognize any of the men?"

Beth looked through. Shaking her head, she stepped back. "Should I?"

"Those are the ones who were looking for you earlier."

Bits of debris drifted down on them as several pairs of boots stomped up the steps to Jacob's porch. Snippets of conversation floated through the floor.

"There was a new couple in town, but they left this morning."

Beth strained to hear what was said next, but she couldn't make it out. However, she had an idea when she saw one of the men pull a gun on Jacob.

She grabbed Cook's arm. "He's in trouble."

Cook took a quick peek through the hole and nodded. Silently, she signaled for Beth to follow her.

They stepped into an older section of the cellar where Jacob stored his wines. Cook yanked on one of the racks, pulling it from the side of the rock wall.

Beth gasped as she raced to her side, hoping to get her out of the way before everything fell.

"Jacob has always been prepared for any kind of trouble." Cook smiled at Beth's surprise. "It's fake."

Her eyes widened as the rack swung freely from the wall, its contents staying in place. With the rack out of the way Beth could see a small hole in the wall, just big enough for them to crawl through.

"We must hurry." Cook urged Beth through the hole first.

The next room was a lot smaller and pitch-black. Beth dragged dank, musty air into her lungs and grimaced.

"Beth, I need your help."

She felt her way around blindly, accidentally stumbling over Cook's kneeling form in her haste to find her.

"Help me push this rock into place. Just in case anyone realizes that the rack swings out, Jacob had this false front created so no one should be able to tell there's a hole in the wall. Of course he's never had to test it before."

Beth knelt beside her and helped push the rock into place. Once they were done, Cook took Beth's hand and felt along the rock wall with the other.

Beth had no clue where they were or how far they walked, but Cook seemed to know where she was headed, so Beth didn't argue. She wanted out of the cold, dark place as quick as possible. After they had walked quite a distance, Cook suddenly stopped.

"There should be a door here somewhere."

"And what's it made out of?" Beth asked. She was met with silence. "Well, what do you expect me to think? I have seen all kinds of things today."

"It's a regular wooden door."

"Good. Those little doors made out of rock would be difficult to find."

Cook laughed softly. "Help me find it."

"Do I have to get on my hands and knees again?"

"Yes." Beth could hear the laughter in Cook's voice. "But only because we'll probably feel the air coming from underneath it before we actually feel the wood."

"Normal size door?" Beth got down on all fours.

"Normal size door," Cook confirmed.

Beth slid her hands on the floor, hoping she would feel her fingers slip under the door soon. She almost asked about what critters they might run into down here, but changed her mind. If she knew for sure, she'd be too afraid to search for the door because Beth knew she'd find the critter first.

They both stiffened when they heard a sound behind them. Neither breathed for a moment as they strained to hear more, but nothing else happened.

"I found the door," Cook whispered. Sliding her hand up the slightly warped wood, she found the knob. Wrapping her hand around the handle, she twisted and pulled.

The door opened. Fresh clean air made Beth inhale deeply. The musty air was starting to get to her.

Cook moved first, looking though the doorway, she turned her head right, then left, before stepping through. Once she was sure they were safe, she signaled for Beth to follow her.

"Where are we?"

"In the church's cellar."

"Where's Jacob's house?"

Cook led her to a small window just about eye level. "Over there."

Beth stood on tippy-toes to get a clear view of Jacob's house. There was no sign of him, or the men who had come looking for her. In fact the house looked ominously quiet.

"Where's the stable?" She didn't want to jeopardize her friends any further. She had to get out of town as quickly and as quietly as possible.

"Why?" asked Cook.

"Because those men won't stop until they find me. It would be safer for everyone if I left town."

"But Jacob promised."

"I don't want Jacob or you getting hurt because of me." Beth walked to the cellar door. "I've got to go."

"What shall we tell Drew?"

"Tell him I escaped. He'll believe that."

CHAPTER 22

Andrew turned slowly toward the sound that might be heralding his death. How could he have been so stupid? He wondered what Beth would do when he didn't return.

The muzzle of the Colt, pointing at his chest, looked much larger than it should. His gaze traveled up his killer's gloved hand, to his arm, then finally his face. His eyes widened in recognition. "Able."

"Leroux?" He released the hammer before dropping his gun to his side. "I thought you were one of the McCord men."

"They're already gone," answered Andrew. His anger started to grow because Beau had slipped through his fingers once again. He prowled around the room, stopping in front of the row of windows that dominated one side of the library.

"I know. Got here about a half hour ago and found the barracks pretty much empty. Only a few hands remained to keep this place running. Had to assume most of them had already moved on. What're you doing here anyway?" The scrape of leather mixed with Able's words as he put his gun back in his holster.

"Been hearing stories about the leader here. Sounded a lot like the man I'm looking for, so I thought I'd find out for sure. Didn't expect him to be gone though." Andrew looked out the window into the empty yard. "What brought you here?"

"Pretty much the same thing. Heard about this man and thought if I could get a job with him, I could learn about how he operated. Once I was sure he was the one you wanted, I'd try to get in touch with you. But it looks like we were both a little late."

Andrew nodded.

"Any idea on where he went?" asked Able.

"No." Andrew turned toward Able. "But that has never stopped me before."

~

Beth didn't like feeling like a fugitive as she snuck toward the livery stable. Darting between buildings in broad daylight made her feel foolish, but she feared if she tried just walking to it she'd be spotted. She peeked around the corner of the building she leaned against and released a sigh of relief. *Only a little farther to go.* She took one step forward before the voices floated back to her hiding place.

"Well, she's got to be here somewhere. She didn't travel with him to the ranch, she's not in her hotel room, and we searched that old man's house thoroughly."

"What makes you think she'd come here?"

Her heart sank as she listened. They had already figured out she'd try to leave town.

"Think about it. What would you do if you thought someone was following you?"

"Hightail it out of town."

Beth wished she knew who spoke, but she didn't dare reveal herself. They were too close.

"Exactly."

She heard the pounding of boots and the jangle of spurs as the two men headed toward her destination. Getting a horse from there was out of the question now. With a quick glance around, she found the street relatively clear of people.

Beth eased back into the shadows of the alley she hid in, thanking her common sense for telling her to stay out of sight while she tried to get to her horse. Foolish or not, it had saved her this time.

She bit her bottom lip while she tried to figure out what to do next. Should she try to get to her horse and flee, or stay and hide?

She rested against the building, watching the stable while the two men remained inside. It would be better for her to ride the horse Andrew had gotten for her, but she didn't even know if it was still in the livery. She remembered Andrew asking Edward to get the buckboard ready. Did they end up taking it? Would Andrew take her horse as well to keep her where he thought she'd be safe?

After a few mental debates she convinced herself to sneak over to the livery and see for herself if Andrew had taken all the horses with the buckboard. She darted across the street, fearing someone would spot her. Once she made it to the side of the building she hid in the shadows, gulping in air. Her heart beat hard in her chest. If she got caught now, everything would be in vain.

Voices floated to her. Those men were still inside. Knowing she couldn't check the interior yet, she eased her way back toward the corral. Maybe her horse was out there. She bit her lip again when she didn't see her horse. Did Andrew take it or could it still be inside? She wanted to know for sure, but how?

The sound of feet against wooden planks made her back up against the building again. The murmur of voices could be heard, but she couldn't distinguish what was being said. Three men stepped through the back end of the stable and out into the corral.

"Look, the lady you're looking for has never been here. The gentleman was, but he left early this morning taking three of the horses with him. He didn't say he'd be back."

"But you said he brought in four horses and a buckboard."

"Sure, but lots of people leave things behind. The horse he left is old. He probably decided it was too old to make the journey, and his buckboard has seen better days too. He wouldn't get far with the bad wheel that's on it. He left that behind."

So Andrew didn't take the buckboard after all.

"Contact me if the lady or the gentleman come back for them." There was a pause.

Beth peeked around the corner long enough to see one of them pass money to the guy she assumed worked in the stable.

"Sure. Where you stayin'?"

"At the hotel on Main Street."

That was the same hotel they were in. She couldn't go back there either.

She waited for them to go back inside before she inched closer to the pen that held the horses. Now that she knew one horse had been left behind, she knew she had to get it. *But how?* If she went inside, the man who worked there would surely tell the two who were looking for her.

She eased herself around the side of the barn, climbed over the fence and leaned against the side of it. Taking a deep breath to still her hammering heart, she stepped into the cool interior of the stable.

Where's the horse Andrew left behind? None of the animals looked familiar. Did she take this big risk for nothing?

Just as she berated herself for being so stupid, she felt a hand touch her shoulder.

~

Andrew stood out in the main compound, listening to Edward. Although he really didn't pay too much attention to what the youngster said, he did hear Sally was gone again, with no explanation, and that the men they now had tied up in the barn were brand-new recruits who knew practically nothing about their boss or where he might have headed. If they did know, they weren't talking and no threats would get any more information.

He shook his head in disgust. Beau was out there somewhere, and once again, Andrew had no clue where. Gazing up at the ranch house, he wondered if there was anything in the library he could've missed. He and Able had scoured the place looking for a clue on where Beau could have gone, but came up empty-handed.

After asking Edward to go through the bunkhouse for hints on where they had moved on to, Andrew went back up to the main house and walked through the front door.

He stood there for a while trying to figure out where Beau might have hidden information and not retrieved it. The drawers would be too obvious. Andrew knew better than to believe anything he'd find easily.

He sat down in the chair in front of the massive desk. Drumming his fingers, he looked around the room. *Where would Beau hide something like that? And would he remember to remove it if he was in a hurry?*

~

"Thought you'd be showing up sooner or later."

Beth felt her heart leap up in her throat. She'd been caught! Turning, she looked at the man attached to the hand on her shoulder.

"Don't stand there like a ninny." He handed her a set of reins.

Gawking at the leather he placed in her hands, she followed the strips up to a soft tan muzzle. *My horse!*

"I—"

"You better get while you can. Those men will probably be back to make sure you haven't come by. I made them think your horse was out in the corral, but if they talk to anyone else who works here, they'll learn I was lying to them."

"Thank you." She swung up in the saddle. Her dress wasn't the best thing she could wear for riding, but she couldn't be real picky right now Folding her skirt around her legs, she set her feet in the stirrups, clicked at the horse, and trotted out of the barn.

She really didn't know where she should head. She had very little money, and no spare clothing. For now, she just needed to find a good place to hole up for a while.

Maybe there was a farm nearby where she could stop and get a few provisions. Not a lot with the little money she had in her reticule, but enough to get to the next town if she was lucky.

Knowing those men were looking for her, she kept to some of the smaller roads, and a few backyards to get to the edge of town. Without looking back, she kept her horse trotting along as they left town. She hoped she looked like a wife heading back to her home farther out.

After going over a rise and down into a small incline, she realized she'd made it out without anyone knowing it. Although she wanted to whoop for joy, she urged her horse into a gallop, putting as much space between her and the town as she could. She'd worry about where she should go later, once she felt safer.

~

Andrew had been wandering aimlessly around for about an hour, when he found himself back in the room he assumed Beau had used. The rich brocade spread lay in a heap on the floor at the foot of the bed. The bare armoire seemed to beckon him, with its doors wide open. Several drawers were closed haphazardly, tufts of a few forgotten items caught halfway out.

Opening the drawers, he pulled out the pieces left behind, finding rather mundane things like odd socks, one pair of boxers, and a perfectly brand-new shirt still wrapped in brown paper. He smiled as he lifted it out of the drawer. They were the same size, and Andrew knew how angry Beau would be if he ever found out Andrew might have worn one of his personally designed shirts.

A small piece of paper fluttered to the floor.

Andrew bent and picked it up. It was an address, no city, or territory, just the name of a road, with a few numbers written beside it. It wasn't much, but something.

After tucking the new shirt under his arm, Andrew walked down the stairs and out into the yard where Edward waited.

"Let's get these men into town. It'll take most of the afternoon since they'll have to walk." Andrew rubbed his hand against his horse's neck before pulling himself up into the saddle.

"What about Sally and Able?" Edward climbed into his saddle.

"I'm not going to wait for her. Sally will figure out where we went when she comes back." Andrew pulled on his horse's reins to keep it still. His horse never liked to stand still for very long. "Able is heading west to see if he can pick up Beau's trail."

~

Their prisoners had already been tied to a header rope, which Edward held in his hands. They weren't going to like the trek to town, especially behind his horse. Edward knew Andrew would set a quick pace so he could get back to Miss Elizabeth as fast as he could.

It took two hours before Edward heard the first complaint about his horse.

"Exactly what did you feed that thing?" grumbled one man. "It's hard walking behind a horse who leaves piles as big as an elephant."

Edward smiled. Acting as if he didn't hear the man, he continued to pull them along, directly behind his horse.

"Hey, did you hear me? I've ruined a perfectly good pair of boots because of that animal."

"It's not my fault you were at the wrong place at the wrong time. Maybe you should be thinking about what'll happen to you when we get to town, and not about your boots," said Edward. He heard the man mumble a response before falling silent.

Andrew looked over his shoulder at him before reining his mount so they could ride side by side. "I'd say you're enjoying yourself."

"Yep," replied Edward with a grin. "I'm sure glad I don't have to walk behind my horse."

Andrew laughed.

"What will become of these men?" Edward asked quietly.

"Probably nothing. I doubt if they can be held for anything major. I'm hoping they'll have to stew in jail for a night or two though. Make them think twice before they join up with someone else like Beau."

"Will that work?"

"For those who didn't really know what they had gotten into, yes. For the others, no. They'll probably head straight back to Beau and tell him someone's after him."

"And we'll follow them."

"Someone will. At least for a little while." Andrew paused for a moment. "Once we get back and get these men settled in, we'll talk about how we are going to handle having these men followed. There are too many for just the two of us. But if we can get enough people to follow those who I think know more than they let on, then we just might catch Beau."

"Did you learn anything about where he's headed?"

"All I have is a road and some numbers. And I don't even know if they pertain to his hideout. It's not much, but it's all we have right now. I hope Able is successful in finding Beau and getting that information to me." Andrew sat up in his saddle a little as they came to the top of a sort incline. "Someone's coming at us, riding hard."

~

Andrew urged his horse into a gallop down the other side, hoping to catch up with whoever it was long before they found out about the men they had in tow. He lost sight of the rider as he hit the bottom of the gully before he headed up the small rise in front of him. Once he reached the top he stopped his horse. The other rider had vanished.

A frown creased his brow as he looked around. He knew he wasn't seeing things, so where did he go? Were they hoping to ambush Andrew before he got these men into town? Spying a small copse of trees off to the right, he urged his horse forward, straight for the shaded area. As he drew closer he felt the hairs on the back of his neck stand up. Pulling his gun from his holster, he yelled. "Come out with your hands up!"

CHAPTER 23

Beth heard the voice telling her to come out with her hands up. Fear raced up her spine, blocking out everything else, but she promised herself she wouldn't go without a fight. Unfortunately, she had no weapon.

"I give you to the count of ten to show yourself."

The words barely registered as she looked around for something, anything to use. Several tree branches lay about, but unless she could whittle them down in just a few seconds, and learn how to throw javelins in the same span of time they would be useless to her. "Oh, how did I get into such a mess?"

"I don't know, Beth, but you better start explaining right now."

She spun around, fear clogging her throat.

"Andrew!" Her whole body relaxed at the sight of him. Five seconds ago she'd thought all was lost, now Andrew had appeared like a guardian angel. The relief she felt made her knees weak. "What are you doing sneaking up on me like that? You scared me half to death."

The moment he saw her wobble, he stepped to her side. Easing her down onto the grass he knelt beside her. "What foolhardy notion did you get in your head that made you come out here?"

"It wasn't a foolhardy notion. Some men came looking for me. Cook helped me escape through an underground tunnel. I knew I couldn't stay in town without you anymore. Those men were staying at our hotel. I'm afraid they've hurt Jacob, but I don't know for sure. And heaven knows what they'll do to Cook if they find out she helped me."

"Slow down, Beth. You say some men came to Jacob's house?"

"Yes. We were out on the back porch when Cook came by and said some men in town were looking for me." She took a deep breath to slow down her hammering heart. "Jacob told Cook to take me into the cellar. Then he went out on the front porch to wait for them.

"Cook and I could hear their voices." She paused for a moment, trying to recall all that had happened. "There was a peephole for us to look through. Although I didn't get a real good look at the men, I did see them pull a gun on Jacob. That's when Cook took me through the secret tunnel."

"So how did you get your horse?" asked Andrew.

"When we came out of the tunnel, we were in the church cellar. I told Cook I had to leave town." Beth had to smile at her next words. "When she asked me how you'd know where to look for me, I told her to tell you I escaped. I figured you'd know where I'd try to head if I was successful.

"Anyway, those same men were at the stable. They tried to bribe the man working there, but he was the one who let me have my horse. I was able to leave town undetected and have been heading southwest ever since."

"And what would you have done if it hadn't been me who found you?"

"I probably would've been killed." Her voice came out as a squeak. Tears pooled in her eyes. "I left without money or a weapon. That's why I hid here when I first noticed the dust cloud from your horses. I was hoping whoever was headed into town wouldn't notice me right away and I'd be able to hide here until they passed."

"You are the craziest—"

"No. Miss Alexandra has won that distinction." Beth knew her friend had pulled several stunts that made this one look calm.

"Most exasperating, foolishly brave woman I have ever met." Andrew wrapped his arms around her, thankful he had found her safe before anyone else had happened upon her. He didn't want to think about what could have happened if she had gotten past him without his knowledge.

"Please don't be mad at Jacob."

"Beth."

"Please?" She grabbed his arm. "He truly tried to protect me. I don't think any of us expected what happened."

Andrew nodded as he looked into her tear-filled eyes. He should've known Beau would try something like this. "Come on. Let's get back into town."

"But what about those men?"

"I'll take care of them later. First we have a small army to bring to the police in town."

Her eyes widened as Edward came up over the last rise. There were about twenty men walking behind his horse, all tied together.

"Did you capture Beau?"

"No."

She didn't think Beau would allow himself to be pulled behind a horse in such an undignified manner. With Andrew's help, she climbed back on her horse and headed back into town.

~

"I'm sorry sir, but this hotel has been booked up for weeks. No one new has checked in."

"Is there another hotel on this street?"

"No, sir. The Grand is the only hotel on Main Street."

Andrew's gaze slid to Beth, who seemed a bit paler than before.

"I swear that's what I heard them say. They were staying at this hotel," she whispered.

Andrew didn't say anything. He just nodded to the clerk, and grasping Beth's elbow, he led her outside.

"I know. Let's go speak to the man who gave me my horse. He'll tell you the same thing."

"All right." Andrew escorted her to the stables.

"Is the gentleman who was here earlier around? I need to ask him a question," Andrew asked.

"That would be me."

"No," said Beth. "He means the tall man with the beard."

"Sorry, ma'am, but there's no tall man with a beard working here. There's just me and the owner, and his nephew who helps out from time to time."

"But there was another man here. He gave me my horse."

"Which one, ma'am?"

"That one right there."

"I don't know about no man, ma'am. We thought that horse had been stolen." He excused himself so he could start feeding the animals.

"Andrew, I don't know what is going on, but I'm not lying to you. I did get my horse from a man with a beard. I did hear the other ones saying they were going to stay at our hotel."

"Why don't we go visit Jacob and see what he has to say?"

She nodded, allowing Andrew to take her over to Jacob's porch.

Andrew knocked on the door. As he stood there waiting for Jacob to answer, someone from the street called to them.

"You looking for Jacob?"

"Yes."

"You won't find him here. He went out of town earlier today."

"What about Cook?"

"I believe she went with him."

"About what time did they head out?" Andrew turned toward Beth.

"Not sure. Heard tell they went after some lady they were watching after. She ran off and they felt responsible."

"Thanks." He gripped her arm a little harder than he should have and dragged her toward the hotel. "I should've known better than to believe you."

"I am telling the truth, no matter how hard it is to believe. But knowing how pigheaded you can be, I don't even know why I should try to convince you." She fought his hold on her. "Go ahead and believe what you want."

No matter how hard she struggled, he wouldn't release his hold. She knew they must have made quite a scene, but by this point, she was too angry to care. Aiming with deadly accuracy, she stomped a well-placed heel onto his foot. A few seconds later, she was free.

Lifting her skirts, she set a stiff pace for herself, marching straight toward the hotel. Three quick stomps and she was in the main lobby, quickly walking to the stairs. She climbed the steps to the second floor two at a time and had thrown the bolt home just as Andrew made it to the room.

She sat on the bed while he pounded on the door from the hallway.

"Elizabeth, let me in."

"What? You want to be in the same room as a liar and a thief? Thought you were better than that type of person." She watched as the door vibrated from his hammering.

"If you don't let me in there, I'll get this door removed by the hinges."

"Have fun. Tamper with that door and I'll flee through the window." She could hear Andrew grumbling as the pounding stopped. Maybe he was finally coming to his senses.

She waited a few minutes before she tiptoed up to the door. *Was he still out there?* Now that her anger had cooled, she realized how foolhardy she had been. Why did she alienate the one man who'd been able to keep her safe?

"Andrew?"

"Yes."

His voice came from right behind her. Whirling, she came face-to-face with the angriest man she had ever met. She could feel the color drain from her face. How would he punish her?

~

Andrew saw the fear etched on her face. It served her right after lying to him the way she did. Then she had the audacity to lock him out of his own room.

"Why did you lock me out?"

"Because you won't believe me." Her voice was so soft he barely heard her.

"That isn't a good enough reason." He stepped toward her. Her quick step back didn't go unnoticed. "You tell me that you were being pursued, yet no one can back up your story."

She glanced around the room wildly.

Andrew frowned. Where did she expect to flee to?

She raced to the door, trying to undo the bolt she had used to bar his entrance.

He grabbed her hands and turned her to face him.

"You won't run away again."

"I wasn't..." Beth dropped her gaze to her boots. With a sigh, she asked, "What're you going to do to me?"

"I should tie you up and toss you on that bed. Better yet, I should give you the spanking you deserve."

Her head snapped up at his words. "You wouldn't dare."

"Care to test me?"

She shook her head.

He watched her face, noting her slender throat as it constricted in a swallow. She was afraid. Afraid of what he might do to her now.

Good. Let her stew for a while on how angry he was. Maybe that would keep her from doing anything else foolhardy. He really wanted to believe her story, but all the evidence said she lied about how she left town. Turning from her, he pulled his hat from his head and sent it sailing toward the bed.

Out of the corner of his eye he watched as she let out her breath.

"We will dine in one hour."

Beth remained silent.

He whipped around to face her. "Did you hear me?"

"Ye—yes."

This frightened little mouse wasn't the same woman he had grown to know and love. "If you promise to stay by my side and refrain from trying to escape again, I'll allow you to join me for dinner, but if you refuse, you'll stay up here while I enjoy a delicious meal."

"I promise."

"Good, because I'd hate to handcuff you to the bed."

Her eyes widened at his words, but all she did was nod.

The next hour crawled along. Every time he spoke to Beth, she just about jumped out of her skin before giving him a hesitant answer. It made him wonder why she was so skittish. *Did her father beat her?*

He knew her father had kept men from courting her, keeping her very protected as she matured into a young woman, but he had never heard of him mistreating his daughter or his wife. Her reaction just didn't make sense.

At five o'clock, Andrew stood up and picked up his hat. Beth looked up at him expectantly. Without a word, he offered her his arm and escorted her down into the dining room.

They ate in silence. Just the clink of a glass and the scraping of silverware against the plates could be heard.

Her sharp intake of breath caught his attention quickly. First looking at her, he followed her gaze to two men who had just entered the dining room. They looked pretty ordinary.

"Anything wrong?" he asked without taking his eyes off them.

"It's th—no." She dropped her eyes to her plate, but didn't lift her fork again.

"Are those the men you supposedly saw?"

She nodded once.

The two men were brought to a table at the other end of the room. Andrew kept watching them as they ordered, then ate their meal. She could've just picked two men out of a crowd, but she'd have to be a very good actress to get the color to drain out of her face the way it did when she spotted them, and he knew Beth wasn't very good at faking it.

Andrew asked for coffee when the waiter returned. If they were going to sit there a while, he had to make it look good.

The two men had just finished eating by the time Andrew was on his third cup of coffee. Beth had barely touched her first one.

He waited until they headed toward the lobby before following them.

"Drew?"

"I'll be right back." He walked slowly to the lobby and watched as the two men climbed into the birdcage elevator. Once the elevator started moving up he walked over to the desk.

"Did those two men just check in?" he asked.

The clerk looked up. "Sir?"

"The two men in the elevator. Did they just check in?"

"I don't know, sir. They're headed to the suite of rooms that are permanently rented. I believe they come and go as they please as long as the bill is paid on time."

"Thanks." Andrew headed back to the table. So the men Beth had seen really were staying in their hotel. He wondered how much more of what she said was true. If only he could talk to Jacob.

Sitting back down at the table he picked up his coffee and took a sip.

"It looks like those men are staying in the hotel," he said.

"Then you believe me?" Hope filled her eyes.

CHAPTER 24

Beth didn't know what to think when Andrew didn't answer her. She had told him the truth. His not believing her had crushed her more than she'd thought possible. She had moped since he'd accused her of lying. Her father had never made her feel this guilty. The sad thing was she didn't know how to prove it to him. Seeing those men in the dining room was the first ray of hope she had.

She stood when Andrew did and allowed him to escort her back to their room.

Once their door closed, Andrew walked over to the small table and wrote out a quick note. He excused himself from the room.

"Great," she mumbled to herself. What was he up to anyway? She paced the room until he returned.

He opened the door and closed it behind him. After locking it, he turned to look at her.

"Andrew."

"Look, let's call it a truce." Andrew ran his fingers through his hair. "The presence of those men is the first piece of evidence that your story is true. I've just sent a note to Edward to ask him to see what he can find out about them. He might be able to get the answers I need better than me."

"Why?"

"Because I think they know who I am. A fresh face like Edward's might be able to find out something I couldn't."

She nodded, watching his fingers slip through his hair again. There was something about the way the light played on the strands twining through his fingers that had her undivided attention.

Andrew watched her for a moment. Beth wondered why. What was he contemplating so hard? She nervously stepped back when he started for the closet.

He pulled open the door and crouched down.

Beth wished she had the nerve to peek over his shoulder, but didn't dare. She hadn't been able to figure out Andrew's mood since they had returned and didn't want to anger him anymore. Beau had taught her a lesson in uncontrolled anger she'd probably never forget.

He stood up and turned toward her, a small leather pouch resting in his hand. A frown creased his brow as he held out the package to her. "I want you to have this."

"You don't seem to be happy about it though." She didn't reach for the gift. "Why?"

"I think you'll understand once you open it."

Beth hesitated for a moment longer before she took the offered pouch. Lifting the leather flap she almost dropped it as she tried to get away from the offending thing.

"I can't take that," she said as she gingerly laid it on the bed.

Andrew picked it back up and pulled the small derringer out. "You have to."

"Andrew."

"Explain to me why you can't, then." He looked up from the small gun in his hand. "It's the least you can do."

"Papa's brother."

Andrew's gaze slid to Beth, who seemed a bit paler than before. "What about your father's brother, Beth? I don't remember him."

She bit her lip as she eased herself down onto the bed. He was right. She knew he deserved to know the whole story of her fear of guns.

"Papa was from Mississippi, but moved to Jennings when he and

Mama married. His brother was ten years younger than him. The baby of seven children. As the youngest, he was also the most rebellious of the group. He wanted to shake the image of being the baby.

"At least that's what he told me one time when he came to visit." Beth shrugged her shoulders. "The first and last time I met him was when he was on his way out west. Papa couldn't believe his baby brother wanted to go west."

"And I assume he tried to convince him to stay in Jennings."

"You could say that. I remember several heated conversations wafting out the library windows while I played out on the porch waiting for dinner. Papa never knew I was there, but I think my uncle did. He spoke of the arguments he had with Papa later when he found me out on there."

"Spent a lot of time on the porch , huh?"

"Not a whole lot for a young girl to do in the house, unless I wanted to clean. Momma and I normally had already finished our reading, or working on my letters and numbers for the day. So Mama pretended to not see me when I hid out on there." Beth brushed a stray hair out of her eyes. "My uncle would come out after having dessert with Papa fuming about big brothers and how he felt people didn't understand what he wanted for his life.

"He had a grand scheme, you know. He planned on going west and making a name for himself. He wanted to start a ranch and breed the best horses to sell to the government. Papa actually commended him on that dream, but couldn't understand why he couldn't do it where we were or another town near his family."

"You understood though," said Andrew. He leaned against the bedpost. "Didn't you?"

"Yes. He wanted his freedom." She couldn't verbalize her desire for freedom too. Looking at Andrew's passive face, she wasn't sure he'd understand why she wanted that freedom.

"So what happened?"

"One day Papa pushed too hard and my uncle left our house in anger. He wrote me to let us know about his travels, but he never wrote to Papa."

"He wrote to you?" Andrew sat on the bed next to her.

"Yes." She nodded. "He spoke of the big cities he had seen. How the prairie went on and on. Suddenly, the letters stopped. Papa became worried, so he went to the last place the letters came from."

Beth plucked at the bedspread. "Papa came back after a few months. He was quiet, too quiet for us. He never yelled or got angry. Mama was worried. Papa always yelled."

Andrew arched his brow.

"You know it to be true. But he came back just a shell of a man. Nothing affected him. He never bartered for the best prices or argued with customers when they wanted to pay a lower price for something in our store. Mama ended up taking over the store for a while.

"Then one day a stranger came through town. He was from the West. He stopped by while Mama was home fixing dinner." Beth looked up at Andrew. "He was selling the newest six shooter and had hoped to get Papa to carry them in his store.

"I'd never seen Papa hit anyone before. He ended up in jail because he couldn't control his temper." Beth paused for just a moment. "I was at the store helping with the books when he got angry with the salesman. He told him between punches how my uncle died."

Andrew waited for her to tell him.

"He'd gone into some small town where he had hoped to buy land. My uncle had heard the pasture land there was perfect for horses. Papa said he had gone into the bar in town that evening to have a drink and a fight broke out. His brother tried to break it up.

"A Pinkerton agent came into the bar and just started shooting. One of those bullets entered my uncle's head, killing him instantly. Once the agent learned he'd made a mistake and shot an innocent man–" Beth tried not to cry as she told the last part. "–Papa said the agent left a note for the family of the man he had killed. It basically said, 'Sorry, but he shouldn't have been where he was.'"

Andrew now understood why Beth always rushed them away from her house when he did call on her. "What about his hatred of guns?"

"Papa wanted to find this man. Make him explain himself. So he started searching for this agent. He found him about five towns over, sitting in a bar. When Papa tried to confront him, the man stared at him blankly. He couldn't remember the man he had killed the month before. He'd already killed several others since then.

"The agent got tired of Papa's ranting and asked him if he was calling him out. If not, would he kindly move on." Beth smiled sadly. "I think the man surprised Papa so much he backed off. But not quick enough. He watched as that same agent shot some young kid who called him out for shooting a relative. The senselessness of the shooting changed Papa. After he returned, he banned guns in our house. We weren't even allowed to speak of them."

"You went along with this?" Andrew had never known Beth to do anything anyone told her to.

"Of course not. I even had someone show me how to shoot one. But after my run-in with Beau, I learned just how scary they can be." Beth swallowed as she remembered the memories from her kidnapping. "Beau waved his gun around like it was a part of him. And every time the muzzle of that weapon was pointed at me, I feared it would go off. From that point on, I understood and honored Papa's ban on guns."

Andrew knew she wouldn't take the gun from him, but would she return it if he slipped it into her purse? That might be the only way to make sure she had the weapon with her.

"Let's get ready for bed. Maybe we can talk about this a little more then."

Bed. She went for her nightgown as she wondered what the night would bring. Would she spend another night in his arms, or would he treat her like a stranger once again?

Stepping behind the screen, she undid the buttons on her dress, pulled the strings to loosen her corset, and slipped into her nightgown.

Brushing her fingers against the cotton fabric nervously, she hoped for another night like last night. Remembering the feel of his body against hers sent a silent tingle up her back.

Taking a deep breath, she stepped out from behind the screen to find Andrew sitting at the desk, writing.

"I have some things to take care of first. Go ahead and go to sleep. I'll join you in a little while."

Beth tried to hide the look of disappointment on her face as she climbed into bed. She guessed Andrew had added her to his list of conquests and had no further use for her. Turning her back to him, she felt a tear trickle down her nose.

Why did I have to fall in love with him? She sat up. *When did I fall in love with him?*

"Do you need something?" Andrew didn't even look up from what he was doing to ask her the question, for which she was grateful. He wouldn't see her wipe the stray tear from the tip of her nose.

"A glass of water."

"Do you want me to get it for you?" He did look up at her then.

"No. I can get it." She padded over to the pitcher and basin stand. She picked up an intricately cut glass and filled it half way with water. Although she really wasn't thirsty, she took several sips as she padded back to the bed. Crawling back in, she closed her eyes and willed herself to sleep.

~

A soft moan escaped her as she shifted in her sleep. The gentle glide of a hand caressing her body had her aching for more. She could feel the warmth of the hard male chest as her fingers pressed against it.

A feather-like kiss caressed her brow. Another brushed against the corner of her mouth. Beth turned her face toward the lips touching her. That seeking mouth took hers in a deep and sensual kiss that took her breath away. As her tongue danced with his, Beth realized she wasn't dreaming.

The sensations exploding in her body excited her and made her want more. She wrapped her arms around Andrew's neck, pulling him closer, wanting to feel his body against hers. The weight of his body pushed her deeper into the bed. Her legs wrapped around him, trapping him against her. She felt her gown whisper up her legs to her waist, allowing naked skin to touch naked skin. His hard length pressed against her thigh, making her body rock against him.

~

Without a word, Andrew eased her nightgown off her and gazed in wonder at the treasure in front of him. He wanted to sample it all, drinking the sweet nectars her body had to offer. Breaking the kiss, he licked his way down her throat, eliciting small moans and sighs as his tongue touched sensitive points along her neck and collarbone.

Flicking his tongue against the tightened pink bud of her breast, he felt her whole body stiffen as she arched into him. Pulling the rosy areola into his mouth he laved and suckled, knowing he was driving her closer and closer to the edge. He didn't want to send her over too quickly. Tonight he was going to savor their lovemaking.

His hands slid down her body and touched the core of her. He groaned when he found her hot, moist, and ready for him. His mouth abandoned one tip and started his assault on the other, all the while rubbing his palm against her opening, teasingly slipping a finger inside before pulling it out and swirling it around her nub.

She started to shudder in his arms. Placing one last kiss against her breast, he nibbled on the tender flesh above one rib, then another as he worked his way down her body. The indentation of her belly button called to him, making him swirl his tongue in the small crevice as he continued downward.

God, she tastes so good. Never had making love been like this, but then Andrew now knew he had never been in love before. He paused as he thought. He did love her…something he had been fighting since that awful day when he and Trey confronted Beau. Seeing her tied up with Alex had made his heart stand still. That was when he first realized how much he loved her and didn't want to lose her. Something he couldn't fight anymore.

His breath gently blew against her core, causing her to buck uncontrollably. A wicked smile came to his lips at the thought of how she would react to his next actions. He wanted to love her thoroughly until she screamed his name, and he did.

Beth was awash with so many sensations, all of them wonderful. Her hands clenched the sheets as she felt the first brush of his lips against her. Instinctively, she arched up against his mouth, giving him better access. His intimate kisses set her whole body on fire.

She couldn't speak. Every time she opened her mouth, a moan escaped. Beth also realized she was afraid to speak, not wanting to break the spell he had enveloped her in. Her whole body tightened as she rushed headlong into the ecstasy she knew waited for her. Just as she started to climax, Andrew entered her, tearing a scream from her throat. His deep thrusts drove her higher and higher. She felt his lips on her face and her neck. He took a quick nip at her collarbone.

The muscles inside her started to contract around him, making him moan out loud.

Her breath caught as she suddenly felt everything splinter into the million colors. Tears she didn't realize she had shed slipped down her temples. Her whole body shuddered at her release. Opening her eyes, she stared at Andrew in wonder. A shy smile spread across her face when she saw the same look of wonder on him.

Gently cradling her body against his, he silently stroked her hair, and they floated down from the heaven they had found in each other's arms. Resting her head against his chest, she listened to his heart as it started to slow its beat to a normal tempo. The rhythm lulled her into a relaxed state. She closed her eyes as she sighed contentedly and drifted off to sleep.

Beth wouldn't have believed she had drifted off on Andrew, except the sun was already spreading its rays across their bed.

"Good morning," he said as he planted a soft kiss on her lips. "Hope you rested well."

"Yes." The heat of a blush crept up her throat at the thoughts of all they'd shared the night before. The way he had intimately explored her body, and the way she had been thoroughly satisfied as she dozed off. How could she not have slept well?

"Good, because we have a busy day today." He threw back the covers and walked over to his clothes.

Beth swallowed as she watched the best set of cheeks walk away. Her gaze dropped guiltily when she had to admit they were the only pair she had ever seen, but she was sure they were the cutest. Each one had a dimple, and each almost winked at her as he shifted his weight from one foot to the other as he walked. A giggle escaped her.

"And what do you find so funny?" he asked as he turned toward her.

Her breath caught when he turned. Sunlight danced across his muscled chest and stomach. She didn't mean to, but couldn't stop from staring. He was beautiful. The heat of a blush filled her cheeks when he arched one eyebrow at her. Ducking her head, she grabbed her corset and chemise and ran behind the screen.

"Beth."

She couldn't answer him. She was far too embarrassed. His head popping around the screen told her that he wanted one.

"There's no reason to be embarrassed."

Beth hurriedly pulled her chemise over her head. Seeing him naked was one thing, but trying to carry on a normal conversation while she was in the same state was a different matter.

His hand gently cupped her chin, tilting it up so she would look him in the eyes. "You're very beautiful, and there's no reason to be ashamed."

Without dying from mortification, how could she tell him she found him to be beautiful, too, when he pranced around naked in front of her. This was all so new to her. She didn't know how to react. Not knowing if it would last beyond their hunt for Beau made her pause.

"I'm just not used to this."

"I'll let you get dressed in peace." He kissed the tip of her nose. "But we are husband and wife. It's natural for us to see each other naked."

She nodded, knowing her cheeks had to be flaming by now. Finishing with her undergarments, she walked over to her trunk to choose which dress she would wear. A quick peek at Andrew let her know he had already dressed in his black pants and a crisp white shirt. Instead of his customary leather vest, he had donned a embroidered gray silk one.

And she thought he'd looked good naked.

She grabbed her corset and wrapped it around her waist. Once again she needed help. After their last try she wasn't sure she wanted him to help her but he was right there waiting. She went to the bedpost and waited for the torture to begin.

"Okay, so once I thread the eyelets I should tie it off?" He worked as he spoke to her.

"Yes. Then work your way up as you pull it tight." They worked together to get the corset on her properly. She went to her trunk and pulled out a light blue day dress. Beth stepped into her dress, pulled the sleeves up and smoothed down the front of it. Mentally slapping her forehead, she realized she had forgotten her button loop and turned to retrieve it.

Andrew stood behind her with it in his hand.

"Would you like some help?"

She nodded and presented her back. The heat of his hands working their way up her back as he looped the buttons made her warm all over. If he didn't finish soon she'd probably embarrass herself all over again by taking her dress back off and asking him to make love to her again.

CHAPTER 25

The moment he finished buttoning her dress, she stepped away from him. Beth couldn't handle his hands on her any longer. It didn't matter that Andrew gave her a strange look. One second longer and she would've acted on her impulses.

"Thank you." She brushed down the front of her skirt to hide her nervousness.

"Are you ready for breakfast?"

"As a matter of fact, I'm quite hungry."

"I wonder why?" Andrew commented as he offered his arm.

Beth looked up at his face. His knowing smile made her stomach flutter.

"I'm hungry too." His eyes had a smoldering look that made her think he wasn't speaking about food.

She felt a blush bloom across her cheeks.

Her thoughts remained on the look he gave her until they entered the dining room, where Edward waited for them.

"So, did you find out anything yet?" Andrew asked as he held out the chair for Beth.

"No." Edward sat down once Beth took her seat.

She watched the door as they waited for the waiter, grabbing Andrew's arm when she spotted the two men come out of the elevator.

He turned to look and nodded. Leaning forward, he spoke to Edward. "Those are the two men getting off the elevator."

"I've seen them around. In fact, I'm pretty sure they were in the saloon that night you met with those Pinkerton men."

Beth was amazed at the information Edward knew. The young man was as sharp as a tack and had proved it time and again with the information he kept digging up.

"That would explain what happened to Jim." Andrew sat back in his chair. "Can you stay with Beth today?"

"Sure."

"Why?" asked Beth. She was pretty sure she wasn't going to like his answer.

"I'm going to follow them and see what they do."

"But don't you want me to do that?" Edward asked.

"They know you're with me now, so if you got caught, they'd know I put you up to it. I don't want you to get hurt and I don't know what they are capable of. I'd feel better if I was the one, just in case."

"Andrew."

"Beth." He turned toward her. "I promise to keep myself well out of sight. You stay with Edward, okay?"

She wanted to argue with him or beg to accompany him, but the look in his eyes stopped her. Silently, he asked her to trust him and to do what he said. She nodded. A smile spread across his lips just before he stole a quick kiss that left her weak. Before she could catch her breath he was gone.

She stared at Edward. "So now what do we do?"

Beth looked around the outside of Jacob's house, hoping to find some sign of life. "Nothing."

"Ma'am?"

"Sorry, Edward. I was hoping Jacob would be back by now."

"We have knocked, ma'am."

"Yes, we have. I guess we should head back to the hotel and wait for Andrew."

"Yes, ma'am." Edward's smile had a definite look of relief in it.

They walked back toward the hotel, but Beth found she really couldn't keep up with the small talk Edward tried to engage her in. Her mind kept wondering what was happening to Andrew and if he was all right.

She didn't even realize someone blocked her path until she walked into him. Looking up, she felt the blood drain from her face. It was one of the men who had been looking for her the day before.

~

Andrew stepped up to the corner of the building and peered around it. The two men he'd dubbed Tweedledee and Tweedledum stood near the stables conversing. A few seconds later, they split up. Dee headed toward the stable, while Dum headed toward the mercantile.

"Great." Now he had to decide which one he was going to follow. Well Dee was probably going to check on their horses, so Andrew decided to follow Dum. Ducking from alley to alley, Andrew wondered what the man was doing. He stopped at just about every window to peer inside.

The repeat of a gun, then a loud scream pierced the air. Andrew lost Dum in the crowd when the man went to see what had caused all the commotion.

A woman stood near another alley sobbing and pointing.

Someone else stepped into the alley. "Call a doctor. There's a man in here, and he's been shot."

Andrew circled the crowd. The man who had stepped into the alley recognized him. "Hey, mister, I think it's your friend."

He wanted to deny it. Edward was with Beth, but Andrew knew he had to look to be sure. He felt the instant relief from the blaring sun the moment he stepped into the alley. A cold knot formed in his stomach the moment he spotted Edward lying on the ground.

"Damn." He'd followed the wrong man.

~

Beth wanted to kick herself, which at the moment was impossible. The man who had shot Edward had trussed her up like a mummy. She had tried to wiggle out of the ropes he had wound around her, but they were too tight for her to move. The filthy rag he'd shoved in her mouth had made her want to gag, but now gagging was the furthest thing from her mind. She was scared. Petrified was more like the emotion rolling around inside her.

The buckboard she had been dumped in slowed down after they had fled the city about half an hour ago by her best estimate, but the ruts and dips still took their toll on her already battered body. Where was this man taking her?

And what was Andrew thinking? She also worried about Edward. The young man had taken a bullet trying to protect her. He had better be all right, or her kidnapper would be sorry he had ever laid eyes on her.

The pounding of a horse in pursuit overpowered the creaking and groaning of the cart and Beth. Her heart beat a little faster. *Had Andrew discovered what had happened so fast?*

The wagon stopped and waited for the rider to catch up.

Her heart sank. If it were Andrew, she would have been in for another wild ride. It must be the other man.

Neither paid her any attention as they conversed. As much as she tried, though, she could only catch small snatches of their conversation. Something about taking her to some hideout and their boss.

Beau. They were going to take her to Beau.

Ice-cold fear filled her veins at the thought of Beau having her at his mercy. He would kill her.

The two men stepped up to the back of the buckboard.

"Idiot! We're supposed to return her in good condition. What would the boss say if he saw her like that?" A rough hand grabbed her chin.

"Look at the bruises on her face. He'll think we beat her when he sees her."

"What'd you expect me to do? She's a hellion. Look at me scratches," he said pointing to his face.

Good, she thought. *At least I did a little damage.*

"Her claws did that when she tried to get away. That was the only way to keep her subdued." He turned to look at her. "Let's just kill her and be done with it. The boss did say she couldn't escape at any cost."

"Loosen the ropes."

"Come on. We don't need the trouble of transporting a woman." The man leered at her. "We could have a bit of fun, then kill her."

"Remember what happened to the last man who failed him?"

The man blanched. "Then you do it. I don't want to get too close to her."

The newcomer climbed up on the back of the buckboard. "Ma'am, if you promise to behave yourself, I'll loosen the ropes and take that gag out."

She nodded. After the threat she heard from the second one she knew she had to tread carefully. No one would hear her if she screamed, and trying to escape while they were so far from any town would be downright stupid. Beth needed them right now, so she would behave.

The gag came out of her mouth first, which started a coughing fit from all the fibers the cloth left behind. Water trickled down her neck as the man held a canteen to her lips. She drank the water greedily, hoping to get rid of the dryness in her mouth, as well as the foul taste from the rag.

The ropes around her body came off next. Her hands and feet remained tied, but at least she could move them around a little.

"Thank you." She grimaced at the pain that lanced through her.

"You're welcome, ma'am."

She wanted to ask why they did this, and beg them to return her to Jefferson City, but they'd expect that too. Instead she asked. "Name?"

She rubbed her throat a little, wishing it didn't hurt as much as it did.

When he didn't answer her, she shrugged. "Then you're Idiot One and you're Idiot Two," she croaked as she pointed at each of them in turn. At least her throat was starting to work a little better.

"I ain't no—" said the man who had tied her up.

"Those names will work just fine, ma'am. We need to be moving again." He joined Idiot One in the front of the buckboard just before he shook out the reins and got the horses moving again.

Beth grabbed the side of the buckboard, wishing she'd been given a chance to get her gloves before they took off. Wincing at the splinters that dug into her hands, she was grateful she could at least balance herself and wouldn't be thrown around like a rag doll.

Once the wagon lurched along at an even pace, she eased herself down and searched for all the splinters she had picked up, pulling the ones she could out with her teeth.

Looking at her battered hands, she wished for some salve. Her reticule was near her feet. Something her captures hadn't noticed or chose to ignore. Although she knew it held her gloves, some money, and a small sewing kit, she wasn't sure what else still remained in the purse. She had crammed so much into it when she'd first left home, she had been constantly pulling things out to make room for some of the newer essentials she needed.

She dug inside, hoping to find the needles so she could try to dig out the splinters when her hand hit something small and hard. Her brow furrowed as she tried to figure out what it was. Wrapping her hand around it, she felt her blood run cold. Andrew had slipped the small pearl-handled revolver in there before she woke up this morning. She wasn't sure if she wanted to kick him or kiss him. He had gone against her wishes, but now she had a weapon to protect herself with. All she had to do was figure out a way to escape.

~

If Edward said he was sorry one more time, Andrew thought he just might kill him. "It's not your fault, so stop blaming yourself."

"I should've never let her talk me into going to Jacob's house."

"Edward." Andrew rubbed a hand across his face, trying to regain his composure. He had wanted to hightail it after Beth the moment he realized what had happened, but they would be expecting that and he couldn't try to take them on alone. He needed help, so he had to have patience. "They were after Beth. One way or another they'd have gotten her."

"Then let's go get her back." Edward struggled into a sitting position.

"Hey, now. I just finished sewing that hole up, don't you go and do something stupid like ripping the stitches out," yelled the doctor when he spotted Edward trying to sit up.

Andrew pushed him back onto the table. "You have to rest. Tomorrow we'll leave, but for today, do everything the doctor tells you to let the healing process begin. I need you to be well. If you push too hard, too early, you won't be worth a thing."

Edward's expression told Andrew he didn't like it, but he nodded as he lowered his upper body back on the table.

"Doc, once you think he's ready, take him to the Golden Nugget Hotel." He turned toward Edward. "I'm going to my hotel and see if I can get inside the rooms those men stayed in."

Andrew patted him on the uninjured shoulder before he stepped out of the saloon Edward had been taken into. He wondered what Beth was thinking and if she was okay. If anything happened to her because of him, he'd never forgive himself.

His walk to the hotel was a blur. In the lobby he paused for just a second before he crossed to the desk.

"I need to speak to your manager." The young man stared at him for a few moments before stepping away from the counter and ducking into a small room off to the side. "Can I help you, sir?"

"I need to get into the rooms on the top floor." Andrew pulled his Pinkerton ID out of his pocket. Being undercover didn't keep Beth safe, so now he was going to use his position to his best advantage.

"I can't let you in there, sir."

"If you don't, I'll go to the police and get them to make you. A young woman has been kidnaped by the two men who occupied the rented suites. If you don't let me in there, you can be considered an accomplice."

The man paled at Andrew's words, which is what he had hoped for.

Tugging on a chain, the man pulled his keys out of a pocket as he stepped around the desk. "This is highly irregular, sir, but I'll take you up there."

Good. Maybe this way he could get an idea of where they were headed.

~

The room was a mess. It didn't look like anyone had been up there to clean for days. Andrew's hope took flight. If no one had cleaned in a while he had a better chance of finding some clues to lead him to Beth and to Beau.

He walked to the bedrooms. The thick Prussian rug cushioned the sound of his heels as he stalked back. Pulling a pillowcase off of one of the pillows, he proceeded to stuff every scrap of paper he found into it.

"Sir?" said the man who let him in the room.

"This could be evidence, which I'm taking into safekeeping." He continued through each room, opening drawers, and rifling through the dressers and cabinets for anything that could be valuable. He found several blank pads, but could tell something had been written on the pages that had been torn off. He threw them in with the rest. By the time he had gone through every room, the pillowcase was burgeoning with paper. He prayed it had what he needed.

"Thank you for your time." He turned on his heel and walked out of the suite without a backward glance and headed toward his own room.

The moment he closed the door, he unceremoniously dumped everything onto the bed and proceeded to go through every single piece of paper.

He had weeded his way through a third of the pile when he heard a knock on his door. He frowned when he opened the door.

"Thought I told the doctor to send you to your hotel. What're you doing out of bed?" he demanded as he allowed Edward into the room.

"Helping you find Miss Elizabeth." He eased himself down on the bed with the mountain of paper.

"You need to rest." Andrew frowned. Edward didn't look like he should be doing anything but sleeping. His face had no color, and his eyes had a glassy look to them.

"I'm fine. Besides, I can't rest knowing Miss Elizabeth needs our help." Edward looked at the scraps of paper everywhere. "What's all this?"

For a few seconds Andrew thought about sending Edward back to his room, but he gave in when he realized that he did need Edward's help. "I got it from the room those men were staying in."

"Think there's anything there that will give us information of Miss Elizabeth's whereabouts?"

"I'm hoping."

"Then let's get started."

Andrew nodded. Grabbing a handful of paper he went to the desk and spread them out. Not knowing what to look for made the job harder, but it had to be done. "Look for anything out of the ordinary. A street address or a name."

Edward started to weed his way through the ones on the bed.

As he discarded pieces he let them flutter to the floor.

When they finished, the floor was littered with the unwanted pieces. Andrew took the ones Edward saved and added them to the ones he had saved. Looking over the papers, he frowned. There wasn't a lot.

"Most of what I found were lists of items they must've picked up while they were here. Including some women's clothing, food, blankets, and an extra horse," said Edward as he slid down the bed to move closer to the desk.

"What is this?" Andrew pointed to a piece of paper that had a few numbers jotted down, then some letters that didn't spell out anything.

"Don't know. But I thought it fit the unusual category. There's another one like it, with a different set of numbers and letters." He dug through the strips of papers to find the other one.

Andrew laid them on the desk and compared them. Each had four sets of numbers, and up to six letters. There was another paper with Andrew's and Beth's names plus their hotel room on it. A fourth piece of paper had a first name. *Jim.*

The fifth looked like it had some sort of makeshift map in it, but the landmarks didn't make sense to him. Yet. The sixth one he kept had the name of a town. *Wichita.* Then there was the notepad. Andrew took a piece of burnt wood from the fireplace and ran it across the piece of paper, leaving the letters from the note above readable.

Andrew fished in his pockets until he found the other paper he had found. The information was the same. It was someone's address, he was sure now, but where did they live? If it was Wichita how far out where they?

Folding the papers up neatly, he looked over at Edward, who looked even paler than before. The poor kid could barely keep his head up. "Will you stay here while I go and check out a few things? I'll be back in an hour or two."

Edward nodded and stretched out on the bed. He was asleep before Andrew left the room.

Andrew walked across the busy street to the bank. His first guess was that those numbers were to a safety deposit box. He wanted to be sure. In the hot interior of the bank, he looked around, trying to figure out who he should ask.

"Sir? May I help you?"

Well, that answered that question for him as he stepped up to one of the bank managers.

"Yes. I need to know if these could be a safety deposit box number."

The man arched a brow at Andrew, but looked at the numbers anyway. His brow crinkled as he gazed at the numbers. "Not to this bank, sir, but they sure do seem familiar."

Taking the paper back, Andrew thanked the man before leaving the building.

The bright sunlight made him squint. He hadn't gotten anywhere with the bank. *Who else would recognize these numbers?* He thought about it as he walked back to the hotel.

He found Edward still asleep when he walked in the room. Spreading out the papers, he looked at them again. The information he needed had to be in front of him. It just had to.

CHAPTER 26

Beth wished she had a pillow and a nice soft bed. In fact, anything would be better than sleeping on the cold, hard ground. Her two captors had thick blankets and their saddles to rest their heads on. All she had was her arm and a ratty old blanket that had been stuffed up under the seat of the buckboard.

She was freezing. They refused to light a fire for fear of being spotted and the temperatures had dropped since the sun had gone down.

Not being able to sleep, she stared up at the canopy of stars above her head. The night sky was beautiful. Too bad she couldn't really enjoy it.

A soft snore floated over to her. At least someone could sleep.

She rolled over onto her side, hoping to find a comfortable spot, but found several rocks biting into her hip instead. She sat up, grumbling under her breath and clutching the threadbare blanket to her shoulders.

This was ridiculous. She needed a warm, comfortable place to sleep. Her gaze cut to the buckboard. As uncomfortable as she had been when she rode in it earlier, she knew it would at least be rock free and she just might find it a little warmer since the sides would block the wind that blew up from time to time.

After one quick glance at her sleeping captors, she was up and creeping toward the back of the buckboard. She tried to crawl onto it, but found it just a little too high. Beth ended up having to put her back up to the lip and pulled herself up by her arms, her fanny plopping onto the hard wood. The whole thing creaked and groaned as she tried to find a comfortable spot, and she was amazed neither man woke up.

A sigh escaped her lips as she finally settled down and started to drift off to sleep.

~

The next morning came very quickly. The sound of their yawns broke through the light sleep she had fallen into.

She rubbed her eyes and watched the two men break camp quickly. Without a word they climbed up in the front of the wagon and continued on their journey.

With a strong grip on the sideboards, she looked across the barren land. Her hopes started to sink as she surveyed the openness. No one would be able to sneak up on them. If Andrew were following, he'd be spotted too quickly to rescue her.

A load rumbling filled her ears. It was her stomach. Crawling toward the front of the wagon, she tapped one of the men on the shoulder.

"Excuse me, Idiot Two, but do you plan on starving me to death?" She knew she really shouldn't talk to these men this way. They could ignore their boss and straight-out kill her, but that would probably be better than the fate that awaited her.

The man laughed. "No, ma'am, we're not trying to starve you, but we have a schedule to keep and we can't be late. You'll be fed as soon as we reach our destination."

Beth slumped down. Her body wanted food, not promises. Too bad she didn't have any food hidden in her purse.

She smiled when she thought about her purse. After making sure her captors weren't paying attention, she slid the gun out and up under the hem of her dress. Then as discreetly as she could, she slipped it up into her pantaloons. It felt a little strange having it constantly banging against her leg, but the weight let her know her gun was still in there, which also let her know the few coins she had tucked away were still there too. Now all she had to do was figure out a way to escape.

And that was the hard part. How could she escape in the middle of nowhere? As long as they stayed away from towns, she was stuck with her captors.

By the time they reached their destination, Beth's stomach was yowling. With one hand wrapped around her stomach, she complained once again. "Idiot Two, I do believe you're trying to starve me. It's been at least three hours since you promised me food, yet I haven't seen a thing."

"We're almost there, ma'am."

The wagon crested a small rise, suddenly revealing a bustling town sitting in the small valley before them.

Beth's heart started to beat quicker. This could be her only chance to escape.

~

Andrew glanced over at Edward, who looked like he was perched up on his horse instead of actually riding it.

"Are you sure you can do this? We can go back."

"No." Edward shook his head. "I want to help."

"You won't be much help if you fall off that horse." Andrew was relieved to see a little color had come back into Edward's face. The boy had been so white when he climbed on, Andrew had been sure he would pass out, but Edward hadn't. That made Andrew proud.

"So where are we going to head?"

"The quickest way to Wichita is by train. There's a small depot to the west of here. If they're trying to get her to Beau before I can catch up, that's where they're headed."

"And if they're not?"

"That's the chance I have to take. I left a note for Sally, since she hasn't gotten back yet, to let her know where we're headed. If she does what I asked her to do, she'll go through some of the smaller towns around here and see if they might've taken a different track."

"Do you think we can catch up with them?"

"If you can move that horse a little faster, yes. The train they should be catching will be leaving in an hour."

Edward made a clicking sound, getting his horse to trot a little faster. He winced with each jarring step the horse took, but didn't complain once.

Andrew felt in control once more. They would reach the train on time, and he would rescue Beth from those men. One thing was for certain, Beau wouldn't get his hands on her.

~

That Beau wouldn't get his hands on her was all she could think about as she sat on a hard wooden bench in the small train station as Idiot Two bought their tickets. Idiot One sat across from her, watching her like a hawk. Beth had the distinct feeling he was just waiting for her to make an attempt to escape so he could kill her where she sat. So she sat primly on the seat, waiting as quietly as she could.

The buzz of other passengers waiting for the train filled the air. One child sitting on the same bench squealed with delight when her mother came back with a sweet treat for her.

Idiot Two sat down beside her and smiled. "Mrs. Leroux, we expect you to be on your best behavior. Please don't try to escape. I sure would hate to put a bullet through your head." He eased his jacket just enough to show her his Colt revolver resting in his holster.

She swallowed hard, but kept her gaze steady. Escaping them was something she had to do, but they didn't need to know that.

The station manager announced the arrival of the train, saving her from having to answer Idiot Two. They stood up together, but so did most of the people in the train station.

Beth walked calmly with her two captors toward the landing where the train would pull up. Down the track she saw the large locomotive racing toward them.

The whistle blew, warning everyone of its approach. Steam chugged up out of the engine as the train slowed down. The wheels screamed against the brakes being applied. A few lurches later, people streamed off the cars, looking for family and friends, or a nice place to eat before heading to their real destination.

Beth felt her knees quake. *It's now or never.*

~

Andrew stood in the crowd of people disembarking as he tried to look at the sea of faces waiting to get on.

"Do you see her?" asked Edward, who stood with his back to him, looking out the other side just in case her captors tried to get on board that way.

"No, wait. Yes. She's almost right in front of us. Let's move." Andrew pushed his way through the bodies crushing around him, trying to get to the junction between the cars. He heard a few angry retorts, but ignored them as he fought his way through the crowd.

The crowd had thinned out when he finally reached the joint where the train cars connected. He and Edward slipped between the cars as new passengers started to file in them. They jumped up onto the connectors and ducked down to keep out of sight. As much as he wanted to let Beth know he was there and was going to rescue her, he feared her captors would see him first, so he continued to hide.

Footsteps grew louder as more and more people entered, filling the seats in the railroad cars behind them as well as in front. He felt his heart slam against his chest as the door behind him started to swing open. They'd be caught if anyone decided to switch cars.

"I don't want to go into the next car. Why can't we sit right here?"

Andrew recognized the soft Southern voice immediately.

"This might be a good place," said a second, very masculine voice.

"I don't like this," said a third.

The door handle jiggled as it was let go and the door slowly closed.

Andrew closed his eyes as he said a silent prayer. That was a little too close.

He silently signaled for Edward to jump off the joint so they could enter another car farther down the track. He didn't want the slamming of the adjoining door to alert the kidnappers to their presence. Their boots crunched across the gravel as they stepped from between the cars.

At least he knew Beth was all right. Now he had to get her away from those men.

They entered the train two cars down. Then moved into the car behind the one where Beth was. Andrew watched the doors in front, hoping to get a peek at Beth and her captors through the grimy windows on the doors that separated their cars. A slim silhouette stood up in the next car. Andrew got up and moved closer. All three got up and moved to the front of the car, then passed into the next car.

Andrew and Edward followed them.

~

Beth moved with a grace she didn't know she possessed, weaving her way around well-dressed passengers as well as the occasional cowboy who smelled like he hadn't taken a bath in a while. If she could just get to the bathroom on the train she just might be able to sneak out a window before the train started down the track.

"Folks, you need to get to your seats. The train is getting ready to move." The loud blast of the whistle punctuated the conductor's words.

"I need to—" Beth blushed. "I have to...oh dear."

"Oh." The conductor patted her arm. "I think we have enough time for that, miss. If your friends will sit down right here, I'll escort you."

"Thank you." She beamed at him. All the while her heart hammered in her chest. This had to work. It just had to.

The conductor took her to the door labeled 'Ladies.' She said her thanks, then stepped inside.

Leaning against the door, she pressed her hand against her pounding heart. She surveyed the room. With a sinking heart, she realized that the window was very small and she might not fit through it, but she had to try.

The two latches that held the window up groaned as she released them. This was one room that didn't have its window open. After struggling with it for a few minutes, she finally eased it all the way down. Now she had to figure out how she could get out of it with her dignity intact. She climbed up on the sink, grabbed the lip, and tried going out headfirst. Then Beth realized her error when she looked down. She was a little too far from the ground to try to crawl out that way.

The train jerked violently as it started to move.

Not caring how she looked now, Beth stuck her feet out the window, shoving her dress through the small space as she inched herself out the window. Once she eased her waist out the window, gravity took over and she started to fall toward the ground. She felt herself get jerked back against the train.

Her crinoline caught on the lock, trapping her against the side. Pulling on the stiff material, she smiled as she heard it start to rip, then realized her folly as she fell quickly to the ground. She rolled for several feet, exposing herself to any passenger who happened to be looking out the window.

~

"Look, Mommy, a lady is doing somersaults. How come you won't do somersaults with me?" asked a young child.

Andrew couldn't help but look out the window to see what the child was talking about. There along the track was a flash of crinoline and pantaloons for the whole train to see. He wondered who in their right mind would jump from the train. Color drained from his face. "Oh, no."

He gripped the door that separated him from the next car and wrenched it open. The clacking of the wheels on the track almost drowned out his thoughts. He repeated the process with the next door. Stepping into the car, he spotted the two men who had kidnapped Beth. They were sitting in the front seats, watching a closed door.

The little minx went into the bathroom and went out the window. Andrew didn't know if he should be proud that she escaped or want to throttle her for doing something so foolhardy. Hopefully she didn't hurt herself. He looked back at Edward who had followed him into the car. "I have to follow her. Can you make sure these men make it to the sheriff in the next town?"

"I'll go after her."

"You're in no condition."

"I can track her a lot better than I can control those two men."

Andrew didn't want Edward to go after Beth. He needed to be sure she was okay, but Edward was right. He also needed to make sure these men were locked up. And he had been wounded a lot worse than Edward was and survived. Edward could do this.

With a curt nod of his head, he ordered, "Get her to Wichita. I'll find you there." Then he turned back toward the two men. The sounds of the train thumping down the track grew to a deafening proportion when Edward opened the door to the back of the car.

Drawing his guns, Andrew pressed a cold steel barrel against the back of each man's head. The temptation to just pull the trigger was overwhelming. These men had cost him so much trouble. It was time they learned not to cross a Pinkerton agent. "Waiting for someone?"

They stuttered an incoherent response.

Leaning down next to their heads, he slid the barrels of his guns up and down their necks as he thought of how he was going to break the news to them. Then he smiled.

"Gentlemen. The little lady has flown. Won't Beau be happy to hear you tell him that?" He heard one sharp intake of breath before one of the men started to bolt from his seat. The soft click of the hammer being pulled back stopped the man in his tracks. He plopped back down into his seat.

"Now, that's a good boy. I have a nervous finger and this could go off if you were to push me too hard. And you don't want to push me at all." Andrew spun his gun in his hand and slugged him with the butt of his gun. The first one slumped down to the floor.

"Next?" He did the same thing to the second man, smiling when both were out cold. He'd have to explain this to the conductor, but he was sure after he did the conductor would help him find a safe place to store these two. Once he had them safely behind bars he'd set out after Beth and Edward. Hopefully, they would find each other and not get into trouble.

CHAPTER 27

Beth lay on the ground, trying to catch her breath. She knew she had to get up and move soon or she could be caught. Placing one hand under her, she levered herself up into a sitting position, feeling the sharp sting of a small rock biting into the palm of her hand.

"Damn." She looked around quickly after swearing, but there was no one to hear her. The small gash welled up with blood. She placed her mouth over the cut and the metallic taste of blood filled her mouth as she wrestled with her slip to tear off a small strip of material.

She wrapped the piece of cloth around her hand and stood up to dust herself off. A small laugh escaped her as she looked down at her dress. She was filthy. Her torn dress didn't look like it could live through another washing. To anyone else, she probably looked like some derelict, which might work better for her. The town the train just left couldn't be too far back, so she turned and started to walk toward it. Beth wasn't sure what she would do once she got there, but she knew she needed a horse.

One thing was for certain. She couldn't stay in the small town.

As she approached the outskirts of town, she slipped down an alley so no one would see her. The moment she was assailed by the stench of garbage, she regretted her choice. After a look around, she pulled the coins from their hiding place and counted her money. There was enough for a decent horse and some supplies.

Tucking a little of the money in her pocket, she walked to the general store. Beth purchased beef jerky, some biscuit mix, coffee, a small coffeepot, a cup, plate, and a fork. Since she had no ammunition, she also bought bullets for her gun. The Western Union sign hanging behind the register grabbed her attention.

"I need to send a telegram," she said as she stepped up to the register with her purchases.

"Where to, ma'am?" The clerk pulled out a pad and a pencil.

"The Pinkerton Agency in New York and it needs to go to Andrew Leroux. I'm going to Wichita to be with my aunt." Beth added her aunt's address to the telegram. She kept gazing out the door while the clerk added up the cost.

The total made her gasp. "Um, can I change that?"

"To what?" He seemed impatient with her, probably because of the way she looked.

"I still need it addressed to Andrew Leroux, but I want only one word. Wichita." She hoped Andrew would understand her cryptic message.

She paid for everything, then headed toward the livery stable. A little haggling got her a decent horse for half of what she thought she'd have to pay. And the man even threw in all the tack she needed plus a small bag of feed. Maybe he felt sorry for her. Then again, maybe this horse wasn't as healthy as she thought.

"Well, too late now." She rubbed the side of the horse's neck. The worn saddlebags had been filled with her meager supplies. Beth placed her foot in one of the stirrups she swung up on the horse and headed out of town.

~

ndrew felt a huge weight lift off his shoulders when the two men had been locked away. He had gained a little information

while they rode the train to the next station, but not what he wanted to know. He still had no clue where Beau's hideout was.

He walked to the mercantile, where he could send for any telegrams that might have come for him. The moment he got the latest one, he'd get a horse and head back toward the town where Beth jumped off the train. He had to smile at her spunk. *Most women wouldn't have tried that stunt.* Although she messed up his rescue attempt, she did get away from two very dangerous men.

He hung around the store, waiting for his messages and hoping it wouldn't take hours before he received them.

"Sir?" The clerk walked over and handed him a telegram. "We received this one right away."

"Thank you." He glanced down at the paper and swore to himself.

Leroux stop. Someone wants to meet with you stop. Will be in Jefferson City today stop.

Who was it that needed to speak to him so badly?

"Can you tell me how many trains come from Jefferson City every day?"

"Two. The next one is tomorrow morning."

"I need to send another telegram." He gave the clerk his information. "I'll be back in about an hour to pick up any other telegrams you get for me."

The young man nodded as he helped another customer.

Andrew walked across the street to the small hotel. Although he didn't want to, he was going to stay the night. He sent a telegram letting the agency know he'd wait until noon the next day to meet with whoever was looking for him, but no longer than that. He had to follow Beth's trail before it got too cold.

An hour later he had three more telegrams. The one from Sally letting him know where she was headed. She had a lead on the hideout, but wanted to see how good it was before giving him any information. The second one from Able, basically said the same thing. And there was one more that had only one word. Wichita. *Beth*...It had to be from her. At least he knew where she was headed. Now all he had to do was catch up with her before she got too far.

Stuffing the telegrams into his pocket, he walked over to the jail where his prisoners were. He had a few more questions to ask them.

He sauntered into the small building, and after speaking to the sheriff softly for a few seconds, sat down at the desk closest to the cells. His spurs jangled as he propped one foot, then the other, on top of the desk.

"Looks like someone mighty powerful knows you."

"Why?"

Andrew looked at the one he had dubbed Tweedledee back in Jefferson City. "Because they're coming to pay your bail."

"In person?"

Nodding, Andrew watched their stricken expressions. "It kinda surprises me too. Most just wire the money and be done with it. But this man? Oh, no. He made sure you were who he thought you were, then said he'd be on the next train here and to be sure you didn't escape before he got here. You know—" Andrew swung his boots down to lean over the desk. "—he must be an awful nice boss to worry about you escaping before your bail is paid. Do you two boys do this a lot?"

"No. He's just…uh…thoughtful that way. Would you excuse us for a minute?" The two men huddled together as they spoke quietly.

Their voices were too low for Andrew to hear, but their sharp gestures let him know they were arguing about something. He hoped it was whether or not they should tell him what he wanted to know.

Tweedledee stepped up to the bars. "We've talked it over, and thought we'd save our boss the time of coming out here. If we tell you what you want to know, will you let us go?"

"Gee, don't know." Andrew rubbed his chin a little. "Your boss seemed pretty adamant about your staying here until he arrived."

"Look. He's not really going to be happy to come all the way out here. You could send him a telegram and let him know you've already let us go." Tweedledum came up to the bars and stood beside his partner.

"But what if he's already left? He won't be too happy to come all this way just to find you gone," the sheriff said. He had walked over to the desk Andrew sat at when the men started talking.

"We'll take care of that for you. We'll meet the train," said Tweedledee.

"We will? I thought—" A quick elbow in the ribs shut Tweedledum right up.

"And how will we know you're not lying to us?" asked Andrew.

"We'll swear on a stack of bibles."

"You two religious men, then?"

The two men looked at each other before shaking their head no.

"Then that won't do." Andrew stood up, pretending he was getting ready to leave.

"I'll tell you why we took that lady. That way you'll know we're telling the truth."

"Well, I don't know if that'll help you." Andrew sat back down. "But okay. Why did you take the lady?"

"The boss has been keeping tabs on you the entire time. He knew about your marriage and that you were looking for him. Your wife would be a bargaining chip to keep you at a distance until he could finish what he started."

"And what is that?" So they did know who he was.

"Control the West."

"And one man thinks he can accomplish that in a few days?"

"Mister, you don't know our boss. In the last three months, he's taken over just about all the gangs in a three-state area. Most of the sheriffs and mayors in a lot of the small towns where the train robberies have been taking place are in his pockets. And he's expanding."

Andrew had to wonder just how far that expansion had gone. If this sheriff was also on Beau's payroll, they'd all be dead men, but he knew he had to take that chance.

"He's also searching for some people. Trey and Alexandra Dalton, your wife, and you, Mr. Leroux."

Andrew didn't blink an eye. "The fact you kidnapped my wife tells me your boss is after me. This is nothing I couldn't figure out on my own."

"We can tell you which trains he's going to hit next."

Andrew named the five shipments of gold and arms that were crossing through this territory. "My guess is he's going after all five. So telling me which ones won't help. Now, if you happen to know where the trains would be attacked and how, then you'd be telling me something I'd be interested in."

"Aw, shucks, mister." Tweedledum spoke for the first time. "We don't know that. You think he'd telegram us that type of information?"

"No." Andrew sat back in his chair. Popping his feet up on the desk again.

"What do you want?" asked Tweedledee.

"The location of his hideout."

"We don't know where it is."

Andrew stood up. "Hope you boys have a happy reunion with your boss."

"I swear, Leroux, we don't know where it is, but we have directions to where he wanted us to deliver the woman."

Andrew gave them a feral smile.

~

Edward scrubbed his face a little harder than necessary, but it helped keep him awake. He couldn't believe he'd missed Beth. Now she was wandering around who knew where. All he could think of was how Andrew would react at the news. He sure wouldn't be happy.

He came upon the town where she had bought the horse about two hours after she had left. Edward tried to get there earlier, but he had been writhing in pain for a while after jumping from the train. Like any graceful human being, he'd landed on his wounded shoulder. The stars he'd seen in his head had rivaled any he saw in the night sky.

By the time he got into town, Beth had not only been long gone, but she'd bought the last horse available. Now he had two choices. Walk ten miles to the nearest farm and see if they had any horses for sale, or wait until someone came into town who was willing to sell their horse. The nearest horse trader wasn't due in to town for another week.

The first place he went was the doctor's. After falling, his wound had started bleeding again. And he wouldn't be worth anything if he bled to death. Next he went to the small hotel and got a room. Then he sent a telegram to Andrew to let him know what had happened.

Hopefully, he'd be following Beth by the morning. If not, he might never find her.

~

Beth sat in front of her meager fire, trying to chew the jerky she had bought. It tasted vile and was hard to swallow.

"Well, that's what I get for wanting adventure." Now she sat watching the stars come out one by one, and jumping at every snap and howl she heard. If she wasn't afraid someone would sneak up on her in the night, then she feared that some wolf would come and gobble her up for dinner. A stick on the ground suddenly became a snake. A snapping tree limb was someone trying to attack her.

The daytime didn't scare her as much. Probably because she hadn't seen a soul in the seven hours she had ridden. She wanted to ride more, but since she hadn't seen any sign of a town, or another person, she didn't want to push her horse too hard. The small stream and the fresh green grass appealed to her and her horse, which she had dubbed Magnolia. The off-white mare seemed to like her new name too.

Magnolia munched on the sweet grass growing near the banks of the stream. Beth took a deep breath, inhaling the scent of the grass, reminding her of calmer moments at home. She got up and went to brush the horse. Beth couldn't afford a brush with her meager money, but had been able to find a piece of a small sapling she could use for a while, and Magnolia didn't seem to mind much.

"So, where are we going to head tomorrow?" Beth asked her horse.

She got a snort and a stomp of a hoof in response.

"West it is." The same direction they had been heading in since they left town.

~

Andrew stood on the platform, waiting for the train from Jefferson City. He still didn't know who wanted to catch up with him so badly, but he only had a few minutes' wait to find out now. He could hear the whistle blowing in the distance.

The train eased its way into town, blowing soot and spitting up gravel. People started to pour off the train. All around him came squeals of delight when someone spotted a loved one stepping down from the cars. Once he thought he would be trampled when a young man spotted one of the young ladies disembarking. Must have been his bride at the way he scooped her up and swung her around.

As the people leaving the train started to thin out, he wondered if maybe the telegram had been wrong. Or perhaps whoever was looking for him had missed this train.

He did watch the crowd, making sure he wasn't being set up, but didn't notice anything out of the ordinary. Andrew spun when he felt a slight tap on his shoulders. There, standing in front of him, was his worst nightmare.

"Good morning, Mr. Boudreaux," said Andrew.

"Don't you 'good morning' me." He thrust a small opened package into Andrew's hands.

Curious, Andrew peered inside. Reaching in, he pulled out a beautiful pocket watch.

"Very nice. Yours?"

"Open it."

Andrew looked at William for a moment before doing as Mr. Boudreaux asked. Color left his face when he read the inscription.

"I can—" That was all he could say before a big meaty fist smashed into his face, knocking him unconscious.

CHAPTER 28

Andrew's jaw hurt like hell and he could taste blood in his mouth. For a few seconds, he couldn't remember what had happened, but the shadow of Beth's father brought it all back to him quickly.

"Mr. Boudreaux, I can explain this."

"You can explain why my daughter married you without my permission?"

"Yes, sir." He didn't know if William would believe him, but he had to try. "To protect her, sir. I couldn't travel with her and have people talk. Which would you prefer? Our marriage, or people thinking your daughter was a loose woman because she traveled alone with a man she wasn't married to."

Andrew thought William would punch him once more, but the man ran his fingers through his hair instead.

"My baby girl." He looked at Andrew accusingly. "How could you do this to my baby girl?"

Andrew remained silent. He knew his answer to the last question would probably win him another punch.

"So where is she?"

He swallowed hard as he wearily eyed William's big hands. "Um… there was a problem."

"What sort of problem?" William's eyebrows drew together in a thunderous look.

"She's been kidnapped."

"Kidnapped?" He grabbed Andrew by the collar and lifted him up.

Andrew didn't like feeling like a rag doll in this man's grip. "Could you please put me down?"

"Tell me she's all right."

"She's all right. Just not with me right now." Andrew glanced at the ground several inches below where his feet dangled.

"When are you going to rescue her?"

"I have, so to speak." He wanted to groan when he saw that thunderous look on William's face again. "I arrested the men who kidnapped her, but she escaped them at the same time. Right now she's on her way to Wichita."

"By herself?"

He gave a stiff nod.

William shook him in anger. His face turned beet red, and his mouth opened several times, but no words came out.

Andrew had to clamp his hand on his hat to keep it from falling off his head. "If you're quite through." He wanted to sound dignified, but his words came out more like a croak. William had a tight hold on his throat and slowly squeezed the air out of him. Suddenly coming to his senses, he released Andrew, who fell to the wooden platform in a heap. With as much pride as he could muster, Andrew stood up and dusted himself off.

"Mr. Boudreaux, I'm sorry. But your daughter was quite ingenious in her escape. She locked herself in a bathroom aboard the train and slid out the window. I have someone tracking her, and he'll contact me as soon as she's found, but I have every faith she'll come to no harm. She has proven herself many times to me." Saying it out loud made Andrew realize he truly believed the words he spoke.

"And why aren't you out there right now?"

"I'm going after her today. I would've started yesterday, but I had to wait for you." Andrew knew better than to goad Beth's father, but he just couldn't help himself.

"If you'd been doing your job right, she wouldn't be out there on her own right now."

Andrew stepped up to William, stopping only inches from his face. His fists clenched so tightly he could feel his nails cutting into his palm, but he didn't care. One more comment like that and he would strike Mr. Boudreaux. Everything else be damned.

"Hear me, Mr. Boudreaux. I've already kicked myself up one side of this town and down the other for what happened to Beth. I should have never left her alone. But I also know that one way or another those men still would've kidnapped her. Their boss would've killed them if they'd failed." Andrew glanced at the jail. "They'll probably be killed because they lost her. Beau Manning is the one behind this. So if you're going to blame anyone, he's the one you should be angry with."

"You love my daughter, don't you?"

"I'm leaving in one hour. You better go ahead and get your return ticket." Andrew didn't respond to the question. He didn't want to think about the feelings he had for Beth. It would interfere with his job.

"Are you going to answer my question?" William laid one large hand on Andrew's shoulder, forcing Andrew to look the man in the face. "Ah."

Andrew frowned as he shrugged off his father-in-law's hand. "And what does 'ah' mean?"

"Never mind."

Now he knew where Beth got her infuriating ways. "Mr. Boudreaux."

"I'm going with you."

"No, sir."

"You can't stop me."

"I can do to you what I threatened to do to your daughter when she refused to go home. Tie you up and put you on that train."

"I am not a simple female. You and I know I could best you in any fight."

"Your daughter is no simple female either, sir. In fact, she's just like you," Andrew grumbled. William was right. He couldn't win a fair fight with this man. He was too big.

"Thank you, I think." William laughed. "Now let's get moving. Every second I think of Elizabeth out there by herself makes me very nervous, and you won't like me when I'm nervous."

Andrew stared at the man. He *was* just like Beth. "And if I refuse to let you come with me?"

"I'll follow you."

"You and your daughter are cut from the same cloth." Andrew ran his hand through his hair. He knew he wouldn't win with William any more than he had with Beth. "I need to see if any more telegrams have arrived for me. Then I'll be ready."

~

Beth leaned over the bucket, scrubbing her dress. Her back ached, her hands were raw, but her only dress was finally clean.

"Mrs. Leroux?"

Beth turned toward the soft feminine voice. Before her stood a girl, barely nineteen and already married with two children. She felt ancient next to the young woman.

"Thank you for letting me wash my dress, Mrs. Croft. And for a place to sleep these last few days." Beth stood there, draped in a dress three sizes too big. A hand-me-down from Mrs. Croft's mother.

Beth had stumbled across the small farm three days earlier. This young mother needed help so badly while her husband got the herd ready for market, Beth volunteered to help. In return, she got a soft bed, free meals, and a chance to clean her dress, plus a promise of a fresh mount when she left.

"Oh." The young woman blushed. "You've been such a big help to me, I don't know what I would've done without you. But I came to tell you that my husband is riding out with the herd tomorrow and he's offered to take you as far as Kansas City."

"Oh, that would be wonderful! Thank you." Once she got to Kansas City, she would head to Wichita and her aunt. She shook out her dress before pinning it to the clothesline. "The laundry is all done. Is there anything else you'd like me to help you with right now?"

"If you could watch the children? I want to take my husband some lunch." A soft blush filled her cheeks again.

"Of course." Beth followed the young woman back to the house where a three-year-old and an eighteen-month-old played in the small yard behind the house.

The pounding of hoofbeats vibrated against the ground.

Beth peeked around the side of the building to see who had arrived.

"Ma'am."

"May I help you?" Beth noticed her young friend now held a rifle in her hand.

"I'm looking for a woman. A friend of mine. She got separated from me and I heard she headed this way." The man's steely gaze swept across the house and the barn.

"We don't get too many visitors here, sir."

Beth was grateful the stranger couldn't see her in the backyard. She didn't know who he was, and even though he could be a friend of Andrew's, but she wasn't going to take any chances.

"Why would a woman be traveling this far from town? You might do better if you looked for her in Russellville. That's where most of those traveling through stop at."

"Just left there, ma'am. They haven't seen her either." He pulled on his reins and turned his horse around. "Thank you, ma'am. If you do see her, let her know she has friends waiting for her in Wichita."

"I'll do that."

Beth watched as the man rode off, wondering who would be waiting for her when she got to Wichita, besides her aunt. She didn't like the finger of dread that snaked its way around her spine.

~

Andrew looked at the telegrams he had picked up. One was from Edward, letting him know he hadn't caught up with Beth yet. Knowing Beth, he might not be able to either. The other one was from Sally. She was supposed to meet with her contact in a day or two and hoped to have more information for him.

He sent one more, letting his office know he was moving again and he would contact them when he had a chance. After paying for the telegrams, he added them to the growing pile of paper in his shirt pocket, then headed out to his horse.

He wanted to sigh as he spotted Beth's father, patiently waiting for him. He didn't need the man around. In fact, William would probably slow him down. But Andrew had already tried to shake him twice now, and the man had stayed right on his heels. So he might as well make the best of it.

They rode out in silence. Andrew didn't have a lot to say to his father-in-law. That wasn't true. He wanted to know why his daughter had seemed so afraid of him when he got angry. She had said she had only seen her father hit another person once, but...the question of beatings begged to be asked, but Andrew didn't know how to broach the subject with the man.

He wasn't sure if he really wanted to know the answer if he did ask it.

They rode along for several hours before William finally spoke. "You're brooding, boy. Spit it out."

"I'm not brooding...just trying to figure out where Beth might have headed."

"We both know she would've gone one of two ways. Either back home or to her aunt's, and since her aunt's a lot closer now, I'd bet on the latter. Now tell me what's eating you."

Andrew really didn't want to have this conversation out in the middle of nowhere.

"You're as weak as my daughter."

"Your daughter isn't weak! She's the strongest woman I know. Whether you like it or not she has blossomed into a beautiful, intelligent woman."

"You think I don't know that?" William tilted his hat up a little on his head. "She was happy and looked forward to what her life would be like until she was kidnapped by Beau. I don't know what happened because she would never talk about it, but it changed her. She didn't leave the house anymore, or complain about having to work at the store. She jumped at loud noises and heaven forbid someone sneak up on her. Those screams shook the rafters."

"That's why you sent her to her aunt's? To make her become the person she was before?"

"We hoped she would relax if she was away from home. Everywhere she looked she seemed to see ghosts. Her aunt was willing to help us and sent the telegram so Beth wouldn't fight us on it."

"That was smart thinking."

"It was. We were trying to figure out how to get her to go when the telegram came. It was the perfect excuse."

Andrew looked at him. It was perfect. A little too perfect. He had to believe she was safe. He couldn't handle it if anything happened to her.

"Do you have your sister's address?"

"Sister-in-law, I don't know the actual address, but I can wire my wife and get it from her."

"Let's do that at the next town." Andrew stared ahead. "I want you to know that I've seen the old Beth. The one that will argue with you if she thinks you're being pigheaded. The one who sees the wonder of distant vistas and the stars at night."

"The watch."

"Excuse me?"

"That watch showed me that my baby girl was starting to resurface. She's been sweet on you for years. Even though you made a big mess of this I want my daughter happy."

"I see." Andrew adjusted himself on his saddle. "Um, I told her we'd be married in name only, and she was free to get an annulment once she was safe from Beau. I didn't want her to feel trapped in a marriage she didn't want."

"What?" William shook his head. "Then you're a bigger fool than me. No woman wants a marriage of convenience. They want to be loved. If she thinks you married her just to protect her, she'll ask for that annulment just to keep her pride. Whether she really wants it or not."

CHAPTER 29

The saloon was grimy, and the bodies all around him smelled of sweat and coal dust, but it didn't really register. Edward was at his wits' end. He had searched high and low for Beth and had found no sign of her. He'd even contacted a few of his old friends to help, but no one had seen her. He hoped she wasn't lying dead somewhere. Just the thought made him shudder.

He took a sip of the cheap liquor, feeling it burn its way into his stomach. Maybe in a couple hours, the questions that had been running through his head would stop for a while.

What should I do now? Wait for Andrew? Or keep looking for her? He hated the helpless feeling he had, knowing he would be smarter waiting for Andrew. But also knowing that Beth's very life could depend on whether or not he found her.

He knew it was time to send another telegram. One he really didn't want to send.

Beth was saddling Magnolia when her hosts walked into the small well-built barn.

"Mrs. Leroux?"

"Oh." She patted the horse before stepping out from the stall, the fresh hay muffling her steps as she turned to face them. "I decided to go ahead and get going."

"I thought you wanted to travel with me."

"Jeb." His wife touched his arm softly. She turned to Beth and asked, "You heard that man today, didn't you?"

"Yes." Beth looked down at her feet. "I guess you figured out by now that the man was looking for me."

"Kinda figured that, yes," said Jeb.

"I'm not a criminal." She looked up at them. "I am being hunted, but I didn't break any law. There's this man who's trying to hurt me."

"Then why do you want to ride out all alone? That man could be waiting for you," said Jeb.

"But that's why I'm leaving alone. You've been so good to me, yet I could bring you all kinds of heartache for just being here." She could feel the tears welling up in her eyes. "If I were to travel with you, Jeb, and that man were to catch up with us somehow, he could kill you just so you won't fight when he tried to take me with him. I couldn't live with that."

"I'm a darn good shot."

"And most of those hired to look for me are gunslingers." Beth shook her head. "It wouldn't work out."

"I know a way."

Beth looked at Jeb's wife.

"What are you thinking, Lily?"

"You'll see." Lily gestured for Beth to follow her to the house.

An hour later Beth stood in front of the mirror, hoping Lily's plan would work. She wanted to laugh at the simplistic costume she now wore. The dress she wore earlier was back on her, but instead of it being three sizes too big, it now fit. Lily had dug out an old pair of Jeb's long johns and proceeded to stuff them with scraps of cloth she had in a trunk. She also had pulled out an old hairpiece from the trunk and plunked it on Beth's head. The gray, ratty thing had seen better days, but it did cover Beth's hair. The final thing Lily did was add some pancake makeup she had purchased a few months before.

"Now let's see if this works." Lily clasped her hands together. "The men should be coming in from the pasture soon. Most have seen you enough to be able to recognize you, so if they don't with all this on, you should be able to use it to stay hidden from those men chasing you."

"I hope you're right." Beth followed Lily down the stairs to the dining room. The first people she saw were the children.

She smiled at them.

The three-year-old quickly ducked behind her mother's skirt, while the eighteen-month-old started to bawl.

"Well, it looks like the disguise works on the children," commented Lily.

"All too well," grumbled Beth. She didn't realize the children might be frightened of her if they didn't recognize her. Before she could say a word though the men started coming through the back door. Each came to an abrupt halt when they spotted the stranger standing next to the lady of the house.

"Come on in, gentlemen. Dinner is ready. Hope you don't mind if we have company. This here is an old friend of my mother's. Mrs. Smith."

"Ma'am." The men in the room all said it about the same time as they pulled their hats off their heads. Then they slowly filed into the dining room.

Beth kept her face straight. It seemed to really be working.

The meal was a little awkward, but more for Beth than anyone else. She feared discovery at any time. Her face and body might be hidden, but she couldn't disguise her voice. Luckily most of the questions directed at her were answered by Lily. If the question required a yes or a no answer Beth merely nodded or shook her head. Finally the meal was over and the men said their good nights before they went to the bunkhouse.

Beth stood there nervously as Jeb turned back toward her. He looked her up and down, shaking his head and smiling ruefully.

"It worked, didn't it?" asked Lily.

"I'll say. I didn't recognize her right away and only figured it out because Beth didn't come down for dinner like she normally does." He wrapped his arm around his wife's waist. "And I know no one came to visit us today."

"There's only one problem," said Beth as she pulled the wig off her head. "How am I going to get away without speaking all the way to that fort near Kansas City?"

"Hmm...Can you speak a little softer maybe? Or a little deeper? I doubt if you'll be talking with the men too much, but it would be difficult to not talk at all," said Lily.

"I guess I could try."

"You don't have much time, Mrs. Leroux. We leave in the morning."

"Are you sure you want me to travel with you? I can head out on my own." Beth played with the wig in her hand. She really would like to travel with them if no one discovered who she was. No one would suspect she'd head to Kansas City. They'd all expect her to head straight to Wichita.

"I'd feel better knowing you were with us, at least for a little while. Once you get to Kansas City, you might be able to hook up with a family or two heading to Wichita and you won't have to travel by yourself." Jeb laid a friendly hand on her arm. "Those men are looking for a woman by herself, so you'd probably do better if you stuck with a group as much as you can."

Beth had to agree, but could she be lucky enough to find someone to travel with that wouldn't see through her disguise and be willing to travel with a stranger?

~

Andrew pulled his hat down lower on his face, but nothing would stop the dust from filling his nose and mouth. He hated these little dust storms that blew through the plains. They didn't happen often, but he had been through enough of them in his travels to know this one would last a while. He just hoped they wouldn't get turned around while they tried to travel.

Mr. Boudreaux wanted to stop, but Andrew had convinced him to keep going. Beth was out there all by herself and he had to find her.

His heart had sank when he got the telegram from Edward. The boy hadn't been able to catch up with Beth. He was waiting for Andrew in Clinton.

Mr. Boudreaux's horse plodded along behind his, its head down. Andrew knew the horse didn't want to be out in this weather any more than they did.

William wasn't fairing very well either. His silk brocade vest was deeply encrusted with sand and dirt, and the jacket he wore did little to protect him against the elements. The first thing Andrew was going to force the man to do when they came to a town was buy proper clothing for the rest of the trip.

They continued to move into the wind. Andrew wouldn't be surprised if his face was bleeding from the sting of the million tiny specks slamming into his face. Even with his handkerchief wrapped around his face, he could feel them biting into his skin. Within fifteen minutes, he could feel the wind starting to lessen. They had made it through the worst of it. Hopefully, it would die down as quickly as it had started.

"Do you think Elizabeth is out in this?" William's words were muffled by his sleeve, which he held up to his face.

"I doubt if this storm reached her," Andrew commented, his own voice muffled by the crusty handkerchief tied over his face. "Let's start looking for a rise of some sort so we can see where we are. If we're lucky, we might be able to spot a town or a farm nearby."

It took two hours and several small rises, but sure enough, a small but thriving farm spread out below them. Andrew looked over at William before urging his horse down the slope to the farmhouse. It looked pretty empty, but he did spot a little activity out near the barn. Stopping his horse, he slid to the ground and grabbed his reins. He didn't want to frighten the people here and knew approaching on foot would make them feel a little more at ease.

"Hello?" he called. Would he see a face or a shotgun first?

To his surprise, he saw a slip of a woman, carrying a rifle across her arm. From the way she held it, he knew she knew how to use the weapon.

"We don't get many strangers here." Her grayish-blue eyes looked from him to William, who still sat on his horse.

Andrew tried to mentally will the man off his horse, but he wouldn't budge. A well-placed whack against the leg did get his father-in-law's attention though.

"We're just passing through, ma'am."

"Yes. We're searching for my daughter," William said.

"William."

"And your wife," he sighed.

Andrew rubbed his hand across his face. That wasn't what he meant. He wanted to keep their search quiet. Not knowing who he could trust made him suspicious of everyone.

"Perhaps you'd like something to eat before you head on your way. My husband's men will be coming in for dinner soon. There's enough food for everyone."

"That would be mighty fine, ma'am," said William. He smiled at the scowl he saw on Andrew's face.

Andrew trailed behind William and their hostess. This was not what he wanted. Continuing their search was what he wanted.

Although he tried to be civil while they drank coffee, he found he didn't really want to talk. If he opened his mouth he'd end up yelling at his father-in-law for causing this delay. They couldn't afford it.

His silence didn't seem to bother the man, who chattered like a magpie. "New Orleans is a beautiful city. But I'm happy we don't live in it."

"Where are you from, Mr. Boudreaux?"

"A small town south of the city. It's called Jennings. Very pretty area."

The young woman's eyebrow arched. "And what kind of work do you do, sir?"

"I'm a store-keeper." William puffed his chest out. "It's been in my wife's family for several generations."

Andrew rolled his eyes. This was the same store he wasn't good enough to run.

"Andrew Leroux, I expect you to show better manners to this lovely, young lady. Is this how you treat Elizabeth? If you want to stay married to my daughter, you better start acting like a gentleman."

"You're Andrew Leroux?" asked their hostess.

"Yes, ma'am." A frown creased his brow. She acted like she knew him. *But how?* "You've heard of me?"

"In a way, yes." She sipped her coffee. "Could I ask you a few questions?"

"I guess." He leaned back in his chair. Had they come across one of the hideouts without realizing it?

"Tell me about your wife."

"My wife? Why?"

"Andrew! You're a guest in this lady's house," protested Jacques.

"Yes, and Beau has spies everywhere. How do I know she doesn't work for him?" he demanded, angry at himself for letting the words blurt out of him before he could stop them.

"I do believe we'd be dead or captured by now, don't you?" William said.

Andrew really wanted to wipe off the smirk that crept onto his father-in-law's face, but instead he just grunted.

"What would you like to know about my daughter?" asked Jacques.

She looked at Andrew, then William, before answering. "I'd like to know what she looked like."

"Pretty as a picture."

"I think she means hair color, eye color, height." Andrew sighed. "She's about five foot five. Brown hair … it's got a little bit of a curl to it. Brown eyes with small flecks of gold in them."

"They do not."

"I noticed them too, Mr. Boudreaux."

They turned to look at her.

"She's been here?"

"Yes," said Lily. "She stayed here for several days, helping me around the house."

"When did she leave?" asked Andrew, excitement building in his voice.

"About a week ago."

Andrew stood up.

"Mr. Leroux, your wife is in very good hands. She's with my husband."

"Excuse me?" His whole body started to shake. *Beth with another man, and his wife didn't seem to mind?*

"My husband went to Fort Scott with a delivery of horses. Your wife went with him and some of the hands from the ranch. She said she had to get to Wichita to see a sick aunt. She also worried about someone finding her."

"She's in a lot of danger. Does your husband realize that?" asked Andrew. He didn't mean for his voice to sound as sharp as it did, but knowing she was out there with a bunch of strange men scared the hell out of him. *What if one of those men worked for Beau?*

"Yes, he does. In fact, your wife tried to convince me and my husband to let her head off on her own, but Jeb wouldn't hear of it. He hopes to get her to Fort Scott safely and arrange for an escort to take her to Wichita." Lily took another sip of coffee. "And we disguised her."

"Enough so she won't be spotted easily?" asked Andrew.

"Yes. It was tested quite thoroughly before she left here. She's safe for now, Mr. Leroux."

"Ma'am, I hope so." If Beau figured out her disguise no one would be safe.

CHAPTER 30

Misery. That was what Beth felt.

Sweat trickled down her forehead, but she didn't wipe it away. Her hands stayed clenched in her lap.

She stared at the coffeepot in front of her. Too bad she couldn't pour that inside her clothing. It might give her a little reprieve to her dilemma. She itched badly. Earlier, without thinking, she'd inched her hands toward her face and started to scratch before she realized what she was doing and yanked them back down into her lap.

She had to resist or the scratching would take over. She itched everywhere. Some parts itched so much it made her sweat from the effort of not scratching. The desire to rip off her costume and just scratch herself raw rippled through her. Anything to ease the agony she felt.

It had started a few days after they'd left the ranch. The long johns made her skin itch a little, but it was the rags stuffed inside it that really irritated her skin. Yet she couldn't reach the itch through all the padding, and she had tried just about everything she could think of, including rubbing her back against a tree like a bear. The men's laughter when they caught her stopped that quickly.

What she needed was some privacy so she could scratch every itch she had. But that would only make matters worse for her. Thank goodness, they'd be at Fort Scott today. Then she could shed the disguise and take care of her itches.

Jeb signaled for everyone to mount up.

Beth dashed the untouched cup of coffee that sat at her feet and headed for her horse, the mantra of 'I will not scratch' running through her head.

~

Andrew wondered about Edward's brooding silence. He and William had detoured to Clinton before heading to Fort Scott. It had added two days to their trip, but now that he had a trail to follow, he should be able to catch up with Beth.

"You all right?" he asked.

"Yes," came Edward's clipped answer. Their horses trotted along while a heavy silence hung among them. "I'm sorry. I just feel like I failed you."

"Edward, you didn't fail me. You were there when she jumped off the train. She's smart and very resourceful. She happened across the right people who could offer her protection for part of her travel. Anyone else would have been too afraid. I'm proud of her." Andrew pulled his hat off his head and wiped his brow. "Shoot, if William hadn't been with me, I doubt I would've learned where she was headed right now."

"True." Edward smiled. "I just worry about her out there all by herself."

"I do too, but she has taught us that she can take care of herself. We'll catch up with her, I promise." Andrew urged his horse into a faster trot, hoping what he said was true.

They stopped that evening for a few hours' rest, but continued to push themselves and their horses as hard as they could to shorten the distance between them and Beth. If his calculations were right, Beth would have gotten to the fort just about the time they had left the farm.

Two days ago. Hopefully, Beth had stayed in town for a day or two to rest before she headed out. But since she never did what he expected, he refused to get his hopes up.

About midafternoon the next day they started to see signs of the fort. Farmers with livestock and their wives with canned produce or dainty lace items were on the road now, slowly headed to Fort Scott.

Andrew heard one wife berating her husband for jostling the wagon. She was afraid her prized canned peaches would spill all over the lace she'd brought into town for a friend. If the man hadn't been so embarrassed by his wife's outburst, Andrew would've laughed out loud. The wife reminded him of Beth. He could see her getting madder than a wet hen over something like that too.

The humor he saw in the couple faded when he thought about Beth. What was he going to do if he couldn't catch up to her soon? William seemed to have every faith in him, but Andrew knew how crafty Beth could be when she needed to. He bet he could walk right past her and not know it if she had the right disguise. The hustle and bustle grew as they got closer. People were standing in a line to get inside the fort itself.

Andrew groaned. This could take hours. Precious hours he didn't have. Urging his horse forward, he asked Edward and his father-in-law to stay in the line. Then he swung around and moved up to the gate.

"I'm sorry, sir, but you'll have to wait in line with the rest," said a young soldier.

"And I intend to do that, soldier. If you give this to your commander." Andrew handed the young man a slip of paper.

The young man opened it up, looked at the information with wide eyes, and signaled for a runner to come to the gate. "Give this to the captain right now."

The runner nodded and headed for the captain's office.

Andrew tipped his hat and trotted his horse back to where Edward and William stood. After making sure the young guard knew where he stopped, he slid down and waited patiently for the officer to seek him out.

It didn't take long.

"Mr. Leroux?" The captain walked straight up to him.

Andrew nodded slightly.

"What is the meaning of this?" The captain shook the piece of paper angrily.

"I'm not quite sure I understand the question, Captain."

"Oh, horsefeathers! You sent this to me so I'd come out here looking for you, instead of you waiting for your turn with the rest of these fine folks."

"I came here to speak to you, but with this long line, I could find you gone by the time I reached your gate. Something my superiors would frown upon if that were to happen."

"What is so urgent you couldn't wait until you cleared the gate to speak to me?"

"Not here, Captain. Can we walk?" Andrew handed the reins of his horse to Edward, letting the other men know by his gesture that he expected them to stay in line.

"This had better be good, Leroux."

"What I have to say will only have two reactions. Total shock or a gun pointed at my head."

The captain fell silent at Andrew's remark. They walked away from the crowd of people to a nearby copse of trees.

"I'm waiting." The officer turned toward Andrew, arms crossed over his chest.

"Does the name Beau Manning mean anything to you?"

"Nope." The captain pushed his hat back on his head.

"How about the McCord gang?"

"Thorn in my side. Those people have been wreaking havoc around these parts for several months. Why do you think we have all these people wanting in our gates?" he asked as he gestured at the line.

Andrew scanned the line of people. When he first got in line he thought most were in line to sell their wares to those in the fort, but this time he noticed a lot had all their possessions with them.

"These people don't feel safe in their homes anymore. Every one of them has lost something to the McCord gang. Their farms, their livestock, a family member…the list is endless.

"Where am I supposed to put all these people? I can't send them away.

The McCord gang has made a big mess in this area, and I'm the one who has to clean it up."

"Then you know where they are."

"Not exactly." The captain rubbed his jaw as he turned to look at the people again. "They're somewhere near Wichita. I've sent three scouts out to find his hideout, but those men have never come back."

Andrew waited for the captain to continue. He looked over the sea of people hoping to find safety within the walls of the fort. He knew as well as the captain that he'd probably sent those men to their death, unless Beau had a generous day and offered to let them keep their lives if they worked for him. But even if he did, it would just be a matter of time before they'd end up dead anyway. Beau never really let anyone get away from him. "So why did you mention the McCord gang anyway?"

"I'm going after them."

"You'll need fresh mounts." The captain still stared at the people waiting just outside his gate.

"Food and travel gear as well." Andrew turned toward the captain. "I also have a big favor to ask."

"You need men? Done. I can send ten of my most seasoned with you."

"Thank you, Captain. I could use the men, but that's not the favor. I'm looking for someone."

"A woman," added the captain.

Andrew instantly became weary.

"What type of woman you looking for? I don't approve of such things, but a man has needs."

"No." Andrew started to laugh. "I'm looking for a particular woman... one who passed through here in the last few days. Should've come in with a horse trader."

"The only horse trader we had come through here recently is Jeb. He has a small farm near Russellville. But I don't remember him having a woman traveling with him."

"You're sure?" That was the man Beth should have been traveling with. Lily never told him how she was disguised. He didn't force the information out of her because he knew she was just protecting Beth.

"The best person to speak to is our purchaser. He probably would know." The captain directed him back to the fort. Calling to one of the sentinels, the captain asked for their purchaser.

Andrew stood outside the massive wooden gates while someone searched for the man in question.

A young man barely twenty came racing out the main gate, skidding to a stop in front of his captain. He saluted and slapped his arms against his thighs as he snapped to attention.

"At ease, Corporal. Did you buy horses from Jeb this week?"

"Yes, sir."

"Anyone come riding in with him?"

"His men, sir. Oh, and some old lady. She pretty much kept to herself though."

"When did they get here, Corporal?" asked Andrew.

"Two, maybe three, days ago."

"Do you know if the old lady stayed?"

"I don't know, sir." The boy's brow furrowed.

"What is it, son?" asked the captain.

"Nothing really, sir. Just strange, that's all." He looked at Andrew. "Someone came into town looking for a young woman. They also asked about two men. One of them they were looking for fits your description."

"Someone came in asking about me? What did he look like?" Andrew didn't like the feeling of dread snaking up his spine.

"Older man. He was traveling with a woman. Heard him call her Cook."

"How long ago was that?" *Jacob? Out here?*

"Couple of hours."

"Which way did he go?"

"Sir, I wish I knew, but I've been so busy trying to help these people find food and a place to stay, I didn't really pay attention."

Andrew nodded as the captain released the corporal to go back to his duties. "Captain, I'd like to take you up on those men."

"Fine. I can have them ready to travel in an hour." The captain gestured for Andrew to accompany him back to where Edward and William waited.

"I'd rather travel light." Andrew hoped the officer would go along with his plans. "Beau Manning is the leader of the McCord gang, and he's expecting me. If I ride into Wichita with a bunch of soldiers, he'll just sneak out of town. If I go in with just the few he already knows about, Beau will probably confront me, not thinking I could do him any harm. I need the men, but I also need the element of surprise. I'd like them to join me after I get to town and figure out where Beau is holed up."

"How're they going to know where to meet you?" He glanced over at Andrew as they neared the crowded line.

"Have your men stay out of town, but have one go in to speak to the minister. I'll leave word there where they can meet me."

"All right, Leroux. But be forewarned. I'll be traveling with my men. We need to take care of this menace as quickly as possible."

"Yes, sir. Thank you, sir." Andrew spotted his friends.

"Will you be staying?"

"Not sure. It depends on if I find that old woman here."

"Friend of the family?"

"You could say that."

~

Andrew frowned as he stared ahead. Something about the man's silhouette seemed familiar. Then he spotted the woman standing with him. Shouldering his way through the crowd, Andrew tapped the man on the shoulder and waited for him to turn around.

"Drew!" Jacob smiled at the sight of him. "Thank goodness. Cook and I have been looking for your wife since she took off."

"Good luck. She's eluded everyone so far," Andrew grumbled as he took Jacob's outstretched hand. Against his better judgment he, Edward and William had stayed in the line to enter the fort so they could get some much-needed supplies.

"Oh dear," commented Cook. "I knew those men frightened her too much."

"What men?" His father-in-law walked up to Andrew just in time to hear Cook's comment.

Cook clammed up at the sight of the stranger.

"Jacob, Cook, this is William Boudreaux. Beth's father." Andrew crossed his arms over his chest. The rest of this conversation should be good. William knew how to get the answers he wanted.

"You mentioned men. What men wanted my daughter?"

"I…um..." Cook looked at Jacob. "Andrew had to leave town for a while. Jacob and I promised to look after her for him until he came back. While she was with us, we got a few visitors. Don't know who they were, but they frightened Beth bad. She said she had to leave town."

She turned toward Andrew. "I went back to Jacob's when I knew it was safe and told Jacob what had happened. He demanded we go and find Beth and bring her back before you returned from McCord's Way, but we weren't successful."

"How about you?" asked Jacob.

"Finding Beth, yes. Finding Beau, no."

"But I thought you said—"

"Andrew lost her again after that," interrupted William.

"I did not lose her." Andrew pronounced every word, trying to control his anger. "She was kidnapped."

"Ha!"

"Where are you staying?" Andrew chose to ignore William. It wouldn't look good for him to strike his father-in-law in public anyway.

~

The plodding of her horse lulled Beth to sleep, but trying to doze in the saddle wasn't easy. She found she got more kinks in her neck that way.

Beth was traveling pretty quickly. If her information was right, she should be seeing signs of Wichita within the next day or two.

She was really looking forward to seeing her aunt. Once she was safe in the woman's home, she'd be able to shed her disguise. Maybe scratch for a day or two and relax. As much as she hated it, her disguise had done a great job of hiding her. Very few people would even talk to her. Her smell probably had something to do with that. She hadn't bathed since she'd left Jeb and Lily's farm.

As the hours and miles rolled by, she kept hoping to see some sign of life, but it was just her, her horse, and the few wild animals she saw from time to time. Wichita seemed like some elusive dream. Always just a hair's breadth away.

CHAPTER 31

Beth entered Wichita two days later, feeling like the bottom of her shoe. She ignored the children who ran beside her horse, shouting hateful words at the bedraggled old lady, and the mothers who scolded those children when they heard them. All Beth wanted was her aunt's warm house.

The farm was farther out, closer to the small town of Delancy, but she had to pass through a good portion of Wichita before she could look for the trail she remembered her family following on visits to her aunt's house.

She didn't care about the stares and odd looks she received. Nor did she answer any of the questions thrown her way. Aunt Martha was all she could think of.

Her stomach growled at her. Absently, she withdrew a piece of beef jerky from the dwindling satchel she had and started to chew.

Slowly she made her way through the city. She breathed a sigh of relief when she was finally out in the open again.

A small brook gurgled nearby. Sliding out of her saddle, Beth led her horse over to allow her a chance to drink. "We're almost there, Magnolia." In the end, she hadn't been able to part with Magnolia, and since the horse had rested enough at Jeb and Lily's place, she'd decided to keep her only friend.

"Aunt Martha's house should be on the other side of that small hill." She rubbed the horse's neck. "If it isn't, I think I'll break down and cry."

After her horse had her fill of water, Beth climbed back up and aimed for the hill. There, nestled in a small valley, stood her aunt's farmhouse. With a glad cry, Beth urged her horse into a gallop.

Before the horse even stopped, she swung off and ran up the porch steps. Her brow crinkled at the lack of activity. Opening the front door, she called her aunt's name. The drawing room was empty, and so was her aunt's sewing room. Maybe she was out in the barn.

The soft click of a gun made her stop and turn around. Color drained from her face when she saw who stood in front of her.

"I've been waiting for you."

~

Andrew drank his coffee without really tasting it. They were just outside of Wichita and he hadn't caught up with Beth. He hoped she was safe, but feared she wasn't. Not knowing drove him crazy.

He had sent Edward to town to pick up any telegrams that might be waiting and give his message for the troops coming from Fort Scott. They could have all gone into town but Andrew feared they'd be spotted. While he waited he pulled out the small pieces of paper again. It was the first time he had looked at them in a while. He smoothed out the two that had the same numbers on them. The ones that looked like street addresses.

William sat down next to him. "Good coffee, no? This'll put hair on your chest."

"Then I hope Beth hasn't drank any of your coffee." Beth had complained his was strong, but it didn't hold a candle to William's.

His father-in-law laughed. "What you got there?"

"Not sure. Found one of them in the room where the men who kidnapped Beth stayed. The other was from the McCoy ranch." Andrew handed one of the papers to him.

"Isn't that the ranch Beau was at?" he asked as he took the papers.

"Yep."

William sipped his coffee as he looked at them.

Edward came into view. Andrew stood. Good, now they'd be able to get moving again.

"Mr. Boudreaux received a telegram," Edward said as he slid off his horse.

"Nothing from Sally?"

Edward shook his head. He handed the telegram to William, who opened it and read its contents.

"Can I see your papers again?" He looked at Andrew, telegram fluttering in his hand from a slight breeze.

"Sure." Andrew handed one of the scraps to him. His father-in-law's solemn expression worried him. The hairs on the back of Andrew's neck stood up. He had a feeling he wasn't going to like what he heard next.

"This is Martha's address." William held out the telegram. "I thought these numbers looked familiar but wasn't sure until my wife sent me her address."

"Martha? You mean the aunt my wife has traveled all this way to see?"

"Yes."

All three men started moving at the same time.

"You left a message with the minister?" Andrew asked as he swung up into his saddle.

"Yes, sir." Edward did the same thing. "I did that after I requested all telegrams to be sent here."

"How far is your sister-in-law's house?"

"A few hours." William settled in his saddle before he picked up is reins. "Why?"

"Because we need to see if that's where Beau has been hiding out all along." Andrew clicked at his horse. "Then we need to wait for our support. As much as I want to go charging in there I know better. When Beau is captured again he won't be escaping."

~

"Come, my dear. Is that any way to act toward an old friend?"

Beth stared at Beau. The whole thing was a trap. How could she have been so stupid?

"Not speaking to me? Really, Miss Elizabeth, I think it would be in your best interests to be nice to me." He gestured to one door.

Beth felt her heart plummet when she saw her aunt tied to a chair with a gun pointed at her head.

"But first, I think the lady needs a bath." He wrinkled his nose in distaste. "Definitely."

Beth had thought about hiding behind her disguise until Beau had lifted the wig from her head and thrown it into the fireplace.

"Take her to the master bedroom and make sure she has lots of water. It'll probably take a lot of soap and water to get her clean." He gestured for two of his men to help her up the stairs. "Oh, and if she refuses to bathe, shoot her."

"I will not bathe with these two men in the room with me, so go ahead and shoot me."

He turned toward her and gave her a slimy grin. It made Beth's stomach roll.

"If you don't allow them to be in the room, then I'll have to come up and make sure you take that bath. Is that what you prefer?"

Her skin crawled at the thought. Without saying a word, she turned on her heel and headed up the stairs.

"Let the old woman help her, but don't let either woman out of your sight for a minute," Beau added as an afterthought.

Beth paced the floor of her aunt's room while she waited for the men to bring up the tub. She should've known this would happen. Beau knew their every move. How could he not know she was headed here?

She jumped when the bedroom door swung open.

"Aunt Martha!" She rushed to give her aunt a hug.

"Elizabeth, you shouldn't have come here." Martha squeezed her tight for a moment before stepping back an arm's length.

"I know, but when I got your telegram..."

"What telegram?"

Beth gave her aunt a strange look. The loud clanging of the tub as it banged against the walls interrupted her train of thought. She waited for the two men to wrestle it into the room and set it in the middle of the floor.

"Wait." Martha jumped in front of them before they could set it completely on the beautiful wooden floor. "Please, let me get the rug."

She retreated to a small closet before the two men could protest and brought out a rag rug. Rolled together from old bits of clothing, linens, and such, the rug was just large enough to fit under the tub.

Beth helped her unfurl it and place it on the floor. She gave a sad smile when the men sat the tub on top of the rug. Aunt Martha was trying to protect her beautiful floors even though Beau was probably destroying the rest of her home without thought.

Hot water came next. Beth felt herself salivating at the thought of scrubbing all the dirt from her skin, but she couldn't get undressed in front of these men.

Martha patted her arm and got some clean linens from the closet. After directing Beth to one corner of the tub, she held one of the sheets up to block the men's view while Beth disrobed.

A splash and a sigh later, Beth was neck-deep in the hot water. Martha handed her soap and a cloth, which she used to scrub every inch of her body. After washing her hair a few times she stepped out and allowed her aunt to wrap another sheet around her. The tub was emptied and refilled with fresh water, and Beth repeated the process. She started to feel truly clean after the tub had been filled a third time.

"Aunt Martha, why did you ask me 'What telegram?'" She ran the soapy cloth between her toes.

"Because I didn't send a telegram."

"But we… Oh." Beth wanted to scream. It had been a setup from the beginning. If she had only stayed home, this wouldn't have happened.

She continued to wash herself in silence, knowing anything she said would be repeated to Beau.

"Child, you need to come out of there now. That man has no patience. If you don't emerge from this room, he'll come up here after you."

Beth nodded. Martha wrapped her in another clean sheet and had her sit in a chair.

"I can only offer you one of my dresses. The rest have been used for other things."

"Actually, I have a dress in my saddlebags. It might be a bit wrinkled, but it's clean." She looked expectantly at one of the men, hoping he would go and get her bag. Aunt Martha was three inches shorter and about fifty pounds heavier. Beth knew she'd reveal far too much of herself if she wore any of her aunt's clothing.

One of the men finally moved. It took him a few minutes to retrieve her bag and dump the contents on the bed.

"Where's your corset?"

"That's the one thing I couldn't fit in there, Aunt Martha. I thought I'd be able to purchase one once I got here."

"Well, I should have one of my older ones here. It might not be the latest fashion, but it should fit you." Martha went to the closet and started rummaging through. "Ah, here it is."

Beth took the corset and set it on top of her meager pile of clothing. Behind the sheet Aunt Martha held up, she dressed as quickly as she could. Expecting her dress to hang on her frame, Beth was surprised to find it a little snug. With her aunt's help, she buttoned the back of her dress and pulled her hair back into a bun.

"Well, I'm not ready for a cotillion, but it should do. Don't you think?" asked Beth as she slid her boots back on.

"You look beautiful, my dear."

Beth jumped at the sound of Beau's voice. *How long had he been standing there?*

"Beau, it isn't very gentlemanly of you to sneak up on me like that."

"True, Miss Elizabeth, but then, you and I know I'm not a gentleman, don't we?"

Beth swallowed hard.

"Come, my dear. I won't hurt you. Yet. First, we're going to have a nice dinner. I'm sure you haven't had a decent meal in a while. Then we're going to sit on the porch and wait for your husband to arrive. He should be here just after dark."

~

Andrew stared at the ranch house, looking for some sort of movement. "I wish we could be sure."

"Martha had a thriving farm," said William. "This lack of movement isn't normal."

"I need proof." Just as he said it Beau stepped out onto the porch. He slid down behind the small rise they were hiding behind. Now he had what he needed. "Edward, I need you to go back to town and give the minister an update. Let them know we're at the farm and that Manning is here as well. They can't come charging in. Have them meet us at that rock formation about a mile back."

"How do you plan on coordinating all of this?"

"We don't know if Beth is here yet, but I don't plan on doing anything until we have everything we need. If she is there and her life is in danger we'll have to rescue her without the backup we need, but I'm not going to let Beau try to goad me."

"Is capturing him more important than rescuing my daughter?"

"My heart stopped when he kidnapped her before. Just the thought of her with him makes my blood boil. But Beth knows as well as I do that we need to stop him now, and we need to lock him up so he can't do this again."

"Too bad Beth doesn't know that," William said. "You never told her you loved her, remember. She's going to think you're just doing your job. And, Leroux, if she wants to come home with me, I will take her."

"She's my wife."

"Then prove it to her."

~

The first one to arrive was Able.

"You got here pretty quick."

"Saw your man Edward go into the church earlier and was curious as to why he didn't go to the sheriff. Once the minister believed I was here to meet you he relayed your message so I figured I'd go ahead and ride out here and ask." Able leaned back against one of the rocks. "You got a problem with that, Leroux?"

"No. Just a little nervous, that's all. Don't know if I can trust the sheriff, especially this close to Beau's hideout."

"You sure he's here?"

"Yes. He stepped out on the porch a few minutes ago." He peeked over the ridge for a moment. "I'm not sure if Beth is there though."

"Why isn't Beth with you?" Able asked as he looked at William. "And who is this?"

Andrew watched Able for a moment before responding. "Beth and I got separated. She has been heading to her aunt's ranch since then."

"Can I assume the ranch we're watching is her aunt's?"

Andrew nodded. "And this is my father-in-law."

Able watched William for a moment but didn't comment on his presence. "Anyone else coming?"

"Yes." Andrew wondered what he should reveal to this man. With Beth's life at stake, he didn't feel safe laying all his cards on the table. "What've you learned?"

"Your man is holed up at some widow's house. Now I know that it's Beth's aunt's ranch. Something's going on too. I've seen a lot of activity in the last day or two."

"How long have you been here?" The man sure knew a lot if he'd just gotten into town.

"Awhile." Able opened a flap on his saddlebags and brought out some jerky.

"Seen any new people around?" Andrew didn't like his evasive answer.

"There're always new people there, but I did see something out of the ordinary. Some young woman showed up there two or three days ago. Didn't see her leave, but haven't seen her around the house either. And an older woman showed up earlier today."

All Andrew could do was nod. That older woman was probably Beth. He didn't reach her in time. Rubbing a hand over his face in frustration, he wondered how he was going to pull anything off with her right in the heart of the trouble.

A distant clopping of horse hooves put everyone on alert. Silently, they pulled their guns and braced themselves for an attack.

~

Beth picked at her food. The rich cream sauces on all the food made her stomach roil. It had to be her nerves. Sitting across from Beau at the dinner table didn't give her much of an appetite.

"Come, my dear, you must eat. You never know which meal will be your last."

"Are you threatening me?" She looked up at Beau. The one thing she refused to do was let him know she was scared.

"Why, I'm just being honest." He speared a big chunk of meat dripping with the cream sauce and put it in his mouth with a flourish.

Beth knew she was going to lose what little she had eaten if she didn't get away from the table soon.

"Beau, I'm not feeling well. Guess all the excitement has gotten to me. May I be excused?"

"No! You may not be excused!" His fist slammed against the table. "You will sit there like a proper lady while I eat my food."

"Beau, I really need to be excused." Beth could feel the color drain from her face.

He continued to glare at her, as if contemplating whether he should beat her or just go ahead and shoot her.

"Look, if you're going to shoot me, do it now, because I'm getting up from this table and going outside where I shall get violently ill. Unless, of course, you want me to do it here, all over your beautiful dinner." She stood up and marched out to the porch. Just as she cleared the steps, she doubled over and emptied her stomach into the bushes. She was so busy feeling embarrassed, she barely heard her name being whispered.

Rubbing her hand against her forehead, she hoped whoever was out there would leave her alone. If it was her Aunt Martha, she knew she'd be treated like she was on her deathbed. Something she didn't want.

"Beth." The voice was a little louder.

"Go away," she whispered back.

"It's me. I've got to talk to you."

"Well, 'me,' I'm not really up for company right now. Can't it wait?" Her stomach seemed to be settling down. Taking a deep breath of the night air, she straightened up and looked out into the night.

A sharp gasp escaped her as someone appeared in the bushes a few feet in front of her. Beth couldn't see who it was, but the voice did sound familiar.

"Um...You really don't want to stand there."

"Just listen for a minute. You have friends here to help you. I'll try to get in touch with you again. Just go along with Manning as long as you can."

The screen door squeaked as it opened.

"Miss Elizabeth, if you're done, come back inside." Just the sound of Beau's voice made her stomach lurch once again.

Taking another deep breath, she spun around toward him and walked back into the dining room. As long as she didn't have to watch him eat any more of his meal, she figured she should be all right.

The table had been cleared when she sat down again. Beau stared at her over the rim of his coffee.

She didn't like the way he was staring at her, but refused to be intimidated. A steaming cup of coffee sat in front of her. After adding just a touch of sugar, and deciding against the cream, she took a hesitant sip. "Good coffee."

"You can thank our new cook." Beau sat back in his chair as dessert was brought in.

Beth hoped it wasn't too rich. Rich food wasn't agreeing with her tonight. Her jaw dropped open for a second before she remembered herself and snapped it shut. Now she knew who was whispering at her earlier.

"Here's dessert, Mr. McCord." The accent was new, but Beth recognized Sally instantly.

Beth had only one question. *Why was she here?*

CHAPTER 32

Had Beau figured out they were there? Or was this the men they were waiting for?

"Be ready, but don't shoot unless I give the word," Andrew whispered. Holding his gun in front of him, he stepped out from the safety of the boulders.

"Leroux, is this the proper way to greet guests?"

"Captain." Andrew dropped his gun to his side, relief washing over him. "You know I can't be too careful."

"And I don't want to suddenly find myself riddled with bullet holes." The captain dismounted. "I brought thirty of my best men. They've set up camp a little further back."

"Thank you." Andrew led him to the rest of his group. After quick introductions, they all sat down.

"This is all you have, Leroux?" Disappointment laced the captain's words as he looked around at the four men and one woman sitting around the campfire.

"No. Every Pinkerton man in three states is on his way here to join us." Andrew gave him a weary smile. "I just don't know when they'll be here."

"Is this how you run things, Leroux? On assumptions and maybes?"

"No, sir. But you know time is of the essence. Manning is expecting me to strike. The longer I wait, the bigger his army will be."

"So what plan do you have?" The captain accepted the cup of coffee Edward handed him.

"My idea is quite simple. I'm going to walk in there and ask Beau to surrender."

"And what about my daughter?" asked William. "You going to let her fend for herself?"

"That's where the captain here comes in. He's going to be the one to rescue Beth while I keep Beau occupied."

"That's suicide!"

"If it'll make sure Beth is safe, I don't care," Andrew said to William.

"You'd give up your life for her. Why?"

Andrew really didn't want to answer the question. But he had to. He looked straight at William and said, "I love her."

~

Beth laid in her bed, wide awake, long after the rest of the house had gone to sleep. Heavy clouds obscured the light that would normally illuminate the room.

Why was Sally here? Was she truly the spy Andrew thought she was? Even though he'd never said anything, Beth could tell he'd been suspicious of Sally. She just never knew why.

And what had happened to Andrew? Beau had forced her out on the porch after dinner, but Andrew never showed up. Just remembering how angry Beau had gotten sent chills down her spine.

When he realized Andrew wasn't coming, he had grabbed her by the throat and threatened to squeeze the life out of her if she didn't tell him where Andrew was. True fear had coursed through her veins when she didn't have an answer for him. Beth also knew she would be sporting the bruises on her neck for several days from his painful grip.

A whisper of sound put her on alert. Someone was in her room, but it was too dark to see who it was. Wishing she still had her gun, Beth grabbed her pillow and prepared herself for an attack.

The moment she felt a hand on her arm, she grabbed her assailant, yanked the person onto her bed, and proceeded to try to smother her assailant with the pillow.

Whoever it was struggled fiercely for a few moments before giving up the fight.

The moon peeked out from the clouds for a few seconds, just long enough for Beth to realize she had a woman pinned to her bed. Sliding the pillow down a little, she stared into Sally's green eyes.

"What're you doing here?" Beth snapped quietly as she pulled the pillow off Sally's face.

"I came to check in on you," Sally answered softly.

"In the middle of the night?" she whispered back as she gave Sally some room. "I could've smothered the life out of you and would've had to explain your body."

"I don't think that would've happened." Sally sat up. "Where's Andrew?"

"I don't know. He and I got separated." Beth didn't want to tell her about the kidnapping.

"Separated? How?"

"Never mind that. What are you doing here?"

"My contact. He was able to secure a job for me, so I could be on the inside."

"Does Andrew know this?"

"No." Sally gave her a sad smile. "I know he thinks I could be his leak because I wouldn't tell him everything, and because I'd slink off in the middle of the night, but I couldn't help it. My contact has a very precarious position here with Beau. I couldn't jeopardize that."

"You going to tell me everything now?"

"I can't. You're safer not knowing everything."

The floor outside Beth's door squeaked, silencing them for a few minutes. They stared at each other, wondering if someone outside the room heard their hushed voices.

"I'd better go. I'll try to let you know when I hear anything."

"Beau was sure Andrew would show up tonight," Beth blurted. "So he must be near."

"I was told to pack up the kitchen tonight. My guess is we're being moved to the hideout."

"Is there any way we can leave Andrew a message to where it is if we're moved before he gets here?"

Sally stared at the bedroom door for a minute. "I'm not really sure where the hideout is, but I was told it would be a long ride. I was to make sure everyone would have a cold lunch. Do you have anything you could use to leave a trail?"

"Beau took everything I had." Beth looked around the room to see if there was anything there she could use. "Too bad I don't have a horse like Edward does. You remember the fragrant trail it left behind."

"That's it." Sally hugged her. "I've got to go, but I'll make sure Andrew has a trail to follow. Don't you worry."

~

Andrew propped one foot against a rock as he sipped his coffee the next morning. Able had already left. The man never stayed around long enough for Andrew to truly question him. Since Cook had taken over their meals Edward felt obliged to make sure she had enough supplies. He had headed to town an hour earlier. The boy worked far too hard.

Andrew scratched his rib cage as he straightened up. Sentinels had been set up all along the way so they'd know when someone approached, but Andrew knew today would be another one of waiting. He planned to go and spy on Aunt Martha's house, but also knew more and more of his men would be showing up to help. He needed every one of them to pull off his idea, so he wouldn't be able to watch the house long.

The smell of another fresh pot of coffee brought him back to the fire for a third cup.

"That Cook makes weak coffee," complained William as he walked up to Andrew.

"It's fine," answered Andrew. "Just because you can't stand a spoon upright in it doesn't mean it's bad."

"Ha." William dashed his coffee against the rocks surrounding the banked fire. "You have more men coming. Word says at least a dozen on their way."

"How far?"

"They should be here quickly. One of the captain's men spotted them a few minutes ago." William smiled at him. "Hear they looked pretty ragtag, but doubt they belong to Beau."

Just about that time they heard the sounds of hoofbeats. Once again, everyone drew their weapons and waited, not knowing if their visitors were friends or foe.

The first approached them on horse, noting Andrew's gun. "Coffee and bullets, Leroux. You always did like to be a little different."

"Sam." Andrew put his weapon away. "I could smell you a mile away. You still avoiding bathwater?"

Several of the other men who rode up behind him chuckled.

"Now you know why we let him go first. We figured his smell could be our best weapon against attack," said another man as he rode up.

"Simmons. Good to see you."

"You too, Leroux. This where we'll get Manning?"

"Yep." Andrew shook hands with the men. "Thank you for coming. There's a lot to do, so let's have some coffee as I explain what I need each of you to do."

~

Several hours later, Andrew hid in a small copse of trees near the small garden Aunt Martha had behind her house. As close as he was, he could see everyone clearly. Beth paced in an upstairs room. Although he knew she was now in Beau's hands, Andrew felt a strong wave of relief knowing she was still alive and healthy.

An older woman sat in a chair near the window. That must be Aunt Martha. He committed her features to memory so he could describe her to his father-in-law. If this was his sister-in-law he would know by Andrew's description.

He hadn't seen Beau yet, but there had been a lot of activity as Able had mentioned. It looked like Beau was getting ready to move everyone and Andrew knew he had to get Beth out before he did. He just prayed that those who were supposed to watch the house, like he was doing now, would be able to follow them if they did move before he was ready to attack and let him know where the new hideout was.

If not, Beth could be killed. A thought he refused to let take root in his mind. Beth would make it, and he would do anything it took to make sure she did.

A quick glance at the sun told him it was almost noon and he had to get back.

~

The sun had already dipped below the horizon when Andrew put his plans into action. Once he was sure everyone knew what to do, he rode up to Aunt Martha's house, alone.

The house was eerily silent. No lights shone through the windows. Without a second thought, Andrew slid off his horse and shouted at the house.

"I know you're in there. Come out and show yourself, Manning." Although he knew he was too late, Andrew hoped Beau was lying in wait for him. The only sound that greeted him was the crickets.

"Damn." He walked up onto the porch, his boot steps echoing in the silence. The front door opened with a squeak. Methodically walking through every room, Andrew proved to himself that everyone was gone. Now he had to start all over again.

Three sharp whistles brought everyone from their hiding places.

"Looks like he's already hightailed it out of here. Have any of the men I sent to follow him come back yet?"

"A couple, but they won't be doing you any good," said the captain. He pointed toward two horses. The bodies of their riders were draped over them.

Andrew pinched the bridge of his nose. Those men there were the best trackers around. There was no way Beau would've just stumbled across them, so that meant someone had tipped him off. *But who?* No one knew the full layout of his plan but him.

"Hey, Leroux, you better come here and see this."

"What did you find?"

"Look."

Andrew crouched down and looked at the ground. His brow furrowed when he picked up a button. "Is this what you wanted to show me?"

"Yep. Followed them for about a mile before I came back."

Andrew rolled the button between his fingers. "Have you told anyone else?"

"Nope. Thought you'd like to see this first."

"Good man." Andrew slapped him on the back. "Keep it to yourself. In the morning, follow the trail and see where it leads."

"Yes, sir."

They made good use of the house since no one was occupying it anymore. Andrew took the room Beth had stayed in, hoping to be just a little closer to her for the night. The Spartan room held very little of her essence. He did feel a fleeting smile dance across his lips at the remnants her disguise.

What a sight she must have been in it.

He could almost envision her in the outfit, pretending to be an old lady, beating people with her cane when they didn't move fast enough.

God, how he missed her. He didn't realize how much he had come to rely on her opinion until he could no longer get it. Or how much he looked forward to her side of the arguments. She might be headstrong, but he found it an admirable quality in her because she always made him look at the problem from another angle, and most of the time it allowed him to make a better decision.

Most of all, he missed the way her eyes would light up whenever she saw him. It made him feel special, like he was the only man in the world.

He lay down on the bed, getting tantalizing whiffs of roses. He knew he wouldn't be getting any sleep tonight, but knowing she would be safe in his arms by tomorrow gave him a little more hope.

He closed his eyes, forcing his mind to relax.

To his surprise, he didn't open his eyes again until the sun started to peek in the room. Just as he sat up and rubbed the sleep form his eyes, William came in with a steaming cup of rotgut.

"Yours?" Andrew eyed it warily.

"Yes. I couldn't handle another pot of Cook's so sweet-talked her into letting me make this."

"I would have liked to see that." Andrew took the offered cup. He grabbed his vest with his free hand and shrugged it on before reaching for his boots.

"A scout is waiting for you downstairs."

"Thanks." Andrew had wanted to go himself but he wasn't the tracker this man was. It took all his discipline to remain behind so the scout could do his job.

"What time is it?" Andrew finished off his coffee.

"Just about dawn." William took his cup while Andrew put on his boots. "Cook has started breakfast if you're hungry."

The aroma of fresh baked bread and bacon sizzling in the pan filled the air by the time he got downstairs. She knew she wouldn't be much help getting Beth back, but felt the least she could do was make sure they all had food in their stomachs. And since Beau had left a lot of food behind, Andrew agreed with her. Grabbing a biscuit and another cup of William's awful coffee, Andrew headed outside to the barn.

"Did you follow the trail?"

"As far as I could. I found the hideout, and you're not going to like it. They've taken over a mine."

"A mine?" He didn't know of any mining in this area.

"Bet it's an old nickel mine," said William.

Andrew turned to glare at his father-in-law. "What are you doing out here?"

"She is my daughter." He crossed his arms over his chest. "Besides, you knew I followed you."

Andrew couldn't argue with him. He had known the man shadowed him but he didn't try to shake him. William was right, Beth was his daughter. He had a lot at stake too.

"I remember reading about it a few months back in *Manufacturer and*

Builder. Some men out here claimed they'd found high quality nickel, but that was near Russell Springs."

"And someone here probably tried to find some, then abandoned it when it didn't produce. Just the type of place Beau would look for." Andrew felt like banging his head in frustration. Nothing was going according to plan. "Have the men saddle up."

He was going to have to alter his plans a little, but hopefully they'd still work. Besides, what else could go wrong?

CHAPTER 33

Beth wanted to scream. She'd been tied up and dumped in some little shed with her aunt and another elderly woman hours ago. The three women stared at one another. It was difficult to talk with cloths stuffed in their mouths.

Beth's anger got the best of her and she started kicking the walls of their small prison. The dust that started drifting down from the roof stopped her quickly when it fell in her eyes and nose.

All three started coughing, but with the rags in their mouths, breathing was very difficult.

No one came to their rescue.

Wouldn't Beau have a fit if they all died because they couldn't catch their breath? Beth really tried to control her coughing, but found it impossible. Not being able to draw in a clear breath made her vision start to dim. She knew she was going to die.

A tear slid down her cheek. There were so many things she didn't get to do. She'd never told Andrew she loved him, and she would never get to apologize to him for all the trouble she'd caused him.

Hands. She felt hands touching her. Had she already reached the Pearly Gates? The rag was ripped from her mouth. Then she felt sweet, fresh water surge down her throat, which caused another fit of coughing, but this time she could draw air into her lungs. Slowly, the world righted itself.

Sally sat in front of her, hands on her thighs. Someone else was helping her aunt and the other woman. "Trying to kill yourself?"

"I was—" Beth had to stop while another coughing fit took over. "—trying to get out of here."

"Trying to knock down the walls isn't the smartest way to do it."

"What would you have done?" Beth glared at Sally. "Sat here meekly while Beau decided your fate?"

"Probably not. Give me your hands." Sally worked the knots loose so Beth could wiggle her fingers. "I'd release you, but Beau is on his way. Don't think he'd be too happy to see you free."

Just as she offered Beth some more water, Beau strode in.

"Miss Elizabeth, I can't leave you alone for a minute, can I?"

"I don't like being trapped in here."

"Well, you'll have to stay here for a little while longer while I get your rooms ready." He turned on his heel and headed out the door.

"Where are we anyway?" Beth asked Sally, her voice barely above a whisper.

"Some mine. Look, I have to get back. I'm supposed to bring you a meal in an hour. We'll talk again then." Sally hurried out the door, leaving the water bucket and ladle for them.

"Are you all right, Aunt Martha?"

"I'm fine, my dear."

"How about you, ma'am?"

The woman nodded. She cowered in her corner, jumping at the slightest sound.

"There's no need to be afraid. We'll be rescued soon."

"You believe your Andrew will follow us here?"

"I pray he will, Aunt Martha. If he doesn't, we are in trouble."

~

In his hiding place, Andrew watched Beau as he exited a small tool shed. As soon as he entered the mine, Andrew put his plan into action. He and five other men converged on the shed, hoping to free Beth and whoever was with her before trying to capture Manning.

His heart soared when he found Beth, unharmed but bound, in the small building.

"Oh my God, Andrew, get out of here! It's a trap."

Her words were punctuated with the sound of the hammer of a gun being pulled back.

"Hello, Leroux."

"Manning." He turned around to face his enemy. His brow furrowed when he spotted Edward standing behind Beau. Why wasn't the boy doing anything?

Beau must've read his thoughts. "I have to thank Edward here for helping me with your capture."

Andrew shot Edward a glare that could have melted a glacier.

"I'm sorry, Andrew, but I had to." He looked at Andrew for a moment before breaking eye contact to stare at his shoes. "He already killed my pa and threatened to kill my ma if I didn't bring you and Miss Elizabeth to him."

"Then this was all some elaborate setup," Andrew said flatly. Edward had told him his mother had been killed, but the third woman must be her. Edward had lied to him. At least now he knew who had leaked all the information.

"I wish I could take credit for all of this," said Beau with a dramatic sigh. "But it was just dumb luck. Edward's woeful story was true in the beginning."

"I did run away from him, but only after he said my ma and I weren't worth keeping around. I had to prove to him we were worth keeping. When I heard there was a Pinkerton man on the train, I thought that might be a way for me to prove myself to him." Edward continued to stare at his shoes.

"Beau didn't even know I'd hooked up with you until we ran into the first man after Mrs. Leroux. He spotted me in the first town you saw him and he told Mr. Manning. When Mr. Manning learned who I was with, he threatened me. If I didn't tell him where you were going and what you were planning, he'd kill my ma. I didn't even know Ma was alive until he threatened me. I had to do what he said."

"It was perfect." Beau gave Andrew an oily smile. "I knew your every move, and you trusted Edward so much you revealed every thought you had to him. Like a good little boy, he gave it to me, so his precious little ma is still alive."

"But it's not like you to keep unwanted baggage around, Beau. Why didn't you kill Edward's mother right away?" Andrew found it odd Beau hadn't disposed of the woman and just lied to the boy. Not his normal style.

"She actually begged for her life. Then I found myself without a cook, so her life was spared again. At least until now." Beau smiled. "I have you and a new cook, so once again, I have no need of her."

"Take him." Beau pointed to Andrew. "Tie him up and put him with the women."

Andrew was forced to his knees, then had his hands bound behind him.

"We'll talk a little later, but first I must reward Edward for doing such a good job."

The door slapped shut, leaving him with the three women.

"Andrew, please don't be—"

"Do not lecture me on how I should be feeling right now, Elizabeth Boudreaux Leroux. Of all the people I have been suspicious of, Edward was never on the list." Andrew pounded his head against the dirt floor. "How could I have been so stupid?"

"Andrew! You're going to hurt yourself!" Beth hitched her way over to his side.

He rolled onto his back, watching the cracks in the wall. A shadow hid the sunlight that had been streaming in. As he suspected, someone, probably Beau, stood outside listening to their conversation.

"You couldn't have known Edward was working for Beau," she said.

"I should've figured it out. Beau knew our every move." He sighed loudly. "Are you and the ladies all right?"

"Yes." Beth gave him a confused look. "Beau has been a gentleman so far. But I fear that will change now he's got what he wanted."

"And what is that?" He looked at Beth, making sure he had her attention before nodding his head ever so slightly.

"You." She turned to look in the direction he indicated. A quick smile and a soft nod let him know she saw the shadow too. "He plans on killing you."

"I figured that." Andrew sat up again.

"We have to escape," said Beth.

"And how do you propose to do that?" He contorted his body, forcing his arms under his butt and pushing backward so he could move his arms forward. In order to escape he needed them in front of him.

"I was hoping you'd be the one to have the answer to that."

They talked about nonsense for two hours while Andrew drew pictures in the dirt. At first the women had ignored his doodles, at least until he swatted Beth with the small stick he had been drawing with. "Ow."

He pointed to the ground.

"That hurt."

He glared at her while he tapped the ground. She finally sighed and looked down. Andrew wanted to kiss her when he saw comprehension dawn on her face. As they continued to speak about nothing, he drew pictures to let her and the other ladies know about his plan.

The hinges of the door squeaked as the door opened, and a quick sweep of his foot destroyed the drawings before anyone could see them.

Beth sat next to him, shuffling her feet a little to remove any thing he might have missed.

"Come." Their guard stood at the door, rifle aimed at Andrew's midsection.

Andrew stepped forward.

"Your lady too."

Beth just stared at the man. "If you don't come out, I'll have to shoot your man." The guard raised his rifle to his shoulder, now aiming at Andrew's head.

She looked at Andrew. At his nod she stood up.

"That's a good girl."

Andrew feared she would rise to the bait for a moment when her mouth hung open at the man's audacity, but she stepped outside without saying a word. Her tight-lipped look betrayed how hard she fought not to retort.

They were ushered, at gunpoint, to the mouth of the mine.

Beau stepped out of the shadows to greet them.

"I've contemplated the best way to take care of you two. First, I thought to kill Andrew while making Beth watch."

"The last time you tried that, it backfired on you," responded Andrew. "This little slip of a woman was able to escape and the other was able to knock you out so you could be captured."

Beau turned beet red, his body rigid. "That will not happen again." He took deep breaths. "Then I thought I'd have you watch Miss Elizabeth die before I kill you," Beau continued a few moments later, as if Andrew had never spoken. "But I've come up with the perfect ending for your life, Leroux. Miss Elizabeth will be the one to end it."

"No." She stepped backward, banging into one of the guards. "You can't make me."

"Give her your gun." Beau pulled a long knife from his boot and sliced the ropes from Beth's hands before sliding it back into his boot.

Andrew wondered if Beau had truly thought this one out. Beth would never be able to pull the trigger. Her dislike of guns was too strong. Besides, what if Beth turned the weapon on Beau? She could shoot him and end this whole thing quickly.

"I know what you're thinking, Leroux, but Miss Elizabeth can't hurt me." He opened his shirt to reveal a heavy chest plate beneath. "Bullets can't penetrate this."

He grabbed Beth around the waist, and taking the gun from the guard, forced it into her hand. Beth shook her head as she fought him, trying to pull her hands out of Beau's grasp.

"Come, my dear, whether you pull the trigger or I do, the killing weapon will still be in your hands." Beau grabbed her hands, pointing the weapon at Andrew's heart.

"No," she shrieked. Pulling her hands from his grasp, she smacked him in the eye in her effort to free herself. The gun fell to the ground.

Beau didn't think, he just reacted, backhanding her and knocking her out cold.

"You will pay for that, Manning." Anger glittered in Andrew's eyes.

"And how do you plan on making me pay? You don't have the upper hand, Leroux."

Not yet, but if everyone was doing their job it wouldn't be long. Andrew just wasn't sure if he and Beth would live long enough to see Beau taken into custody.

"Bring a horse and some rope." Beau pointed to one of his men. "Now."

The young man scampered off, returning a few minutes later with the requested items.

Andrew frowned. His agents were supposed to secure the mine as soon as Beau was outside while the captain and his men secured the perimeter. If they didn't hurry and finish their jobs he just might dive for the gun on the ground and shoot the man himself. "Death by hanging will be appropriate, don't you think?" Beau fashioned a noose and tied it around Andrew's neck. "That was what the government was going to do to me if they'd convicted me."

Andrew tried to answer, but the rope was too tight. He was having trouble breathing.

"Cat got your tongue, Leroux? Or are you finding it difficult to breathe? Oh dear, I must've pulled the rope too tight." Beau watched as Andrew felt his face turn red. Sweat started to pour down his face.

"Oh, very well. I'll give you a chance to catch your breath." Beau loosened the rope just enough to let Andrew draw a small breath. Signaling to two of his men, he had them lift Andrew and sit him in the saddle of the horse.

Andrew didn't like the feeling of impending doom as he watched one of them throw the other end of the rope over a sturdy tree branch.

"Make sure the rope is short enough to do the job." Beau smiled at Andrew. As soon as his men stepped back, Beau raised his arm. "Any last words, Leroux?"

"You won't get away with this, Manning. Killing me will only bring more agents here. The agency knows where you are now, and what your master plan is. They won't stop until they've killed you."

"By the time they learn about your death, it'll be too late. Your words don't frighten me, Leroux. Prepare to meet your maker."

Andrew closed his eyes, praying for a miracle and wishing he'd told Beth how much he loved her.

Everything started to happen in slow motion. The sound of the slap against the hindquarters of the horse, the pounding of his own heart in his ears, the surge of the horse as it jumped forward, leaving him swinging in the cool breeze.

As the rope tightened around his neck, crushing his windpipe and squeezing the air out of him, Andrew wondered if anyone's head ever just popped off their shoulders during a hanging. The pressure he felt building up in his sure felt like it could explode any minute.

Small pins of lights danced in front of his eyes. Opening them one last time, he gazed at Beth, still crumpled on the ground. At least she didn't have to see him die.

The last thing he heard was two shots ringing out.

CHAPTER 34

Beth stifled a groan as she started to come to. The hard ground pressed against her face. Small rocks cut into her skin. She sat up and looked around. Her face lost all its color when she saw Andrew dangling from the tree.

Two loud cracks sent every man standing diving for cover, including Beau. Andrew jerked in the wind like a puppet. She noticed his hands were bound in front of him seconds before he fell in a heap onto the ground.

"Get him now," Beau shouted at the two men closest to Andrew as he stumbled to his feet. "You three get over there and see who fired those shots."

Andrew struggled with the rope around his neck as he staggered toward Beau. He reached Beau quickly, long before any of the men could move. Tackling his nemesis, Andrew pushed him to the ground and started to pummel his face with his tied fists.

Two of the men started to rush to Beau's aid, but were stopped in their tracks when the repeat of a rifle was heard.

"Don't go any further."

Beth looked in surprise at the man who rode up on his horse. Dressed in his captain's uniform, she recognized the commanding officer from

Fort Scott. *How did he get out here?*

The whole area was suddenly filled with soldiers, each pointing their weapons as they relieved Beau's men of their guns and rifles.

A growl erupted from Beau.

Beth stared in horror as Beau reached into his boot to grab his knife. Sunlight glinted off it as it made a deadly arc toward Andrew.

Andrew dove to the left, avoiding the blade by inches and losing his hold on Beau. They leaped to their feet, circling each other as each tried to find an opening.

No one paid any attention to her.

There at her feet was the gun Beau had tried to force her to use. With shaky hands, she picked it up.

Beau lunged at Andrew. The blade sliced through the air once more, aiming straight for her husband's throat.

Beth swallowed hard. Andrew's life was more important than any fear she harbored. She aimed and pulled the trigger. Smoke danced in front of her face as the bullet flew to its mark. She watched as the blade slipped from Beau's hand.

He turned toward her, a ghastly hole in one side of his head.

Beth feared he would come after her next. She raised the gun and prepared to fire again.

"No need, daughter."

Beau flopped to the ground.

"Papa?" She flung herself into her father's arms, grateful she didn't have to look at Beau's wound again. Her whole body trembled in the wake of her fear for Andrew. Leaning against her father, Beth felt a little lightheaded. The steel arms of her father supported her as she slipped into unconsciousness again.

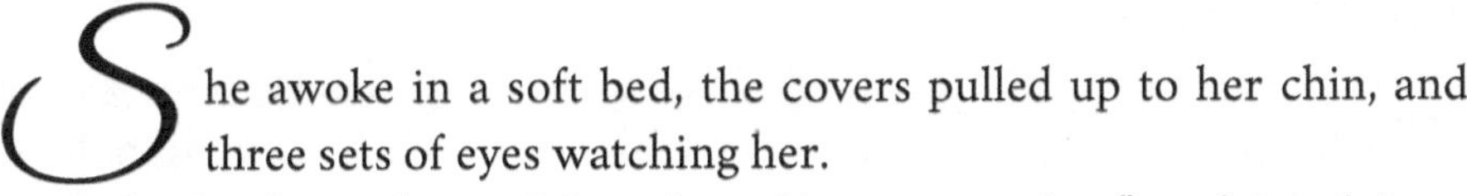

She awoke in a soft bed, the covers pulled up to her chin, and three sets of eyes watching her.

"Oh, thank goodness! I feared you'd never awaken," exclaimed Aunt

Martha. She sat on the bed next to Beth, resting her hand against the cold cloth on Beth's forehead.

"You did give us quite a scare, Elizabeth. You've been out for several hours," added her father.

"Beau?"

"He's dead." Her aunt patted her hand.

"And I killed him." Beth felt the tears slide down her face.

"You did what you had to do, dear."

Beth turned away from her aunt. She really wasn't in the mood for being patronized.

"We'll stay here for a few days. Let you gather your strength. Then we'll head home," her father said.

"Home?" She looked over at Andrew who had kept his distance.

Instead of contradicting her father and demanding she went with him, he kept quiet. His brooding silence made her uneasy. *Was he going to walk away this soon?*

"Yes. I've sent a telegram to your mother, letting her know it was all over and we should be home within the week."

Beth put her hand on her chest. Oh no, she was going to be sick She could feel it creeping up inside her.

"Whatever you say, Papa." Throwing back the covers she dashed for her chamber pot.

A loud slam jerked her attention to the bedroom door for just a second before her stomach started to heave.

Her aunt ran to her side while her father stared at the bedroom door Andrew had slammed behind him.

"I'm going out for some fresh air," said William.

Beth waved her hand behind her, hoping he'd be gone before she could embarrass herself further.

"Too much excitement, my dear."

"I'm not sure about that, Aunt Martha. I've been feeling like this for days." She rested her head against the wall.

"Why don't you rest a little and see if you feel any better."

"Whatever you say," she mumbled as she climbed back into bed. Maybe a little rest would do her some good.

~

Andrew jerked on the cinch as he tried to tighten it for the fifth time.

"You're lucky that horse hasn't decided to kick you where you stand," remarked William. He stood just outside the barn where Andrew worked on saddling his horse. "If he doesn't, maybe I will."

"Leave me alone."

"The way you're leaving my daughter alone?"

"Leaving her?" Andrew whirled on him. "She's already made the decision to go home with you. I'd say she's leaving *me*."

"Is that what's got you in an uproar? Elizabeth didn't really hear what I said to her. That is her normal answer when she's distracted." William took a step closer. "If you want her to stay with you, you have to talk to her or I will take her home with me. Once she's on that train, you'll never see her again."

"Is that a threat?"

"That, Andrew, is a fact." William took the horse's reins. "So get back into that house and straighten this out with my daughter."

"Not right now." Andrew took the reins back. "I need to make sure Beau's hideout has been secured and all the men have been arrested." He also needed time to figure out how he would convince her to stay.

"Don't take too long, Leroux."

Andrew nodded as he swung up on his horse. He passed the porch where Aunt Martha stood on his way out.

William shook his head and he climbed up the steps to the porch. "That boy is thick-headed."

"He'll come around. Right now we have more pressing matters." Aunt Martha wrung her hands. "Elizabeth is very sick."

"I'll go get the doctor."

~

"You must be wrong, Doctor," said Beth as she clutched the blanket to her chest.

He chuckled. "I know it seems frightening right now, but you'll do fine."

"A baby?"

"You're a healthy, young woman." He patted her hand. "There's nothing to be afraid of."

The doctor stood up and spoke with Aunt Martha for a few moments before taking his leave.

"Where's Andrew?"

"Um…I believe he went into town," Aunt Martha said.

"He's left?" She swung her feet to the floor and stood up. Beth grabbed the bedpost for a moment before laying out her dress. "How long ago?"

"About the time you got sick, my dear."

Beth felt her cheeks heat up at the reminder, but she'd have to get used to it. She had a few more months of that happening before it passed.

Dressing in record time, Beth marched downstairs to where her father waited for her. His worried look softened the anger she felt boiling inside.

"I'm fine, Papa." She looked up into his troubled eyes.

"So the doctor said." He touched her cheek. "But should you be up?"

"I'm not sick, Papa."

"But earlier..."

"Isn't unusual for a woman in my condition." She waited for her words to register.

"In your condition?" Shock filled his face. "Elizabeth?"

She nodded and smiled. "Now, where's Andrew?"

"Probably in town. He mentioned something about making sure all the loose ends were tied up where Beau was concerned."

"I need to talk to Andrew, Papa," she said.

"I'll go get your aunt's wagon and take you in."

~

Beth and her father stopped at the sheriff's office first and learned Andrew had headed to the bar.

She stood just outside the bar, watching him talk to Sally and Able. Other than the nasty red welt around his neck from the rope burns, he looked perfect to her. His hair could use a combing, and his clothes looked a little rumpled, but he still stood tall and proud. It took her breath away.

Would he want her now that it was over? Or would she return home to bear a child on her own? She hesitated and listened to a little of their conversation from the doorway, trying to work up the nerve to go in and confront him.

"Well, Leroux, looks like everything worked out in the end," said Able, who sat across from Andrew.

"Too bad I didn't figure out it was Edward until it was too late."

"Unfortunately, I was part of the reason Edward ended up betraying you," Able admitted.

"Why do you say that?"

"He knew I supposedly worked for Beau and probably thought I had standing orders to kill him if he didn't do what Beau wanted. I don't think he would've followed through if I hadn't kept showing up."

"Beau had his mother and threatened to kill her if he didn't tell Beau everything." Andrew pushed his hat back on his head. "It had something to do with the first man I ran into from Beau's gang. The one you shot."

"Yes. About that. I couldn't let him reveal who I was. He would've ruined everything."

"You had to kill him?" asked Andrew.

"Suffice it to say that sooner or later it would've come down to that. I knew he would cause a threat to your wife's life and my position, so I did what I had to do." Able propped his elbows on the table. He pulled a few pieces of paper from his pocket and laid them on the table. "Remember these? We figured out what they were."

Andrew stared at the little scraps of paper he had given Able.

"The letters stand for the railroad. The four sets of numbers are the time and location of planned robbery."

"You think they're still going to rob the trains?"

"Yes. Beau had foolproof plans and made sure they'd be followed no matter what. We ride tonight to finish this. You with us, Leroux?" asked Sally. "Since this has been your mission, I thought you'd want to be part of the finishing touches."

Beth had heard enough. She turned on her heel and stomped away from the saloon. Not really caring if her father followed or not.

~

"Somebody's sure making a commotion," commented Able as he peered out the window.

Andrew turned his head in time to see a very angry Beth stomp by. He choked on his coffee.

"Oh no." Andrew stood up. "How long was she there?"

Sally shrugged, taking a sip from her cup.

Without another word, Andrew grabbed *his* hat and headed outside.

"What about helping with the train robbery?" asked Able.

"I think he's got more important things to worry about right now," chuckled Sally.

Andrew raced down the street, trying to catch up with Beth. He had to explain. Beth had already swung up on the buckboard when he reached her.

"Beth," he panted.

"Get out of my way." She glared down at him.

"We need to talk."

"No, we don't." Beth pulled on the reins, making the horses dance a little in place.

"Yes, we do." He had to back up from the horses or risk being trampled.

"Mr. Leroux, your mission needs you. Don't worry about me. I can take care of myself." She shook out the reins.

Andrew wanted to tell Beth he'd take care of her, but she didn't give him a chance.

"Remember what I told you, Leroux," shouted William as they pulled away.

"How could I forget? You promised me I'd never see her if I let her leave without me," he said to the air as he dashed his hat on the ground. How was he going to convince her he loved her? If he went back to her aunt's house she'd be too stubborn to listen, and he couldn't use his usual tactics to get her attention. Then he looked up. That wasn't exactly what William said. He said if Beth made it on the train Andrew would never see her again.

A sly smile stretched across Andrew's lips. He'd just have to make sure Beth never made the train.

~

Beth stood in silence as she waited for the train with her father. They had argued constantly about her returning home with him, but she'd refused. Although she was legally married, she knew she wouldn't be able to face their friends and neighbors, or the questions they might whisper behind her back.

She would stay with her aunt Martha until the baby was born.

Then she would decide what she wanted to do. Of course, her father was furious, but she refused to budge on it.

A flash of light slashed across her eyes, blinding her for a moment. She winced at the brightness. Then it was gone.

"You all right?"

"Yes, Papa. I'm fine." Beth had to smile. His concern for her welfare since he'd learned of his grandbaby was so sweet, and so unlike him. She knew this child would be spoiled to death.

"I saw that wince."

"It was just the brightness of the day."

"Perhaps you should go and sit down for a while. A woman in your condition..."

"Has been through this many times. Really, Papa, nothing is wrong." The light flashed again. This time it was much brighter. It was starting to give her a headache. "But perhaps I should go sit down for a moment."

Her father escorted her to a small bench against the building.

"Stay right here while I get you something cool to drink."

Beth sighed and rested her head against the wall as her father hurried away. A soft noise caught her attention. Straining to hear the noise again, she tilted her head a little.

The train wouldn't make that kind of noise, would it?

She stood and walked to the edge of the platform, shielding her eyes with one of her hands so she could get a better look down the tracks.

Beth heard a high-pitched shout before she noticed the charging horse coming right at her. Before she got a chance to react she was swept up and slammed down on a pair of well-muscled thighs and the horse wheeled around and charged back the way it came.

She started fighting the moment she got her breath back. "Let me go!"

"Not until you listen to me."

"Andrew Leroux, you have no right!" She struggled harder, only to find his grip tighten.

"I have every right. I'm your husband."

"You only married me to protect me, remember? Those rights don't pertain to you." Beth looked around and felt her heart sink. She had no clue where she was. "You can't do this. Papa will come after you."

"I don't think so, Beth. He knows about our marriage, so he knows he can't interfere." Andrew slowed his horse down as they reached a small rise. "We should be far enough away by now." He urged his horse down to the edge of a small creek.

"Far enough for what, Andrew? One more tryst before you move on to the next town?" She turned to face him.

"I'd recommend you let me have my say, Mrs. Elizabeth Leroux, before I do what I've threatened to do from the beginning," he growled. Andrew let her slide down from the horse.

She started pummeling his leg the moment she hit the ground.

"Damn it, Beth." Andrew launched himself at her and knocked her to the ground. In one swift motion, he had her hands pinned up above her head and her legs immobilized by his. "You will listen to me."

She renewed her struggling.

Andrew used his whole body to pin her down. Their faces were inches apart. He looked into her eyes. She knew she couldn't hide it and that he saw the pain and fear she felt. She didn't want her heart broken any more than he did.

"Beth." Keeping her hands pinned with one of his, he used the other to brush a few strands of hair away from her face. "You didn't give me a chance the other day."

"You're the one who slammed out of my aunt's house," she snapped back.

"Only because when your father said he wanted to take you home, you said yes. What was I supposed to think?"

"Oh, that." Beth broke eye contact. "Well, I was preoccupied then and wasn't really listening."

"And what had you so preoccupied?"

"Will you get off me?"

"No." He shifted his weight, though, so she wouldn't take the brunt of it. "Are you going to answer my question?"

She looked back up at him but didn't answer. Beth knew if she answered his question now she'd never know if he truly loved her or stayed with her out of duty.

Reaching into his pocket, he pulled out the watch she had bought him. William had given it to him after they had worked out their differences.

He snapped open the lid and read the inscription. "I will always treasure the joyful days we had together."

She paled as he read the words. A single tear slid down her cheek.

Andrew cupped her chin and made her look at him. "Did you mean it?"

"Every word," she whispered.

"Then stay with me. I want our marriage to be real."

"Just like that." She tried to buck him off.

"What is wrong with you?" He rolled off her and got to his feet. "Do you want to fight me? What happens if I win?"

Beth sighed and shook her head as she sat up.

"Then what do you want?" Andrew ran his fingers through his hair. "Good Lord, woman, do you know what I went through when you disappeared? I'd fallen in love with you only to find you gone. Then when I finally do catch up to you, what do you do? Mess up my rescue attempt by escaping the men who kidnapped you. And you weren't the easiest person to follow either." He paced back and forth in front of Beth. "Edward couldn't find you anywhere and I stumbled across your trail accidentally."

"You tried to find me?" *Did he say he loved me?*

"Are you daft?" He stopped pacing for just a few seconds and looked into her eyes. "Of course I tried to find you. And if it hadn't been for your father, I might've caught up with you sooner. Then again, if it hadn't been for your father, I might not have gotten the information about where you were headed from your friend Lily."

"My father?" *He said he loved me!*

"Yes. He showed up wanting to trounce me. He was sure angry over this watch. But then we decided to team up. He got Lily to open up and tell us about your disguise and traveling with her husband to the fort."

"Wait." Beth rubbed her forehead. "You're confusing me. I thought my father went to Aunt Martha's."

"He helped me track you down."

"He never said anything about it."

"Knowing your father, he probably waited for you to broach the subject. And knowing you, you were too angry at me to ask." Andrew crouched down in front of her. "Which is why I brought you out here. You never gave me a chance to explain myself, and what you thought you heard."

"Fine." She crossed her arms. She wasn't going to let him soften her resolve. Even if he did say he loved her. He probably didn't mean it anyway. "Explain."

"I love you. You are the most important thing in my life, and I want you to be part of it. Always have. I know what you're thinking. You think I'm some sort of Casanova who has had all these different women and am just saying these words to make you feel better. But, Beth, you were with me. You saw how most townsfolk treat me. What woman would want anything to do with me? Most of the time, I was hiding on the trail somewhere trying to catch a criminal, not whiling away my time in some fancy hotel room waiting for the bad guy to come to me. That's only in those dime novels. Having you with me taught me I don't like being alone."

"Andrew." His words had touched a place deep in her. Tears started to fill her eyes.

"Let me finish. When I had the chance to marry you I took it, but I didn't think you'd go along with it if I told you the real reason I wanted to marry you, especially after knowing how so many look at the work I do. I used the protection idea to make you feel safe." He searched her eyes. "I had no idea you'd think I didn't want the marriage.

"Shoot, I was dumb enough to think I could convince you otherwise once we took care of Beau. I only met with Sally and Able today because I was still trying to figure out how to talk to you. Sometimes my best ideas come to me when I'm thinking about something else. I hadn't planned on going with them. But you were there, hearing everything the wrong way and stomping off before you knew what was going on. When you rode away, my heart broke into a thousand pieces." Andrew wiped away a stray tear that had escaped her eyes. "Then I remembered what your father said, so I kidnapped you."

"You're making a habit of it, Mr. Leroux," she sniffed, not able to stop the tears. "What did my father say to make you kidnap me again?"

"He told me once he got you on that train, I wouldn't be able to see you again, so I had to make sure I spoke to you before you got on the train."

"Why didn't you just come to Aunt Martha's house and talk to me?"

"Would you have talked to me then?"

"No. I was too angry."

"That's what I figured too. This was the only way I could think of to get you to talk to me without your father running interference."

No wonder her father had fought with her to go home. He knew Andrew would come after her.

"I don't want an annulment, I want to be your husband, Beth. For real and for always. I want to fill each of your days with joy, just like the watch says. To tell you you're beautiful morning, noon, and night. To love you with all my heart."

"Oh, Andrew." Beth jumped up to her feet and flung herself into his arms, knocking them both into the dirt again. She laughed and cried as she tried to express her feelings. "You left Aunt Martha's without a word…and when I needed you most. I wanted to hit you so hard, but I've been too sick to worry about it, but the doctor says that will pass. Don't know what it will be yet, but I'm so glad you'll be there. Oh, Andrew, I love you!"

He had no clue what she'd just said, but just held her until the tears subsided a little. A hiccup and a watery smile let him know she was all right.

"Now, what's this about you being sick?" he asked.

Beth looked at the ground. *Would he bolt when he heard this bit of news?* She mumbled her answer.

The only word Andrew could make out was *baby*. "Baby!" He grabbed her arms and held her at arm's length. "Beth?"

There was that watery smile again.

He pulled her to him and held her like he wasn't going to let her go. "A baby."

Beth snuggled against him. Her heart sang with joy.

~

They rode into Aunt Martha's yard arguing.

"I am not going to allow you—"

"Andrew Leroux, you will not start dictating to me. Women have been having children for thousands of years, and riding horses to get around." She slid down from the horse and jammed her hands on her hips.

Andrew spotted William sitting on the porch on a rocker. He swung down from the horse in silence.

"You going to answer my daughter, Leroux?"

Beth turned toward her father. She was all smiles when she spotted him. "Papa! I thought you'd be on your train home by now."

"Not when I didn't know where you had gone off to." He stood up.

"But you knew where I'd be, Papa. Didn't you?"

He watched her for a moment, then walked down the stairs. “I had my suspicions, but waited around to be sure.”

“Why didn’t you tell me, Papa?”

“You didn’t ask.” He stepped up to her and rested a hand on her shoulder.

“Papa.”

“You sure you want this, Elizabeth? He can’t offer you much.” William searched his daughter’s face.

Beth looked at Andrew, who stood tall and proud beside her, ready to fight the world for her if need be. The thought made her smile.

“I don’t want much, Papa.” She went to Andrew’s side and slipped an arm around him.

“Leroux, if she ever comes home crying because of something you’ve done, I’ll break every bone in your body.”

“Yes, sir.”

Beth hugged him as her father turned and headed inside. “The rest of my family isn’t like this, you know.”

“Glad to hear that.”

“Wait until you meet my grandpa.” She gave him a sly smile. “Papa is a pussycat compared to him.”

“As long as you are by my side, I can take on anything.” He pulled her close and captured her lips with his. A sigh escaped them as they parted. “Pussycats, huh?”

“Meow,” Beth purred before lifting her face for another kiss.

~

ABOUT THE AUTHOR

Writing for Barbara Donlon Bradley started innocently enough, like most she kept diaries, journals, and wrote an occasional letter but she also had a vivid imagination and wrote scenes and short stories adding characters to her favorite shows and comic books. As time went on she found the passion for writing to be a strong drive for her. Humor is also very strong in her life. No matter how hard she tries to write something deep and dark, it will never happen. That humor bleeds into her writing. Since she can't beat it she has learned to use it to her advantage.

www.barbaradonlonbradley.com

~

Also Available

Love Is...
A Portrait in Time
A Quest For Love (coming 2019)

www.ingramcontent.com/pod-product-compliance
Lightning Source LLC
Chambersburg PA
CBHW031111030726
47496CB00002BA/488

* 9 7 8 1 6 8 0 4 6 7 2 5 3 *